MONSTROUS AFTERMATH

Monstrous Aftermath

Stories in the Lovecraftian Tradition

W. H. Pugmire

Hippocampus Press

New York

Contents

Within Your Unholy Pit of Shoggoths 11

Your Weighing of My Heart.. 17

The Tomb of Oscar Wilde 21

These Harpies of Carcosa.. 27

An Ecstasy of Fear... 31

Darkness Dancing in Your Eyes 61

Beyond the Wakeful Senses... 65

Ye Unkempt Thing... 71

Half Lost in Shadow.. 83

Circular Bone 91

Jester of Yellow Day... 93

This Splendor of the Goat... 97

Monstrous Aftermath.. 127

An Element of Nightmare... 135

Some Unknown Gulf of Night... 145

Fungi from Yuggoth, *by H. P. Lovecraft*.. 247

Acknowledgments.. 267

This book is dedicated to Paul Maclean.
Cthulhu fhtagn!

MONSTROUS AFTERMATH

Within Your Unholy Pit of Shoggoths

Leaning against the brick wall, I sucked at my exotic cigarette and then blew perfumed smoke at the orange moon. But Doris would not be silent, and I was growing annoyed. To entertain myself, I sucked again at my cylinder of narcotia and exhaled; and the cloud of smoke that poured from my mouth shaped itself outlandishly, suggestively. I moved my eyes to see if she had noticed my feat of subtle wizardry, but her own orbs were glued to the leaves of her little book. I spat, hurled the butt of my fag to the ground, and crushed it beneath my heavy boot. "You read like one entranced," I complained.

"It's the secret poems that he wrote during his marriage. They were found behind a false wall in the Crowninshield place when it was undergoing restoration two years ago. The style is so different compared to the poems in *Azathoth and Other Horrors,* and there is a kind of fearful timidity in the expression of dark wonders, as if he were writing of forbidden things. Why are you sneering at me?"

"Not at you—at your gullibility. You are the victim of an elaborate hoax, I fear. Why would anyone want to publish the poetry of a forgotten poet, who is only remembered by some few occultists in this dreary town? Who is this publisher, and why haven't they published an accompanying volume of Edward Pickman Derby's finest work? No, this is a jest played upon your little coven."

She leaned against my shoulder and turned the pages of her silly book. "These were written during his marriage to the priestess. Some

11

of them express a crazy kind of eroticism. I think Asenath introduced him to lots of sex magick."

Rudely, I snatched the book from her and flipped through its leaves. "It's not even poetry in places. Look here, pages of prose."

"That's his prose-poem sequence, 'Pit of Shoggoths.' It concerns an area near Chesuncook Village in northern Maine. Read it carefully, Simon. It describes the roads he traveled on, the places stopped at. A casual reader would think it little more than a series of Nature vignettes, celebrating beautiful landscape. Actually, it's a kind of poetic road map that tells the way to a sacred spot hidden deep within the woods there. I'm thinking of inviting some of the others to drive with me and find the spot, do a little ritual there in memory of the poet. Why don't you come?"

"With your dreary little band of cultists? No, thank you. I find Arkham witches too pretentious. My one reason for coming to this boring town was to investigate the book sale at Miskatonic Library. I have found some few fascinating old volumes, and now I will depart."

"Well, if the idea of being with the others annoys you, we could go there alone." She reached for the book and I surrendered it to her. "It's a haunt you've never visited, right? Who knows what traces of necromancy we may find there?"

I feigned boredom; but I actually did feel a kernel of interest, inspired by some queer passages from what purported to be Derby's prose-poems. Perhaps I had been overly hasty in my dismissal of the little book, inspired by my dislike of Arkham and its clique of modern occultists, who could not compare with the delicious madness that had corrupted Arkham decades ago, when it was indeed an authentic witch-town. And so I agreed to meet Doris in early morning mist, and I read portions of the book of poems aloud as she drove to Maine.

Riding in cars always makes me drowsy, and eventually I shut the book and closed my eyes. I do not dream as mortals do, but the imagery of the poetry played in my mind. I beheld the Cyclopean ruins sequestered in a deeply wooded realm, as described in what purported to be the 'secret' poetry of a doomed Arkham soul. I descended the vast steps that led down to abysses of nightmare, into vaults where the walls were strangely angled and embossed with alien design. In flowing darkness, I beheld the pale thing that stretched along an altar stone and mewed to a memory of moonlight. And then the car bounced violently, and when I opened my eyes I saw that we had traversed a densely wooded terrain on a road of dirt and sand and rocks. The sky was white with mid-level clouds, and my companion studied both sky and forest with anxious eyes. I sensed the occult instincts that guided her, and which were a source of my attraction to her. Her heritage was rooted in Arkham sorcery, and her power, although not potent, was genuine.

She stopped the car. "We'll walk from here. It won't be far. I can feel the oddity of the air. Do you feel it on your eyes?" I nodded. "I love the sense of neglect and abandonment. It's as if this region has protected itself from prying human eyes."

I nodded again. "There are places that so cloak themselves, in which elements of the Outside are evident, in the earth, on the aether. I have devoted my time on this mortal plane to locating such hidden corners. How delightful to come across one so unexpectedly."

Doris laughed softly. "I'm happy to be your occult compass. Come on."

We vacated the vehicle and sauntered into the wooded territory, walking for quite a while before I noticed the climatic shift. Pausing, I knelt onto the ground and clawed at the earth, then brought particles of sod to my snout. I sighed, then worked at removing my boots. As we resumed our way through woodland, I could feel the arcane properties of the ground on my naked feet. Doris, too, could feel the alchemy all 'round and began to run. Not in the mood to chase her, I kept my steady pace, stopping only when we came to the area that was clear of trees, the dark green vicinity where prehistoric dolmens tilted against one another. The young woman smoothed her hands against one pillar of antique stone, and then she began to undress. I went to her and reached to the ground so as to dig my hands into the dirt, and then I bathed her naked flesh with earth's debris. Grabbing my hands, she guided them to her loins and moaned as I coated her pubic hair with dirt. Quickly she pushed from me, fell to the ground, and began to crawl to a place inside the gigantic structure of olden stones, and I watched as, creeping into some earthen pit, she sank from view.

I entered beneath the stones and began to descend the firm clay steps that led below ground, into a lean tunnel that, turning, led to more steps that took me into an expanding cavern of rocks and sand. Phosphorescent smears on the rough walls helped to give the pit a dim illumination, so that I could vaguely see the altar and its pale occupant. Doris, still on hands and knees, dragged her nude form to the altar and reached to touch the hand of the thing that reclined thereon.

"Come," rasped the creature wrapped in filthy rags, "and suckle my witch's tit. Moisten my nipple with your anxious tongue, and I will teach it rare language. Come."

The creature held out a claw, into which Doris placed her hand. The young sorceress raised herself onto the altar stone and touched her mouth to the flaccid sack that was the other's breast. Turning from the sight, I rested my hand against one of the shimmering patches with which the wall nearest me was stained.

A cracked voice spoke. "They leave their mark, the indestructible shoggoths. Ah, they have shifted through the ground to the womb of earth. But they will return, to melt into one another and feast upon the airy tissue of my lunatic dreams. Oh, my dreams are dim, dying like the light that once frolicked in my eyes. I have fed the elder ones for decades, and my essence is almost used." Her hands reached for the woman who bit into her breast, and she wound her talons into the younger woman's hair. Thus guided, Doris moved over the woman's form until their mouths met. Pushing away from the wall, I glided to the altar and kissed my friend's firm buttocks. She rocked to and fro, and then she rolled over so as to help the wretched hag mount her. Above us, I heard a moan of windsong.

The antique creature cackled as she ground her loins against the other woman's flesh. "Ho, it awakens, the immemorial seraph of the woods! *Iä! Shub-Niggurath!* Take my hand, inhuman thing—my time as servant here is at an end."

I did as she commanded, and she stumbled to the ground. Doris writhed on the altar stone, her pale flesh shimmering in the light of the phosphorescent stains that were the markings of shoggoths, those things that would return and feed anew on her uncanny dreams. Clutching the Antient One, I guided her up the earthen steps, out of the pit. We stepped past the tilting dolmens, into moonlight.

"Oh, the sick moon," the creature chortled. "How long it's been since I have felt its dead light reflected on my eyes. Ah, this evening air. Let me expel my final breath into it and serve as sacrifice to the Black Goat of the Woods." So saying, she exhaled violently, and I watched as her arcane breath spilled from her as unholy mist that shaped itself grotesquely as it drifted skyward. The violent gale assailing us tugged at her rags, shreds of which lifted behind her like daemonic wings. I watched as her eyes sank, replaced by ebony pits. I whistled as her flesh melted and her brittle bones broke apart as dust and ash that was swept away by storm.

I looked again toward the moon and the cloud of mist that drifted to it. Expanding nostrils, I took in the stench that rose from the pit beneath the dolmens, heard the maddening shrieks, and knew that the shoggoths had returned to feast upon the psyche of my friend. Some dark cloud cloaked moonlight, and I sensed that it was a manifestation of the Outer God known as Shub-Niggurath. I raised my wide hand to the dimming image of the moon and made unto it an Elder Sign.

Your Weighing of My Heart

"*The white leaves float upon the air,*
The red leaves flutter idly down,
Some fall upon her yellow gown,
And some upon her raven hair."
—OSCAR WILDE

I moved through swathes of crimson shadow, past figures that were mutated and incomplete, not stopping until I confronted the frowning man who stood beneath an artificial tree. His hand, sheathed inside a dim white glove, held up a morbid mask, and he bent slightly forward so that the mask's frozen lips touched my pomegranate-mouth. The gentleman's nostrils took in the scent of my semi-mortal flesh, my body encased within its tight yellow gown; and as he sucked in my fragrance, one red leaf detached itself from the branches above him and drifted to his face, briefly touching his eye and then continuing its descent. He exhaled, and a spiral of wind, surrounding us, moved the coils of my midnight hair.

Keeping my eyes lowered, I spoke to the mask, avoiding the shifting face of the one who stood so near me. "Those distant drums are maddening; and I wish that you would order those cosmic pygmies to remove the whining flutes from their amorphous mouths, for I do not like the way their din conjures forth a cloud of odd black sigils in the sky. But now I see that the feathery cloud is actually a congeries of traumatized bird cadavers, broken things bent into esoteric shapes the meaning of which I cannot decipher. Their lifeless beaks all point to you, thing of Egypt, and their black forms, silhouetted against the mauve sky, remind me of a text I once glimpsed in the dreaded *Necronomicon*. What is it they would summon, Crawling Chaos, if one could decode and utter their language?"

Yet he, silent and lean and cryptically proud, did not deign to reply. He stepped past me, dropping the peculiar mask and moving smoothly forward as the ebony beasts that followed licked his hands. He raised one palm to the calm sky, moving his fingers until sparks flew from them into the aether. I watched as those flying sparks blossomed with ignition and formed a mad aurora—orange and green and pink and yellow—the hysterical movement of which I felt upon my queerly pale and colorless eyes. I stalked after the thing of antique Egypt and wondered why his crimson attire reminded one of the flow of bloodstain. My pale eyes watched, as his hand lifted once more to the sky, where the display of color darkened as heavy storm cloud in which his electric light-show flashed as streaks of fire. I felt waves of chilly heat rush to me, and inspired by a touch of madness I wound my hands into my raven hair and sank nails into my scalp. I lifted my face to the cloud that followed us, that cloud that was a conglomeration of tortured fowl cadavers from which, now and then, feathers loosened and sank toward the earth. I was thankful, when the heavy rain began to fall, for the tunnel of twisted wood we entered, where low prodigious oaks locked boughs above us, where our way was lighted by the phosphorescence of strange fungi with which those boughs were spotted. Oh, I was thankful for the dusky shadows of the place, for they tainted my eyes and cooled my brain, dispelling entirely the lingering traces of the mad auroras that had colored my liquid orbs. I almost smiled when we came to the clearing and I viewed the ascending flight of seven hundred steps that led to a realm of reality from which I had always been excluded, of which I had learned from the wizard who raised me and had studied deeply of the Seven Cryptical Books of Hsan. I wondered who the melancholy dreamer was that sat upon those steps and held a flute to his mournful mouth with one hand, while his other hand made curious movement to the daemon out of Egypt.

The thing of Egypt ceased his movement and waved away the following beasts, those panthers that hung their heads and vanished into the blackness of the surrounding woodland. I noticed the unusually large upright mirror that had tipped over and reclined on the ground, looking like some frozen pool encased within a frame of white gold. The moon-eyed dreamer's music altered, took on an explicitly somber sound, as the thing of Egypt advanced toward the fallen mirror and stepped onto its polished glass. He smiled at me, looking so like a handsome young pharaoh, and his scarlet robe melted from him, revealing the perfection of his form. Naked, he sank into the shadowed mirror, and I fell onto my knees so as to touch the eerie earth, to claw at it and lift its particles to my face, into which I rubbed the aromatic substance. Specks of sod blurred my eyesight, and so I could not clearly see the one who lifted out of the shadowed mirror, who stepped over the frame of white gold and towered above me. I rubbed my eyes and looked again, took in the half-naked figure in its yellow skirt, the figure that held an Egyptian scale with an ostrich feature in one pan. I took in the muscular body, the bronze flesh, the sable head of a jackal with pointed snout and ears.

I rose, and when I spoke my words were accompanied by the somber music of the dreamer who sat upon the steps. "Ah, thing of Egypt," I uttered. "You come to judge my worth. And yet, how can you comprehend my nature? I exist in an Underworld, yet one that is completely different from your own. My world is a place beyond Time, in a dimension between the landscapes of Reality and Dream. You crawled as Chaos into my world, you trick of Egypt, you thing of Cosmic Void. Like me, you do not belong to any sane or solid place. We are the vagabonds between the worlds, wandering those places where we can never know firm foothold. You crawled to me, thing of Egypt, and intrigued me with your corruption, and I followed you here, to this woodland between the dreamworld and the territory of humankind. How, then, can you pretend to understand my ways, or to judge me by any means? Nonetheless, I will engage in your curious ritual, because you beguile me in ways I cannot understand. There, I split my vestment and expose my breast. Rip your talons through my hide and steal my heart, poor thing that it is. Take it, Anapa (or shall I name thee Nyarlathotep?), and place it is the empty pan of your bronze scale. Ah, see, see! My moist pink heart is lighter than your ostrich feather, and thus it is not meant to be devoured. But how could it not be weightless, a heart that is so hollow? Watch me now, as I reach for that sepia feather and hurl it skyward, to that cluster of bird cadavers that coil as cloud of death above us. Behold, I take up my little heart, poor thing that subtly pulses with a remnant of mortality. I take it up and touch it to your snout, so that you may savor its carnal aroma. I offer it to you, jackal of Hell. Consume it, let it slink down your throat and nestle in your heaving breast, so that you may know, fleetingly, what it means to have a heart. Ah, you shudder so violently that you have lost your jackal masque. Your shifting visage begins to lose its features as you reveal your true semblance. Yet I see it form, Faceless God, that darker void where a human mouth might have existed. I see it stretch in lunacy, that crazy cavity, and I accompany the madness of the lunatic baying that vomits from it!"

The Tomb of Oscar Wilde

And alien tears will fill for him
Pity's long-broken urn,
For his mourners will be outcast men,
And outcasts always mourn.

—OSCAR WILDE

W hy did you bring me here?" I muttered, looking away from the grotesque defacement. "I find the sight exceedingly depressing. Please, let us flee."

But the poetess who signs herself "Celaeno" merely laughed at what she saw as my dramatics. "Don't be absurd, Yakov. What you condemn as disfigurement are the authentic love tokens of countless admirers."

"To mar a poet's grave with graffiti is the opposite of admirable. How many of the fools who have pressed their painted lips against this tomb have ever read 'The Sphinx' or 'The Harlot's House'? Or"—and I pointed a long finger at her—"'The Grave of Keats'? If they want to pay homage to Wilde let them write a poem. But to blemish his tomb in such a manner! I had heard about these ugly lipstick stains, but I had no idea there was such a plethora of them. They have marred this sacred place with their Judas mouths and killed the thing they love. Away, away!" But my companion merely smiled and hummed a snatch of Chopin's somber Prelude No. 24. "Anyway, we shouldn't be here at this ghastly hour, and the last thing I need is to be arrested for entering this place past closing. How you knew about that other gate and the way in which to open it is a mystery I do not wish to think on. No, let us go, Rochel."

"But there's so much more to see. Let's go whistle at Chopin's tomb after we have conjured some magick here." She raised the portions of her black gown that fell from her shoulders toward the earth, looking very much like a winged and mythic beast. I was not enchanted. Some winged thing soared above us in the Parisian sky.

"Conjure? No, no—I do not wish to commune with the poet except through the alchemy of his pages. No specters need apply. I need none of your outlandish witchery in this place. Oscar's poetry is sorcery enough."

She pointed herself, to the sky. "It's Rosh Chodesh, Yakov."

I followed her pointing digit and glanced at the sliver of moon. "I fail to see the significance."

"Do you remember Wilde's 'La Fuite de la Lune'?" Without waiting for my response, she began to sing the opening quatrain as it was set to music by the American composer, Charles Griffes:

> "To outer senses there is peace,
> A dreamy peace on either hand,
> Deep silence in the shadowy land,
> Deep silence where the shadows cease."

As though conjured by her song, a chill crept into the evening air, and a curtain of cloud covered the moon momentarily. The modernist angel on Wilde's tomb became a darker creature, seeming now like some somber sphinx that might at any moment whisper unfathomable riddle. I stood in the deep silence of a shadow-land, where the memory of wilted lives wafted to me on a gentle breeze. Queerly obsessed, a memory of Wilde filtered once more to mind, and I whispered a snatch of his verse: "A beautiful and silent Sphinx has watched me through the shifting gloom." As soon as my line was uttered the clouds melted from before the moon and my eyes were kissed by starlight. "Did you not write you own lines in memory of Wilde?" I queried, my face still lifted to the sky.

"My song, imprisoned in this cave, my skull,
Cannot be uttered by this clumsy mouth;
My lips are thus consumed by poet's drouth,
My song becomes a hymn unuttered, null.
And so I sing with gleam of liquid eye,
A prayer unuttered to the silver moon
As liquid spills from lips of one dull loon
Who aches to warble poesy to the sky.
My mouth is clamped, but now my soul will glide
To ancient moon as ache of silent hymn
In which I pay homage, however grim,
To one whose graceful language never died.
Dear Oscar, take my song as silent token.
It is my gift, however frail and broken."

She finished reciting, glanced at me and shrugged. "Nu, it's rather poor, I know. Someday I'll polish and let it see print—maybe."

I shrugged and smiled, then looked again at the mammoth tomb before us. A faint ache to whisper Kaddish came over me, however lacking I was of a Minyan. I remembered that this was Rosh Chodesh, the minor holiday of the New Moon. And that made me think of Oscar, who had been condemned to oblivion in his final years of mortality; yet like the moon Wilde returned and grew to fullness, so that now he shines in eternal opalescence through the magick of his works and the tragedy of his story. And so I whispered a portion of prayer in Hebrew, which in English would be something like, "You have given to Your People the celebration of New Months, a time for Atonement for all their generations."

Rochel snorted. "Kaphar?" she pronounced in Hebrew. "What, you'd have Wilde repent? Feh. This poet deserves prayer to darker deity. How about this?"

I frowned as she began to recite her hymn to darkness, and yet I could not but marvel at how her small mouth pronounced the arcane language so perfectly.

"Y'ai, Shub-Niggurath! Y'gai h'yeh Aklo shoggoth! Ygnaiih . . . ygnaii . . . Shub-Niggurath!"

Darkness spilled into the sky once more, and wind arose. I watched as the lengthy sections of Rochel's long gown spread behind her like daemonic wings as her hawk-like visage leered at me in moving shadow, and I remembered why she had adopted her pen-name. She continued mouthing the obnoxious language, but now she combined it with Hebrew from a prayer with which I was unfamiliar. The monstrous sound withered my soul and froze my streaming blood.

"My heart!" I groaned. "You have emaciated it with your diabolic art. It withers still, and will soon be a thing of naught. I will wander the earth as heartless fiend, sans passion and poetry. Oh, oh!"

The witch laughed and drifted from my side, to the tomb against which she pressed her mouth among the horrid lipstick stains. I wanted to curse her, but my limbs failed me and I fell to the ground as nameless outlines cavorted in the haunted sky and extinguished starlight. A thing of monstrous mist began to boil in the gulf of night, and I had no doubt that this was the "deity" that Rochel had called with her unholy art. Enfolded by gloom, I dug my nails into the dirt near Oscar's tomb. I saw his engraved name, obscurely, on the stone, defaced by the horrid red smears of lipstick, the animals fats of which caused havoc to the monument's stone and would cause irreparable damage. Gasping, I wept the poet's name.

The air had been tainted with a grotesque stench, a goat-like smell that fell to us from the cloud-like entity that Rochel had conjured in the sky. But now I sensed another fragrance lifted as perfume from the sod on which I knelt. With it another thing arose, a pale round luminescence that seeped upward before the poet's tomb. I watched it shape itself into a semblance that was familiar and reminded me of Beardsley's irreverent illustration, "The Woman in the Moon." Reverently, I removed my clothing and struggled to my feet as nude acolyte to the poet I so adored. His spectral form took on a semi-mortal semblance, and I watched him wink at my companion and then lift his large face to the daemon in the sky. Pursing his lips, the prince of poetry exhaled sublime speech, the poetry of the ages. This magnificent and potent art penetrated the cosmic tempest and swept the paltry daemon from our view. Rochel fondled the jeweled tassel that dangled from the length of pearls around her pretty neck, and although her stance was defiant I could see the wonder that smoldered in the depths of her cloudy eyes as her alchemy was usurped by the Lord of Language.

Naked and heartless, I shuddered. Yet, although I lacked a beating organ in my breast, I still owned memory and mouth. My lips split and I heaved poesy.

"Then turning to my love I said,
'The dead are dancing with the dead,
The dust is whirling with the dust.'"

The poet gazed at me with star-like eyes, and I lifted my arms to him, reeling like a thing composed of mortal debris that might fall apart at his touch. But, oh, his caress was gentle! We danced among the dust of earth to a soft vibration that I seemed to recognize. I knew, at last, that it was the beating of the poet's eternal heart, and the sound of it brought tears to my eyes. He laughed and pressed his ghostly mouth to mine, and then he blew upon my liquid eyes as his hand rested against my breast. Momentarily, he frowned, not sensing the vibration he thought to experience from my chest. His gazing orbs seemed to read the misery of mine own, and thus he moved away a little and reached through his incorporeal frame. When his hand emerged I beheld the solid thing it held—his pulsating heart, which he offered me as gift of sacrifice. I took hold of the warm wet thing that seemed drenched with blood and martyr's tears. I held it to the waxing crescent of the moon, on this holiday of Rosh Chodesh that marks new beginning. I looked at Rochel, who was muttering to herself in Hebrew, and I winked at the sudden tears that had gathered in her eyes. Finally, I swallowed whole the poet's heart and laughed musically as it took root.

These Harpies of Carcosa

I smiled at the canvas on the wall, and felt the shadow of its artist at my left. "It's interesting, isn't it?" I told the fellow without turning to him, not wanting to take my eyes from his painting. "I've never known buildings to look so—tattered. The city itself oozes of self-extinction, although how a city could commit suicide is a perplexing puzzle. There is not a trace of life, except for the two sirens in the sky; and yet they look so fantastic that one guesses that they may be mere figments of twisted dreaming. Look how they hang there in the air, horribly illuminated by the lifeless light of the twin porphyry moons, those globes of ghastly reddish-purple rock. Finally, our eyes take in the figure in its yellow robe, with its pallid artificial face and arms outstretched. I cannot comprehend why his hands should be so crimson."

I turned my head slightly and looked at the artist; and although his eyes were fixed onto his creation, I knew that he listened to my language. "Now," I continued, "there is one minute glimmer of natural light, and yet it emanates from an artificial relic. Do you see it, there, in the corner of the canvas, like something dropped onto the road, forgotten and forsaken? Yes, the brass crown with its synthetic jewels. One feels that it sits in proxy for something more authentic. And that long knife sitting beside it looks so nasty, doesn't it, like some implement designed exclusively for mayhem? It all makes one shiver and wish for movement, for some shifting of starlight or some song of wind. But those obsidian stars in the painted sky do not crawl, of that I am certain; and the air of that deserted city, one knows, is dead and still. And yet—and yet, how *captivating* it seems, this painted image,

27

how it tugs at the brain and makes one wonder how it would feel to weep beneath those black stars, to inhale the lifeless air. However did the artist come up with such an image, one wonders?"

"It's from a play," my companion finally spoke.

"Indeed? And where would one find this play?"

He did not hesitate in his reply, and yet he spoke as one who had lost his way in reality. "I read it in a dream. I read it aloud, and the dream took on solidity. I could hear the waves of the lake breaking on the shore, and when the wind arose I could hear the flapping of the tatters of the King, that flapping that should never be sounded. They had such a strange rhythm, and I tried to sing in accompaniment; but my mouth was dry and my voice was dead, like the lost city that festered all around me. God, the *hard* light of those twin moons, burning their essence onto my eyes! And when I finally awakened, I could still feel that acidic impression on my eyes; and the world looks weird, and its inhabitants look like puppets." He then turned to me, smiled, and chuckled. "Sounds completely kookoo, I confess."

I shrugged and returned my attention to his creation. "The fantastic artist sees the world in singular ways, divorced as he is from the dull world of dreary reality. How far more creative and captivating, to live within a dream."

He turned his gaze again toward the painting. "I really *would* prefer to live there, godless region though it may be. I wouldn't have to pretend all the time. So you like this?" He motioned to the canvas.

"Oh, yes," I assured him, "for I long to live there myself." Bowing to him, I walked to the door and exited the gallery. The sun was beginning to set, and the sky was a gorgeous bouquet of color. I stood there and admired the mixture of gold and mauve and amber, and I felt his shadow blend into my own.

"Are you an artist?" he asked.

"I exist within a realm of Art," was my esoteric response. We walked away from the city, toward the hill that rose before us. It was early spring, and the trees that lined the lane were sweet of fragrance and delicate upon the eye. We had almost reached the apex of the hill when we encountered the murdered thing. The artist knelt before the feline corpse and studied it for a little while as the sun continued sinking; and then he removed the long knife from the cadaver and wiped its blade on a patch of clean grass. How deftly he handled the implement. Rising, he held the knife with hands that were clasped together as if in prayer.

We stood atop the hill and watched the death of day. He shut his eyes for a moment, and then he flinched as his body began to tilt. He smiled sheepishly. "Sorry. I'm feeling a bit faint."

"When was your last meal? Your face looks haggard with hunger."

He shrugged. "I'm an artist."

Reaching into my pocket, I took out a folded piece of paper. "I don't have any money on hand, but perhaps this will aid you."

Putting the knife under his arm, he took the paper and unfolded it. I do not think he understood the Yellow Sign traced on the paper. Folding it again, he placed it in his bosom. The moon rose within the darkening sky, and we noticed the distant artifact that reflected the lunar light. "Ah," I sighed, "it's your brass crown. How golden it looks in this unearthly light." We walked to it, and he bent to pick it up. "Yes," I continued, nodding my head, "it is quite golden, and its diamonds are authentic. Will you don it, the golden diadem?"

How near the white moon seemed to the hill on which we stood. Its dull light shimmered on the crown as he lifted it above him and then placed it on his head. The leaves in one nearest tree began to rustle in the rising wind, and the branches of that tree began to sway. I could not help but warble.

> "Atop the hill he makes his stand,
> In wind that sings a saraband,
> And we uncover
> Lost Carcosa.

> "There are no stars on this strange night,
> Just one strange moon that sheds its light
> Upon our dream of
> Lost Carcosa.

> "See how the moon divides its sphere
> Into twin globes that mock and leer
> Above the streets of
> Lost Carcosa.
>
> "Ah, double globes, grotesque, divine,
> Evoke the ageless Yellow Sign,
> Return of hearts to
> Lost Carcosa."

I moved in little steps to the music of the wind and clapped my hands as he removed the long knife from under his arm and held it before him. Reaching into my bosom, I removed what was folded just above my heart and held it before him, winking. He watched as I unfolded the pallid mask and fastened it to my face. I think he shuddered just a little as the moon began to darken and divide. I watched the division of those spheres and listened to the sound of their wings unfolding. He turned at last to face them.

"They come to adore you, these sirens of suicide. They come to take ye home. You hold the key. Will you plunge it into place?"

I danced toward him and hummed a little song, unable to contain my joy. His length of hair moved in the wind aroused by daemonic wings, and his mouth began to hum in accompaniment to my noise. Lowering his eyelids, he raised the knife and thrust it into his throat. Shouting in ecstasy, I moved to him and caught his flow of blood with greedy hands. Somehow he refused to fall. I stretched out my arms and offered my wet red palms to the creatures of nightmare, and laughed as they floated to me and kissed my offering. Their attention was then caught by the wobbling of his body. Licking their moistened mouths, they flocked to him and caught him by each arm. Bending, I picked up the fallen knife and raised it to their nebulous forms, as they conjoined once more into one solid sphere.

An Ecstasy of Fear

I.

Sarah Paget-Lowe stepped off the train and into fog, a miasma so thick she could not see the majority of the small train depot. She stood and shivered in the chilly air, and then looked up at the sound of beating wings. A hazy shadow drifted over her, the outline of some large winged thing. Looking at the copy of Christina Rossetti's *Goblin Market* that she held, and that she had read during portions of her long journey, she smiled bemusedly. The thin book had dark green boards and its text was illustrated with color reproductions of artwork by the author's elder brother, Dante. Had her choice of the book been a kind of presage, indicating what she could expect in this unfamiliar setting? Two figures approached her from different directions, and she waved a hand to the porter who carried her bags. Then she turned and named the young poet, Akiva Loveman, as he floated to her through the mist.

"I apologize for the fog—it's quite unwarranted; usually our weather is fair and fine. Are these your bags?"

Sarah answered in the affirmative as the train pulled away and disappeared into the brumous cloud that had settled over the valley. She then followed her friend onto a dirt road and to the place where his car was parked. Her mouth curved at the sight of that vehicle. "This is yours, this beautiful relic?"

"Yes, it's a 1928 Model A Ford Sedan. A local fellow sold it to me after I first moved to Sesqua Town. It runs perfectly well. I had new upholstery put in, but otherwise it's mostly original." She watched as he placed her luggage into the back seat of the car. Then he slammed shut the door, turned to face her and held out his hands. "Welcome to Sesqua Valley. I imagine you're exhausted."

"I've never traveled so far by rail. It was a long journey, and I am a little tired."

Escorting her to the passenger side of the car, he opened the door and stepped aside as she bent to enter the vehicle. "I have some nice stew and home-made bread awaiting you, and then you can have a quick bath and sleep as long as you like."

Sarah moaned in pleasure and sank into the soft leather of her seat, trying to fight the temptation to shut her eyes during the brief trip from the depot to Akiva's small house, into which she followed him as he carried her baggage from the car. She laughed, dismayed, as she scanned the cluttered living room in which they stood. "I thought gay men were neat and tidy by instinct. Good lord, Akiva, this place is chaotic! And what on earth is *that?*"

Akiva followed the direction of his guest's stare. "Ah." He walked to the statue and bent to the altar he had built before it. She watched as two squat black candles were lit, and then the poet ignited a stick of incense. He did not turn to regard her as he spoke. "Do you know the work of Bernard Buffet? He was a French painter linked to Expressionism, and illustrated editions of Cocteau's *La Voix Humaine* and Lautréamont's *Les Chants de Maldoror*. There's a rather wonderful print he did of Dante, and when I first saw this statue I thought perhaps it was an effigy of the poet in the Buffet tradition, mistaking the spikes atop the dome for an exaggerated laurel wreath. Since then I've discovered a rumored legend of a dark god of chaos, who is said to wear a triple crown. Little is known of this supernatural being, although its myths are multitudinous, and its aspects are so varied that it has been said to be a kind of shape-shifter. Artists have often depicted it as a haughty pharaoh of elder Egypt."

Slowly he turned to smile at Sarah. "And you now think this is a representation of that deity?"

The poet laughed lightly. "I call it the Nameless Eikon. I burn incense and speak poetry in its honor. But I do not know his name."

"'His'? The attire, as it has been sculpted, seems genderless."

"Men in ancient Egypt sometimes wore long clothing far more elaborate than what women wore. I usually address him as male because the chap I purchased him from did so as well, and he seemed to be an authority on the figure. Well, he hinted of the myths that whisper the legend of the thing. And isn't there something about statues that have their palms facing forward, as this one does? I think I read that somewhere. That strikes me as a compelling gesture, for some reason—as if the thing is waiting for us to kneel before it and kiss the hand that is held aloft. I found it in a local antique shop and purchased it for a goodly sum. It gives the room such a splendid atmosphere, I find."

"I hope you're not being reckless with your inheritance."

"No—no; not that two million is a lot these days. And since finding this hidden spot, my wants are inexpensive. I spend most of my fortune on rare first editions. I do a lot of traveling to bookshops around the country. It's an extremely pleasant existence."

She began to move about the room, walking to a tall oak bookcase that did indeed seem crammed with rare old books. "I'd get lonely for the city."

"You wouldn't if you lived here. It's a fascinating little town. I'm so glad you accepted my invitation." He walked to where he had set down her luggage and picked up her bags again. "Come on, I'll show you your room. I almost never sleep in there. I've turned the smaller bedroom into a kind of office and library area, and I spend so much of my time there that I've installed a little cot."

Sarah followed Akiva into a spacious bedroom. She admired the beautiful antique furniture that gave the lie to his statement about spending his fortune mostly on rare books. "This is delightful, it has a fine feminine air about it. You have a woman's way, my dear." He grimaced at her, although she ascertained that he was, in part, pleased with her praise. Walking to the window, she gazed out of it and frowned. "The fog has yet to lift."

"Have you any appetite? Come on, let's have a bit of food and wine, and then you can bathe and retire. You look travel-worn."

"I can eat a small portion, and a glass of wine would be lovely. I'll bathe in the morning. That bed looks so damn comfortable that I want to sink into it now."

They retired to the small kitchen and she allowed him to serve her a small bowl of stew and a plate of bread that was still warm from the oven, on which she spread delicious garlic butter. As they shared their repast, she studied the young man before her, and he smiled at her investigating eyes. "Do I meet with approval?"

"You've aged." He frowned in response. "Rather, you've matured. You still resemble a very young Rudolph Valentino, albeit with larger ears. Your sleek black hair quite shines, and your profile has never seemed so handsome. I think it's your eyes that have changed—they've lost their juvenile frivolity. They've darkened with experience. This bread is delicious."

He grinned at her change of topic as they sipped the last of their wine in silence, and then she rose from the table and returned to the living room, the aura of which caught her curiosity. Akiva followed her and seemed suddenly anxious. "Do you really find me so changed? Am I not as charming as I used to be?" She turned to him and saw a flicker of his former adolescence, his uncertainty and need to be liked. Walking around the room, she studied the various figurines, the *objets d'art,* the peculiar paintings on the walls.

"You've developed a taste for the macabre."

He shrugged. "I've always had it. It's become more acute since coming here."

"You've been here half a year? How long do you plan to stay?"

"Indefinitely."

"But what's here that holds you?" He shrugged again, yet she thought his eyes were cautious, as if he knew secrets that he could not yet share with her. That was another new element in his personality, for he had been so garrulous with her in the past, sharing his ideas and passions and miseries without hesitation. Suddenly weary, she yawned; and then she went to him and kissed his brow before retiring to her room. It was in the bedroom that she sensed the lad Akiva used to be: here were the shelves crammed with Penguin Classics paperbacks, of which he had been so fond, and here the walls wore paintings that depicted scenes from Shakespeare and Dante and Milton. The atmosphere of the room seemed lighter than that of the living room, where his new and darker nature seemed to lurk. Stepping to a window, she looked out and saw nothing but thick mist. Not bothering to close its curtains, she walked away from the window and went to where her bags had been placed.

Sarah undressed and got into bed, resting her reading glasses on the bedside table next to its ornate antique lamp. Just as she was about to switch off the lamp, Akiva appeared at her door. Quietly, he entered the room and sat next to her on the bed. "This is my newest work," he whispered, handing her a notebook. "It's still very rough, but I thought it might interest you. No, don't look them over now, you're sleepy. Wait for the morning, when you'll be rested and attentive."

"My dear child, you cannot give me this and not expect me to glance at it before retiring. Now, go and close the door. I'm in need of silence and solitude."

He took her hand and kissed it, and then he vacated the room. Reaching for her glasses, Sarah donned them and opened the notebook. Akiva's admirable hand had written out the lines of poetry in violet ink, the same shade with which he penned his correspondence. Sarah glanced at the first two poems, which were his usual kind of sonnet, the form he liked best. They were admirable poems of praise that paid tribute to the beauty of Sesqua Valley, one of which sang of a twin-peaked mountain of white stone that seemed to stand as emblem of the region's unique nature. She then turned the leaf and came upon the curious thing. She read it twice, her forehead furrowed.

"Out of the depths of dreaming came
The antique thing that called my name.
It shook me from my placid rest,
Commanding me to kiss its breast.
My mouth pressed to its marble hide.
New longing was not satisfied.
The pale thing called me brother, said,
'I am the Dreaming and the Dead,

Fallen from distant vortices,
From whirling far-off galaxies,
Past dying suns and chilly stars.
I come to kiss thy psychic scars.'
Looking down I was perplexed
To see the beast was double-sexed.
'Kiss me there,' it spoke to me,
'And penetrate my mystery.'
I did not heed its queer command;
Instead I took its pale hooked hand
And with its talons pierced my eyes.
Through blood and tears I scanned the skies.
I saw the crawling stars that named
Me as their own. Thus I am claimed."

This was like nothing he had written before, and although it was too strange to be understood, its imagery whirled within her skull. Sarah set the notebook onto the wooden floor and shut her eyes. When the pale antique thing crept to her from its secret lair, she struggled mentally to awaken. Instead, she felt the hooked hands that pressed her mouth unto a marbled breast.

II.

Soft light filtered through morning mist and illuminated the valley. Sarah lifted her face to it and shut her eyes, letting the texture of her skin drink in the subtle warmth. This was a nice alternative to the dark troubled dreaming she had experienced during the night. She inhaled the fragrant air of Sesqua Valley as her toes, curling, pushed into yielding earth. The air, as Sarah sucked it in, tasted sweet, almost cloying, as if composed of elements that were of a different nature from that with which she was familiar. As she scanned the surrounding sights, it felt almost as if she had entered into a fairyland. The place was so different from Providence, had such a singular atmosphere. There was an impression of agelessness in the region, and to have entered it was to fancy that one had stepped out of time, stepped into some province that was unspoiled by modernity, although it contained aspects of human dwelling. But even that seemed odd to her: each dwelling that she had looked upon possessed its own bizarre personality, its own peculiarity of design.

Sarah stared past the woodland, to the distant twin-peaked mountain. The stone of which the mountain was composed sparkled in the soft morning light. Like everything else in the valley, this titan of white rock contained its own distinct and curious personality. The tall twin peaks resembled arched pointed wings that sprouted from daemonic shoulders. To fix one's eyes on the mountain was to feel that it could rise at any moment and stalk toward one, crushing one's puny shell of flesh and bones beneath a mammoth hoof. As she gazed at it some shapeless blurred thing, black and winged, rose from it and then descended into the mist that covered much of the woodland.

A hand touched her shoulder. Sarah looked at Akiva and returned his smile. "Enchanted by our local beauty?"

"That is exactly right. Utterly mesmerized. I've never seen so many trees. It's a wonderland of beauty. You're up early."

"I have a new thing I'm anxious to continue working on."

She nodded. "I dipped into your recent work. It's rather odd. It has a quality that I can only describe as 'sinister.' Why does that make you smile so broadly?"

"Because I call these new things the work of my left hand. Living here, in Sesqua Valley, has had an effect on my imagination. I dream differently. Instead of the human noise that I had grown so used to in the city, I now listen to the whisperings of nature, its secret sounds. New sensations have resulted in new poetic visions, an innovative form of expression. Coming here has invigorated me as an artist. I thought, perhaps, it may have a similar effect on you."

The woman laughed lightly. "Ah, because of my taking a break in writing. You think I need a little kick in the aesthetic derrière. No, no. The truth is, I've been much too active, especially since Wilus died. I had no idea that he, too, had a heart condition, he never told any of us. He was my senior by half a year, and when he suddenly died at home I took it as a sign that I would be next. Foolish and melodramatic, I know, but there you are. It's surprised you, my having two books published this year; I've always made it a habit to wait a year or two before writing a new book. What you don't know is that I have three more completed books awaiting publication. Hopefully only two of them will be published next year. I went through a phase of mad productivity, because I thought I would be dead by the end of this year and I didn't want to die without having added significantly to my oeuvre." She looked at him and shrugged. "My doctors tell me that my heart is on the mend. I have thus slowed down, stopped writing. Now I can delve into other things, I can travel a bit if I feel up to it. Best of all, I can be lazy and relax. There you have it."

"Excellent. All I knew was that you told me you had stopped writing for a while, and that distressed me. I invited you here to give you a taste of the inspiration that has recharged my creativity, hoping it could do the same for you. I still hold on to that hope. Sesqua Valley will inspire you in ways that are new and novel."

Sarah shrugged. "I have no intention of doing any work here—or anywhere, for at least two years. But, yes, new inspiration, a new approach—that would be most welcome. I would like the next book I write to be absolutely unique."

"Your work has been so urbane—to the point where you've been described as a female Henry James, the writer who has inspired you the most. You have a knack for outré characters, but your settings lack imagination. I think that the valley will aid your facility for distinctive characterization, giving you a different background in which to drop your freaks and fools." Akiva turned away from her and looked down the road toward the main section of Sesqua Town. "My friend has a charming café that serves the finest French toast I have ever tasted. Let's go." He linked his arm with hers and led her down the dirt road, to the main business section of town. They spent an hour at breakfast, and then Sarah said she wanted to investigate the area.

"If it's going to inspire new work, I need to take it all in and drink the ambiance. I confess I find this little area charming, like something from a 1950s movie set. This town wears an aspect of unreality. Its inhabitants dress in a simple way that is neither modern nor outdated.

I've seen but two cars, both of which are of olden models. The quietude is like nothing I've known—where are the birds? Come, Akiva, show me this remarkable setting."

The poet led her away from the café and onto the sidewalks that were composed of planks of sturdy wood. Sarah drank in the rustic aura of the town as Akiva, in his low voice, spoke of various venerable homes and their inhabitants. Some of the Victorian-seeming dwellings would have fitted perfectly in Providence, for which she was becoming just a little homesick.

"You're frowning," her friend informed her.

She glanced around her before she answered, her eyes catching sight of the twin-peaked mountain. When she looked at him and tried to laugh, her noise was not successful. "I feel as though I've wandered into some alien realm wherein I am unwanted. The beauty of the place is fantastic—and yet one feels guilty soaking it in. To gaze too long a time at that white mountain makes me feel positively sinful, and I ache for my eyes to sink deeper into their sockets in escape. I'm not supposed to be here."

"I remember feeling exactly the same, especially when I began to meet the locals." He paused, as if trying to decide how much he wanted to confess. "You don't want to keep peering at the mountain—it doesn't like to be scrutinized."

She did not heed his mystifying advice. "It looks like some strange slumbering beast. Those incredible arched peaks—they could be wings on a daemon's back, ready to spread and lift the creature into the air. Whatever brought you to this place, Akiva?"

"A book of poems. A rare secret book that outsiders like me were never meant to see. And yet, I don't feel like an outsider any longer, and I'm happy to be here. I've discovered things here that sing to me and seduce me into staying. She is such a one."

Sarah's eyes followed the direction of his hand, and then her eyes grew wide. Across the road, bathing in the morning sunlight, was a magnificent sphinx. Captivated, the woman crossed the road and stood before the gigantic statue, and then she heard Akiva breathing beside her. "No—it's not Greek, as you can tell from the headdress. Too, there are neither wings nor breasts. This is a child of Egypt, where such figures are usually male. The face is amazingly androgynous, however, so you may be excused for thinking it female." She moved so as to look beyond the sculpture, past a low stone wall and into a spreading cemetery, wherein she espied a number of unusual monuments. Akiva's hand stopped her as she began to move toward the area.

"I'll show you the Hungry Place tonight—in moonlight."

"The Hungry Place?"

He held up a hand and nodded, as if to say that all would be explained eventually. "Come, let's wander in the woods. You'll find it charming."

He linked his arm to hers and led the woman away from town, toward the wide expanse of woodland; yet as they approached the area she felt that it would prove impenetrable, unwelcoming. The trees were too unnerving, twisted and ominous; the spaces between those trees were dark and foreboding, and although she espied no creatures in those spaces she felt that they were the haunts of hidden imps. The poet seemed to sense her hesitation and turned to smile at her; he laughed lightly at the expression on her face and then brought her hand to his mouth and kissed it. But she did not like the shape of his lips as they curled in mirth: his expression seemed curiously cunning. He was, she reflected, the author of the weird verse that she had read the previous evening, a tainted soul, strange and perplexing. She knew that he had altered, that his brain had somehow been bent by the influence of Sesqua Valley and her secret ways. But then the idea of her fear, her absurd sense of danger, caused her to chuckle as well. They made no sense, these new apprehensions, these confusions. She really was in need of a rest.

Darkness swallowed them, as they found a pathway that twisted through the woodland. The foreboding atmosphere dissipated. Immediately, Sarah's sense of unease was erased. The shade of the place felt soothing on her eyes as she stepped on ground that was cushioned with leaves and soft mossy earth. The air sucked in had altered and was no longer cloying but refreshing and minty in taste. Somehow, light of a kind fell onto various places, dimly illuminating the woodland and making it easier for her to take in her surroundings. She could not feel a breeze moving through the place, and yet the trees sometimes moved, subtly, as if touched by gust. Black boulders of remarkable size and shape were everywhere, and at one point she and her companion passed a deep ravine, at the bottom of which Sarah could espy a murky stream that reflected patches of fallen radiance.

A distant sound caught their notice, and Akiva ceased all movement. Although his face was encased in shadow, Sarah could sense his distress, and when she touched his arm it trembled beneath her hand. Her mouth parted as she prepared to ask him what it was he feared, but then the music grew in resonance. Eerily compelled, the woman moved away from her friend, toward the mysterious tone. She witnessed the place where blackness reeled, a whirlwind of gloom, within which odd harmony sounded. And then the spinning darkness fell before the figure that stood there, lowering as if to grovel at the creature's feet before melting entirely into the earth. Sarah watched the outline take on a more solid form as it removed something long and lean from its mouth. The only features that were clearly evident were two slanted eyes that shimmered as if composed of liquid mercury. As the figure began to drift toward her, Sarah was kissed by an uncanny thrill of fear such as she had never known, and yet she could not turn away and flee. She had been caught completely. Someone behind her wrapped their arms around her waist, but Akiva remained silent as the beast drew nearer and then stopped. Sarah's alarm sharpened as she experienced the entire trembling of her friend's body as he held her.

"Ah—Loveman, it's you. What curious expressions you both wear. Has something in our wooded realm disturbed you?"

"Yes, your piping. I've never heard anything quite like it. It was more than music—it was like some evocation of lost or secret things, and it aroused a kind of fear that such things might once again be located." She stopped, as if suddenly aware of her words. "Oh dear, what nonsense I'm talking!"

The tall man slipped his flute into an inside pocket of his jacket as Sarah took in his attire, which resembled that of another era. This fellow could have stepped out of the 1930s. His alchemical eyes had lost a little of their brilliance, and they now had to compete with the fantastic nature of his ensembled facial features. She had never met anyone so grotesque, with an ugliness that seemed, in a way, inhuman. Certain characteristics of his face seemed amphibian, but the general outline of the face reminded her of a deformed wolf. His voice was cultured and his enunciation crisp, as if language was something he relished and spoke carefully. Although his hair was mostly covered by a hat, she sensed that he wore it long, in the fashion of a young Oscar Wilde. He cocked his head and smiled at Sarah.

"*Au contraire.* Your words were quite applicable. You have been touched by our local sorcery. I will leave you so that you may revel in the wonder of it all. But don't loiter in the woods overlong, Loveman—at times it so affects your imagination. Your previous howling still echo in mine ears! *Au revoir.*" His smile lingered a few moments longer, and then he turned and nodded to Akiva as he ambled down the path and out of sight.

"That man is a freak. What on earth was he nattering about, your howls?" She turned to her friend, whose face was mostly eclipsed in shadow; but she could sense the fear that caused his eyes to tremble, the fear aroused by the creature they had just encountered. Sarah could not suppress a shudder. "I think I'd like to get out of here," she told her friend as the shadows of the area darkened around them. Taking hold of Sarah's hand, Akiva led her from the lonesome place.

III.

(From the journal of Sarah Paget-Lowe)

My memory has always been quite keen. However, since returning to Providence my reminiscence of those three weeks spent in Sesqua Valley are beginning to blur, to dim. It's as if the valley were trying to remove its images from my mind, to cloud my memory. That's why I've begun this journal of my recollections of my days spent with Akiva, who seems now to have forgotten that such a place as Sesqua Valley exists. Here's the weird thing: something in the nature of that valley and the secrets that it revealed to me seem to have touched my eyes with new perception. I have always found the antiquities of Providence charming. I love the sense of the past that one can feel here from walking down certain streets, no matter how modern the city has become. Now, however, my senses have been enhanced, and I am more and more aware of a different kind of aura here, something a bit sinister and covert. I have found pockets of the past that I never noticed before. Once, while sitting on a tabletop tomb in St. John's churchyard, I heard the wind arising and felt something grasp my hair and press against my ear as though it were some phantom mouth. Disquieting as the experience was, it also rather delighted me. Perhaps this is but one aspect of my new Muse, the thing that has inspired me to neglect the Jamesian novel I've been working on and spend my time writing some delightful horror tales. I read one of these new things to Herbert when he was visiting from New York, and he was riveted. "If you can write a book-full of these things, I'll publish them!" he exclaimed.

I have been followed by a denizen of the valley, I'm sure of it. I noticed it as I was wandering down Benefit Street and stopped to admire a small copse that rises beside an antique house. One small tree that was almost entirely concealed by tall bushes looked so odd that I continued staring at it for quite some time, and then I thought it wasn't a tree at all but something, some creature, disguised as a tree. I thought it was sunlight catching some bits of moss or whatever and illuminating the tiny patches of growth, but then I fancied that the two tiny spots of brilliance resembled a pair of silver eyes. I rushed away!

One of the things I want to make note of in this journal is the transformation of Akiva Loveman. He is such a brilliant poet, and yet he has always been so nonchalant about his work and its reception. His two collections of verse came about only because of my insistence and my showing his work to my publisher. Although those books garnered some very glowing reviews, they sold poorly, and it was shortly after the publication of the second book that Akiva suddenly vanished, not to be heard from until six months later, when he wrote to me from his new dwelling. He had learned that I had been feeling tired and listless and assumed that this was due to writer's block, when in fact I was simply burned out from having finished too many projects in too little a time. And so he invited me to visit him in what he called Sesqua Town and gave me instructions on how to reach the place by train. I hadn't traveled by train for three decades, and it was a pleasant (although overlong) experience. I had, of course, never corresponded with my friend, as we were both living in this beloved city until his sudden disappearance. Aspects of his letter were peculiar. He expressed himself in an unusual idiom, and at times I seemed to be reading a macabre prose-poem full of morbid hints and half-expressed emotions. He demanded that I tell no one of my destination and destroy his letter after having made my traveling arrangements. I did no such thing.

Akiva has changed, in ways I cannot understand. He has always seemed so reserved and serious, living for his art, his love of literature. A new characteristic revealed itself to me during my visit—a coy playfulness. I can best explain this by describing our visit to the Hungry Place, as he called the local graveyard. I've written up the experience as a wee horror story, so my description of it here may become over-literary and fictive in nature. But that's okay. I want to evoke precisely what happened and how it affected us.

My young friend has always been a collector of rare things, mostly fabulous editions of old books. After moving to Sesqua Valley, he began collecting other items, some of them quite curious. For example, he had, on his mantelpiece, a collection of small animal skulls, some of which were quite bizarre. He laughed when I suggested that some of the skulls were fakeries, however cleverly crafted. One thing that caught my attention was a beautiful antique lantern, which he said he had found in a place called Kingsport. It was my interest in the lantern that reminded him of something he wanted to show me.

"There's a mausoleum in the Hungry Place that I want to take you to. It will help you to experience the new ecstasy I feel for fantastic sensations, the stuff that feeds my current verse. It's a place that needs to be visited in moonlight, and the moon tonight is very fine. We'll take the lantern, for we'll need its assistance."

The lantern was on a small cedar table next to the intriguing black statue, and it was before that statue that Akiva made a very bizarre motion. I have said that one of the statue's hands was held away from its body, palm outward. As I watched him, Akiva stood before the statue and began to mutter strange words in a language I did not recognize, although portions of the words seemed Semitic. I was astonished, because I knew that he had forsaken completely his racial and religious heritage. He then touched his fingers to the upraised palm of the black statue, as a Hebrew might touch the casing that holds a mezuzah parchment, and brought those fingers to his lips. Apparently my astonishment was evident, for he turned to gaze at me with playful wickedness shining in his eyes, and then he brought his fingers to my mouth. My kiss was a tender thing.

"Let's go," he told me, grabbing a jacket and leading me outdoors.

We walked beneath the moon and stars, which seemed intimately near in the sky above Sesqua Valley. I noticed, as we walked, how relaxed my friend was, with such a mellow expression on his face. Whatever it was that had drawn him to that mysterious valley, his dwelling there had had an advantageous effect; of that there was no doubt. At one point he began to whistle as he guided me down the dirt road toward town. It was a lengthy walk, and I wondered why he didn't use his car more often, as he had when he picked me up from the train depot. But I had seen very few cars on the roadways, most people preferring to walk instead. The lack of vehicles added to the quietude of the place, which was striking to a city lass.

After a length of time I espied the large Sphinx statue in the distance, looking eerie in moonlight. I was touched, as we passed the statue, with a sense of mild foreboding, feeling as though the sculpted beast had been awaiting and was now observing us as we passed it on our way to the walled cemetery.

What strange apprehension I suddenly feel as I prepare to record this memory. So much of my time spent in Sesqua Valley is fading away, and when I try to remember things all I see in my mind is a kind of haze, a mauve mist. But this one midnight stroll is keen and clear, to the point where I can almost taste the fear it arouses. I remember thinking that the moon had never seemed so near to our planet and that I saw that sphere of dust as never before. The cosmos seemed but a little skip away, as if I could jump upward and follow a trail of twinkling stars into the depths of night. Akiva's mellow mood struck me oddly: it should have helped to relax me, but instead it was a source of anxiety, as if he knew secret things that were not to be shared. He led me to an opening in the low stone wall and we entered the graveyard, which he called the Hungry Place. Very few of the stones seemed old, and on many of them there was but a name and date of death. I noticed a change in the air as we stepped onto the cemetery sod, a chilliness of which I had not previously been aware. Akiva led me past tombs until he reached a statue that stood upon a column of marble.

"This is the man who brought me to Sesqua Town," he whispered to me. "The poet William Davis Manly. I had found a rare edition of his verse in an antique shop in Boston, and I bought it on a whim—or so I thought. Now I feel that I was destined to own it, and to bring it home. The verse affected me deeply, especially the sequence of seventeen sonnets entitled 'The Seventh Sun.' Tucked inside the book was a short epistle to the book's original owner, which mentioned this hidden valley. The more I delved into that book, the stronger was my ache to find this town."

"And this is where the poet is buried?"

"No. I—I don't quite understand what happened to him; people don't care to discuss it with me. I'll find out in time. I need to become more rooted to this soil. Come on, the place I want to show you is up a ways."

We approached a place where many trees enshrouded what I eventually saw was a large mausoleum. Oddly, the closer we got to it, the darker the sky became, and I noticed a vague stench which my fancy absurdly associated with rotting stone. As we drew nearer the edifice, some large winged thing drifted out of the trees and floated toward the twin-peaked mountain, uttering no cry. I had yet to hear any birdcall during my time in the valley, nor had I seen any squirrels or other wildlife. However, as I began to listen, attentively, to the aura of the place, I thought that I could detect a sentience, as if some *thing* was indeed aware of us. I could feel the thing's interest in us, and its appetite. Stopping for a moment, Akiva dug into his pocket and produced a lighter, with which he set fire to the lantern's wick. We climbed the three steps that took us to the crypt's double gates, which we opened together. Inside, we found three immense granite slabs.

"No names or plaques," I whispered. And then I pressed my hand to my forehead and used my other hand to steady myself on the nearest tomb, for I had been overcome with slight and sudden vertigo. "That was weird," I told my friend.

"No, it's a common occurrence in the Hungry Place. The children of the valley never come here, it affects them strongly."

"It?"

"The Hungry Place and its unholy appetite."

"My dear, you're sounding like one of your fantastic poems. Please, talk sense. A little common sense would benefit me in this macabre place. Ugh! Your lamp is casting the queerest shadows."

"The lamp will light our way."

"Our way to where?"

"Below." He moved away from me, toward a back wall, then paused and turned to smile at me, and once again I felt a tinge of fear, his expression was so abnormal. And then Akiva began to sink into the ground, taking the light with him, which increased my dread. I rushed to where he was descending and saw the large pit and earthen steps leading into a depth of darkness, from which an odor of decay arose. Following his light, I cautiously descended the soft steps, which took us into a small grotto. The air grew very thin and dry. I did not understand why the flame of Akiva's lamp had darkened and grown red, casting a crimson pall all around us. I shuddered at the smell encountered in the chamber, and at the disquiet that the stench inspired. Akiva rested his lantern onto a large oblong slab that looked as if it had been made a thousand years ago; and I wondered what on earth could have been interred in so large a sepulcher. I then noticed the two items that rested on the slab of stone and reached for the smallest. It was an old diary or some such thing, and judging from its appearance it was quite aged, a relic of the past. Turning the frayed faux leather cover, I saw a faint script where someone had written a name, which I made out as 'Harley Warren.' The pages of the diary were so brittle that I knew it would most likely split and rip in my attempt to read it, and so I shut the cover and returned it to its place upon the slab. Reaching for the other book, I picked it up, surprised that it was so weighty. It too reeked of age, and yet I could tell it was of a more solid construction. It felt *nasty* in my grasp, moist and squalid, like something that had been retrieved from swampland. Hurriedly, I set it down on the slab and watched as Akiva turned its binding.

"Curious, isn't it? I've never seen such alien-looking and undecipherable characters. Impossible to tell if the pages are printed or if the lines are handwritten. The script is very fine, however foreign. You see that one character, which is oft repeated? Look."

Picking up his lamp, he stepped away from the sepulcher and to one lightless corner. I gasped at the sight of the thing that stood there. Its stone, I sensed, was as ancient as that of the hoary tomb, and I knew that it was a thing of great age. And yet it was almost an exact replica of the black statue that Akiva kept in his living room. It had an identical stance, with the one arm lifted just a little from its body, palm outward. My friend shone his lantern's light on that palm, and I saw the character that had been chiseled upon it, the same strange sigil that had been repeated in the text of the outré book.

Vertigo overtook me a second time, and from beneath my feet I felt a growing sensation, a pulse that could have been the strengthening heartbeat of an atrocious beast. In my growing delirium I imagined that the dirt on which I stood was shifting ever so subtly, spreading so as to pull me downward. Frantically screaming, I rushed from that crimson chamber, up the smooth earthen steps and out of the mausoleum. The moon, so large and yellow, sneered at me as I fled the Hungry Place and ran, panting and full of panic, to my friend's abode.

IV.

She awakened on a bed still made, fully dressed yet rested. Light filtered into the room from the window, and glancing at the clock Sarah saw that it was late morning. At some point in the night she had kicked her shoes off, and so she found where they had fallen onto the floor and slipped into them, and then stalked into the living room. It seemed that she was alone in the house, and this inspired her to investigate the living room and its curios. The spacious room was so crowded with bizarre objects that it did indeed seem like a room inside a cluttered museum or antique shop. Sarah avoided looking at the corner where the black statue stood, for it reminded her too sharply of the weird dream she had suffered in the night, that remarkably realistic dream about visiting a haunted mausoleum with her host. Coming to one cabinet filled with books, she opened one of the glass doors and ran a finger over the soft old bindings. Instinctively, she was looking for a slim volume, and most of the books before her were thick and weighty. One by one, she pulled the thin titles out and opened their covers, disappointed until she found the volume with purple binding. Sarah opened the book and read its title aloud: "Visions of Khroyd'hon, by William Davis Manly." Closing the book, she stepped out of doors and studied the valley, its lush woodland, the titanic white mountain that seemed to sparkle in the light of day. She then opened the volume again and read one poem aloud.

> "Ah, subtle scream beneath disrupted earth,
> Oh, moaning of one mouth beneath the sod,
> The choking of one final cry, the dearth
> Of air spilled forth in prayer to heedless god.
> Allow all breath to cease, allow the stream
> Of mortal blood within to stop its course.
> Allow the liquid eye to dull its gleam.
> Abandon misery, unclench remorse.
> Your ache, so lunatic, is realized.
> You have achieved your fitful mortal goal.
> You have accomplished that so highly prized:
> The valley has embraced your mortal soul.
> You now are kindred with our shadow-race
> As you dissolve beneath the Hungry Place."

It was as strange as Akiva's newest work, and equally disturbing. Where was he, she wondered? Perhaps he had gone to have breakfast in the main section of town. Book in hand, she made the journey to the business area of Sesqua Town and located what looked to be a bar and lounge. Sarah entered the establishment and was charmed by the quaint atmosphere, the feel of the old wood on her eyes, the sense of the past. However, the inhabitants of the place were dreadful, yellowish and gaunt and peering at her with queer pale eyes. She advanced toward the one she recognized, as the others watched her, astonished.

"Have you seen Akiva?"

The grotesque fellow studied her in silence for some few moments, and then his lips curled in what was a ghastly smile. "Sit down, Miss . . ."

"Paget-Lowe. Thank you, I will. Your bowl of fruit is beautiful." She indicated the large bowl that was filled with a colorful array of apples and Japanese quinces, oranges and melon slices and raspberries, apricots and blackberries.

He smiled as he scanned the delectable display, and then he raised one hand and snapped fingers. "Nathan, a second plate, and some of your cherry coffee." He turned his eyes to Sarah. "You'll enjoy it—it's brewed with organic black cherry-flavored beans from Columbia. I discovered it during a stay in Panama. Here we are. Let me select your nourishment. Here are some sublime dates, and this Asian pomegranate is perfection. Let me slice it for you."

"You've not seen Akiva, sir?" She set her book onto the table and watched him at his task.

"Simon Gregory Williams," he introduced himself as he handed her the plate. "Eat, drink. When did you last see Loveman?"

Sarah frowned. "I can't quite remember. I must have been especially tired and gone to bed early last night. I had such a curious dream, about your graveyard."

"Indeed. I'm told that dreams can seem especially vivid in this valley. I do not dream myself." Simon watched her eat and grinned at her obvious enjoyment of the delicious repast. "What brings you to Sesqua Town?"

"Akiva invited me, thinking I needed to get away from Providence. He was mistaken. But I'm glad I came, because I think that being here is having a bad effect on him. He's become morbid. He's started collecting the oddest of things. Last night he made the strangest ceremonial motions to that awful black statue. No, wait, that was a part of my dream. I think." She frowned, confused.

"Your dream was very vivid. You've slept badly. Perhaps a walk would relax you and help to ease your mind. Will you join me?"

Something in his voice captivated Sarah. This grotesque creature had an air about him that was seductive, and she found that she did want to stroll with him. She watched him rise and allowed him to help her out of her chair, and then she followed him outdoors.

"Are you a poet, like your friend?"

"No," Sarah answered. "I'm a novelist. My reputation is that of a feminist Henry James, as I deal with social issues that affect my gender. Did you know that it was this book of poems that brought Akiva to this valley?"

She noticed Simon's momentary frown and almost expected him to snarl. Instead, after a pause, he replied in a low, soft voice. "I have heard whispers of such a circumstance. Loveman has fallen under the spell of William Davis Manly. It has happened far too often. The book was never meant for outside eyes. The incident of its publication has caused us nothing but mischief." He had been muttering to himself, but then he seemed to catch himself and smiled at her. "There is a statue of its author just over there—in the Hungry Place."

Sarah was just about to remark that she had visited the place the previous evening and seen the statue; but then she remembered that visiting the place had been a part of her vivid dream, and this deepened her confusion. "Will you show me?"

Simon frowned. "It's an unpleasant place, but I suppose we can stop there for one moment. Come, follow me." The fellow led the way to the low stone wall that surrounded the graveyard, and to the opening in that wall that allowed passage into the place. Sarah felt a sense of *déjà vu* as she stepped onto the cemetery sod and joined Simon as he stood before a high statue that was mounted onto a three-foot base. "Is this what you saw in your dream?"

"Yes. He resembles you, Mr. Williams."

"We share a similar heritage. Pah, this place reeks—can you not notice the rank odor that has infiltrated the air? Let us depart." But then his eyes widened as they watched the figure that was staggering toward them, the fellow with a fever of madness tugging at his mouth. "Loveman!"

The young poet's appearance was shocking. Whereas once his entire head of hair had been black and sleek, it now wore a small patch of white strands. His dark eyes were sunken into their sockets and rimmed with red, giving him a lunatic look. The chiseled mouth was wretchedly twisted and stained with slaver. His clothing was rumpled and one sleeve was torn at the elbow. As the poet joined them, both Simon and Sarah curled their nose at his stench as they noted the spread of wetness at Loveman's crotch. The young man raised his eyes to admire the statue.

"Yes—yes, that's him exactly. He could be your twin, Simon, except that his features are softer and he wears his hair longer. He has the most beautiful voice. I could have listened to him all night."

"What the devil are you chattering about, pathetic wretch?" Simon demanded.

Ignoring him, Loveman turned to Sarah and took her hands. "You shouldn't have fled. It was fantastic. The slab is large enough, we could both have slept there. Oh, the *dreams!* The heartbeat of the valley took hold of my own palpitation, and we thumped as one. Didn't you hear it as you ran away? Why did you fly? I've experienced such wonders. Oh! I've left my lantern there. Come with me now, and I'll teach you the sign of Nyarlathotep. It's delicious to feel the crawl of chaos creep over one and kiss one's eyes!"

Simon clutched at the lad and turned him. "How do you know that name?"

"Manly taught it to me, when he showed me the Circle of Seven Suns. I liked the way he felt, his soft padded hand in mine. He is far friendlier than you've ever been."

"You've dreamed of Manly?"

"Don't be stupid. Although, come to think of it, he seemed a thing of dream as he drifted to me out of the mauve mist. Manly came to me as I reclined upon the slab in the sunken chamber of the Howard mausoleum. He told me how the Howard family had been among the first mortals to settle in Sesqua Valley, how they began to build the town. They corrupted this place of secrecy and wonder, and awakened the children of shadow." He cast a playful look at Simon. "The first to seep from out the valley's shadowland was a potent fellow, richly daemonic and a very devil. Oh, the deadly tricks he played on those early white settlers who dared to invade the sacred land! They were driven away, those pilgrims, but the valley was forever tarnished, and others come, freaks of peculiar bent. The valley accepted them and their absurd ways. He told me of the mountain, which serves as symbol of the valley's majesty, and of its influence over those pathetic souls who wander into this realm. The mountain adores those who are most bent, as I am, and those are the adopted souls of Sesqua Valley. And then he took my hand and guided me to the Circle of Seven Suns and taught me what ritual to perform once I took my statue there. I was so *compelled* to buy that statue from Leonidas. Now I comprehend why—well, vaguely. Manly marvels that you've yet to figured it out, you're usually so clever, beast. He's been so amused by your 'antics,' as he calls them."

"Sirrah, William Davis Manly vanished from this valley decades ago. His fate remains a mystery. Come, we must remove ourselves from this soil. It has a vile effect and is the cause of your pathetic ranting. Come."

Akiva laughed as he allowed Simon to pull him across the ground and out of the cemetery, followed by Sarah. "You can be such an idiot, Simon. Manly hasn't left the valley. He's dwelling in the second shadowland, the place he's conjured through his sorcery. Haven't you felt his presence deep inside you? He's your brother, so alike that you two almost share a single heartbeat. Haven't you heard him singing to you in your dreams?"

"I never dream. This is all rubbish. You have slept within the Hungry Place and it hath made ye mad. Pah—this is what comes from allowing outsiders to enter freely into our demesne. I have warned the others of this, but things have become so lax. What madness you talk! The Circle of Seven Suns? No such place exists."

Swiftly, the poet turned to Simon and thrust his hand against the Sesquan's face, digging his fingernails into Simon's brow. "This hand has touched the seventh statue, the residue of which has left a paranormal stain. Feel it sink into your bestial hide and find your throbbing brain. Let the Circle conjure itself inside your mind. Feel its image bubble in your diseased brain. Yes, there you go! Isn't it fantastic?"

As she watched this performance, Sarah was overwhelmed with a sense of being trapped inside an absurd dream. Her surroundings, and the macabre inhabitants she encountered in it, disturbed her. Akiva Loveman had altered absolutely, and she did not recognize the man before her now. No longer the shy boy she had known in Providence, the poet seemed to tremble with a subdued inner power that lit his eyes. Sarah was not alone in her astonishment.

"How dare you touch me!" panted Simon Gregory Williams; and yet he did nothing to push the poet from him, and his silver eyes grew more fantastic as Akiva kept his hand on Simon's brow. The beast of the valley was bewildered, for he had been used to his role of intimidation and control, especially within his valley realm. Although his eyes had remained wide open, dream-like images began to filter into his mind. He saw a steep ravine and a descending trail with broad steps of rough-hewn stone. A wide stream cascaded as waterfall over rocks and boulders and fallen trees in an area that Simon did not recognize. "This is mere delusion and delirium," he muttered, and yet he could not escape the image in his mind. In vision, he walked away from the singing stream, to an area beneath the trees and ferns where the earth was smooth. It was there that he visualized the circle of diminutive statues, dark gnome-like figures that each held a sphere composed of pale stone. This vision angered the beast, and he sneered. "This is your imagination only. How dare you try and transpose it onto me with your feeble witchery."

"No," Akiva countered, "the site exists. Manly took me there."

"Enough. I will not listen to your babble of secret places and second shadow-lands. I would *know* if my brother still existed in the valley, in whatever hidden pocket of it. You have fallen under the spell of Manly's poetry, as have others before you. Incredibly, you seem to have spent a night within the Hungry Place, and as a result of this unheard of behavior you are now utterly deranged. Obviously, you cannot withstand the influence of the valley." Simon turned to Sarah. "It would be best for you both to return to Providence and not return. You are unwanted here."

Before either outsider could answer, Simon stalked away. Turning a flustered face to his friend, Akiva cried, "But I *did* visit it, and Manly lives! Let me share it with you." He raised his hand to her face, but she blocked his movement with an arm.

"No, don't touch me." The harshness in her voice surprised her, and she winced at the painful expression in Akiva's eyes. Taking hold of his hand, she brought it to her lips and kissed it. And then she, too, walked away from him.

V.

Sarah was in her room, packing things into her small suitcase, when she heard the commotion in the living room. Going to investigate, she saw Akiva striving to lift the strange black statue. Seeming to sense that she was watching, he turned and grinned at her.

"It's not very heavy, actually. I think I can do this."

"And what exactly is it that you're doing?"

"Manly suggested that it would be appropriate to take this to the Circle of Seven Suns, that maybe it would help to evoke the Crawling Chaos."

The woman laughed. "Akiva, when did you become consumed with all this esoteric jabberwocky? I'm beginning to agree with Simon—you need to escape this place. Come with me to Providence."

"Manly's book was my key, you see, and the valley is my gateway. I've connected with the valley's laureate, and I think he wants to crown me with his laurel. I am destined to become the valley's new poet, to sing her glory as it has not been expressed for decades."

"And why can't Manly do this himself, if he still dwells here?"

"I think he is conjoined to the second shadowland and can rarely leave it, or rarely wants to." He noticed the expression on her face and laughed heartily. "God, you don't understand any of this. How could you? You're far away from Providence, dear Sarah. Look, I don't have time to explain it all now. I need to get this eikon to the Circle of Seven Suns. We'll talk later."

"Let me help you. I want to see this mysterious place that has so upset Simon."

"But—I don't know what's going to happen when I evoke the Crawling Chaos."

"Then it will be a learning experience for both of us. Do you think that thing will fit into your car?"

"Only just. I managed when I brought it home from the antique shop. It's lovely, isn't it? So smooth and black and—potent." He wrapped his arms around the statue and began again to try and lift it. Shaking her head, Sarah went to assist him, and together they moved the effigy out of the house and into Akiva's motor car. Before getting into the vehicle, the poet glanced at the moonlit mountain and frowned.

"What's wrong?"

Akiva squinted his eyes with suspicion. "It's too quiet, like the valley is holding its breath. Usually, when something really dangerous or weird is going on, the valley sends out a signal from beneath its ground, a deadly kind of pounding that alerts the children."

"The children?"

"The ones who have silver eyes, the local tribe, whatever they are. They often refer to themselves as the children of the valley, without ever explaining what that means. I've sensed a lot of things in the months that I've lived here, but nothing's concrete inside my mind. Perhaps after tonight I'll have more answers. Let's go."

They both entered the car, Sarah having to adjust her head so that it would not bang against the head of the statue, which was protruding over the back of her seat. She remained silent as the car bounced on its way toward the mountain. Their road entered a place in the woodland where the trees overhead formed a kind of tunnel through which they journeyed. And then the trees were gone, and the mortals were moving along an expanse of dirt field. The mountain, now very near, hovered over them like some slumbering behemoth. Sarah cracked her window open and cursed. "Ugh, I thought I smelled something vile. What is that stench in the air? It's sickening."

"It emanates from the soil, or so it seemed to on the few occasions that I've visited this area. It's like the ground is cankerous. Look at how yellow the dirt is? The children shun this place. I tried to get my friend Cyrus to join me on an outing here and he freaked out, said something about it being too near the mountain. I think they shun the mountain as well. It's nice to know that there are places in the valley where you don't have to worry about meeting its freakish clan. I think we're almost there."

"You *think?*"

"Well, I confess that last night's all a bit of a haze. But I'll recognize the wooded area once we get there. I'll remember the signposts that Manly showed me."

Sarah could not take her eyes from the bulk of Mount Selta, and something in the shape of the mountain increased her sense of unease. "This place is creepy," she mumbled; but Akiva ignored her, seemingly intent on locating their destination. And then he stopped the car and they stepped out onto the land.. "This is the place. It's not a long walk. Are you sure you want to help me haul that statue down there?"

"I am not yet decrepit," she scolded, opening the vehicle's back door and stooping to pick up the bottom portion of the statue. Struggling, they removed the eikon from the car. Sarah felt extremely silly as they entered the woods, and smiled broadly at what a sight they made. She noted that the vile stench in the air had dissolved and was replaced with a new scent, subtle and uncharacteristic of what she had thus experienced in the valley. There were spaces between the trees and thus bright moonlight illuminated their way. Then she noticed what she thought was an extremely freakish tree.

"Ah, there's the totem. This is the right path," the poet assured her. Sarah gawked at the towering thing as they passed it, having never seen its like before. The object looked skeletal and albinic, and the misshapen faces that it wore appeared to be composed of rotting mold and resembled no living creatures with which she was familiar. From some place beyond the totem she heard the sound of rushing water, and then she had to watch her step as the path began to incline downward and became a series of large stone steps, beside which a wide stream fell over rocks and boulders. Sarah could not understand why the woodland grew no darker as they descended—indeed, the moon, when she glanced up at it, seemed nearer to earth than it had at any other time. She could see the face in the moon, the sight of which chilled her blood.

At last they reached the end of sloping earth. Although the statue was not very heavy, Sarah was tiring. When her eyes met Akiva's, however, she saw that his burned with an almost preternatural ignition. Looking at her, he laughed joyously and showed his shining teeth. "Right over there. Watch your step, there's a bunch of ferns just here. Can you feel the spray from the waterfall? It's like drinking liquid aether. Okay, let's lift him over these sculpted figures and set him in the center of the Circle."

Trying to study the dwarfish figurines as they lifted the black statue over them, Sarah lost her footing, stumbled, and fell onto soft ground. Her end of the statue pressed against the earth, and she let go of it as Akiva wrestled with the thing and put it into place in the center of the ring of stone effigies. The seven sculpted gnomes were grotesque in the extreme and filled Sarah with disquiet. Each creature held a pale white sphere over its dome, globes that caught the weird moonlight and appeared to drink in its luminosity.

"He's here, I think." Before Sarah could respond, she felt a beating beneath her hands, a pulsing from some place under the earth on which she knelt. The air grew chilly, and a mist began to rise from distant places in the woodland, a mauve-tinted mist that grew opaque. Sarah sensed the presence before she saw its silhouette moving toward them through the gathered haze. He was tall and lean, and he exuded a sense of energy and influence. As his features became clearer she thought it might be Simon without his characteristic hat; but then she noticed the distinction between this being and the beast. The gentleman before her was not quite as grotesque as Simon, although his features were just as animalistic. His eyes shimmered like glossy nickel.

"Greetings, Miss Paget-Lowe," the stranger said, bowing his head to her. "Welcome to my realm. Please remain silent as we summon forth the Crawling Chaos. Akiva has been chosen to be the bard of the Outer Gods." Turning to the poet, the fellow took Akiva's hand and smoothed its palm with taloned fingers. He then pierced that palm with one nail and began to etch into the poet's flesh. Sarah thought that she could smell the blood that dripped from her friend's hand onto the earth. She watched the tall fellow smooth her friend's hand with his own, until the drops of blood ceased. Akiva showed her his hand, whereon the sigil that had been carved onto the black statue's hand had been repeated. Moving out of the Circle, the odd one reached into a jacket pocket and produced a red flute, which he pressed against his mouth. Unearthly music filled the air, as did an unearthly reek. Looking up, Sarah observed the darker mist that was falling toward them through the other vapor, the greenish-yellow mist that churned unspeakably as it ceased its descent and billowed above them. From behind that rancid miasma she thought that she could just make out the circles of blistering globes of fire, and she saw the two winged things that sailed to them through the fog, beings that had been replicated in stone in the Circle of Seven Suns. The creatures settled near the base of the black statue, against which they huddled as they brought weird flute-like instruments to their misshapen mouths.

Sarah looked to where the child of Sesqua Valley had been standing, but there was no one there any longer. Another shape stalked toward them through the mist, and Sarah marveled at the black man's regal beauty. She watched the figure drift to where Akiva stood and spoke something to the poet in antique Hebrew. Not rising from her kneeling position, she saw the strange dark one tilt toward her friend and kiss Akiva's eyes, eyes that were suddenly transformed, that grew black and liquid. And then the black man turned to her, drew nearer to her as he made motions to the air, the air that cleared of mist and sour fog. She saw the brilliant moon that cast its insane light onto her eyes, and then she howled as the black man raised a foot and kicked her head violently. Her vision blurred and she could see nothing but a congeries of red and black dots. The sound of insane fluting washed to her and embraced her head for but one moment, and then the sound departed, lifting skyward. When at last her sight returned, she saw that Akiva was trembling before her, his frantic fingers reaching at his black and burnished eyes.

"I am blind! As in the dream I had when I visited the woodland and Simon found me! But this is not a dream! Oh god, I am blind. And yet, I *see,* beyond the blackness, beyond the dead moons. Oh, I *see!"* he uttered, and then he began to howl like some idiotic thing. Gasping, weeping, Sarah rose and clutched the poet's coat. Roughly, she tugged him from that place, up the rugged path and over the stone steps on which they occasionally tripped as Akiva screeched in Hebrew. When at last they reached the car, Sarah opened the passenger door and pushed the poet into the vehicle. Rummaging through his pockets, she found the car keys and rushed to the driver's door. By the time she managed to turn the motor, Akiva had grown silent. He turned his altered eyes to her, and her blood froze as she felt him peer into her paltry soul. "The seven suns," he whispered, and then began to speak poetry of the strangest kind, poetry that contained a kind of alchemy of sound. Sarah listened, entranced, and then she put the car into gear and began to drive. She followed the roadway, away from the twin-peaked mountain, past the center of Sesqua Town, out of the valley. Finding the freeway at last, Sarah pushed on the gas pedal, guiding the car on its way toward Providence.

Darkness Dancing in
Your Eyes

The scent of night evoked him. Enoch Blake awakened and wiped the dust from his eyes. He thought he must have slept longer than usual, for his brittle bones were unusually stiff and difficult to move, and some spider had woven a web between his parted lips. His mouth always remained open when he slept, so as to drink darkness. It was Enoch's little theory that the darkness helped to keep him reanimated over the length of decades in which he semi-existed. Looking around, he saw that much had changed within the chamber wherein his master had worked with spells and philters and alchemy. The mangy room looked as if it had been vandalized, and much of the chemical apparatus had been smashed; books had been removed from shelves and now littered the floor; furniture had been overturned and broken. But some of the room's wrack seemed to be the ravages of time, resulting in discolored wallpaper and brittle window shades torn and tattered. His master's desk remained intact, as did Enoch's favorite thing in the room—the full-length oval upright mirror. The dark glass of that mirror beckoned him, and he lifted his limbs to a standing position; but he did not step too closely to the mirror, for he did not want to be beguiled by its reflected shadow, the reflection that was not his own.

He saw it, there within the glass, a thing of depth and dimension; and as he gazed at the image it began to coil, and by doing so it seemed to pull more shadow into it, so that it expanded and reformed until it aped a human figure. Its danse was seductive—Enoch could feel that movement reflected on his eyes, his eyes on which the other creature saw its own mirror image. Enoch watched, as the figure in the mirror faded, as he could sense the coiled image take over his eyes completely and weave its influence behind his eyes and to his brain. He suspected that this presence was that which remained of his master, the alchemist, who had a penchant for working with glass, with transmuting the components of glass so that it become something novel, something different and outré. Enoch began to feel that transmutation in the chemistry of his orbs, which chilled and hardened, which were transformed from living tissue into something sleek and artificial. He was almost afraid to blink, worrying that the violence of eyelid movement might shatter the crystal of which his eyes were now composed. Exiting the room, Enoch Blake walked into the night. The edifice in which he had served the alchemist had once been an isolated apartment building on a hill above the city, once teeming with occupants; but as those inhabitants became the occult toys of his master, the building became more and more isolated, abandoned, forsaken. For a long time it had been he and his master only who walked the building's dusky corridors; and then his master had gone away, except for that particle of him that existed in the mirror.

The scent of night aroused him; it amplified his sense and filled him with weird appetite. Enoch walked the silent night until he entered the place that took hold of his imagination. Although he was almost vacant of memories, he sensed that he had known this place long ago; for its rotting slabs were familiar, as were its willow trees; and when the wind picked up and moved the limbs of those trees, the sibilant sound was a noise that he knew. Other sounds came to him, or perhaps these were memories of sounds, of things that crept beneath the graveyard ground, muttering to the sod above them. Hadn't he been among their brood, long ago, moving through the burrows they had manufactured, sifting at times through the debris so as to break through the surface and leer at the moon? There was no moon in the sky this night, and the dim stars were very few indeed. He liked the lack of light and smiled at the darkness above him; for darkness reminded him of his master, that alchemist who had found Enoch's special bungalow beneath the graveyard ground and spilled queer salts and liquid onto the earth, stuff that mingled with the mire and, sinking, sifted into the texture of his remains, transmuting Enoch's charnel nature so that he emerged out of shadow, split the stuff of earth, and stood before his master on the cemetery sod.

He stalked upon that sod again and saw the frolicker who capered among the tombstones. He could not ascertain the dancer's gender, for its lowered head was shaved and its uniform of pale linen might have been meant for any sanatorium inmate regardless of sex. When the figure stopped its movement and raised its emaciated face to his, Enoch recognized a degree of lunacy with which he himself had once been familiar, in some epoch of his existence. Thus he approached the mortal and allowed it to look at itself in the mirrors that were Enoch's eyes. The being danced before the daemon, as the sorcery in Enoch's eyes lighted upon the cavorting creature and entered the texture of its tissue, which began to darken as shadow and break apart. Enoch could smell the transmutation, for the dancer was but a whisper away from him; and he was unprepared when one pale and solid hand, not yet transformed into darkness, fell to Enoch's face and smashed into his eye, his eye that broke into tiny shards from the violence of the blow. His vision became so blurred that Enoch could not relish the sight of the mortal's body, now a mound of black spectral particles that sank into the graveyard ground.

Enoch found his way home, to the abode where he had assisted his master when that alchemist had lived, where he served his master still in some unholy way. He wanted to weep for the destruction of his eye, but he was fearful that the gathered tears would wash away remnants of that orb, and so his eyes stayed dry. The building, as he approached it, looked more neglected and lifeless than it had ever seemed to him, like some forgotten crypt that, embracing Enoch, would hide him forever from the mortal world. As he climbed the stairs that took him to the building's door, he could hear the rising wind that sang through crevices of rotting wood, and he remembered a time when he had more of a mouth and could whistle in accompaniment to such wind; but time had withered his mouth so that its lips were now but two flat flaps of thin and useless membrane. It was strange to experience, as he entered the ruined room that had been his master's sanctuary and laboratory, an ache of depression that blossomed as deep despair. Enoch stood in that lonesome place and smoothed what remains of his hands over his face, his throat, his chest. He pressed one hand to the place where once he could feel his heartbeat. Nothing pulsed there now. He remembered how his master would touch the blade of a ritual dagger to Enoch's breast and scratch a sigil into his flesh, and how his heart would grow in strength as the alchemist's lips smoothed against the wound so as to sup upon its wet red nectar.

Movement in the mirror caught his attention. Enoch approached the mirror and stood directly before it for the first time. He saw the squares of polished glass with which the mirror was composed and remembered watching his master manufacture those oblong pieces of treated glass in his laboratory. Enoch watched the dark figure that was not his reflection and sighed at the way that figure danced before him; and he was close enough to the glass so that he could discern the pin-points of cloudy light that were the figure's eyes. Those eyes were familiar, and the sight of them brought memory to Enoch's withered brain. He remembered those times when his master had taught him the alchemy of danse, had taught him how ritualistic movement could conjure impossible things. And so he lifted those white things that had once been hands and clacked their talons together, and moved in time to the rhythmic noise. And he could feel the dark thing in the mirror reflected on his eyes, the one that was whole and the one that was shattered. Overwhelmed by memory and emotion, Enoch brought one talon to his breast, to the place where he had once been able to detect his heartbeat, and nearly toppled when he detected yet again a slight palpitation. Ripping his talon through his thin tissue, Enoch etched a remembered sigil and could not keep from weeping as he saw the slim stream of blood that seeped from the wound. He wept, violently, and the shards of his shattered eye broke free and fell onto the floor; but he did not care, for the dark figure in the mirror reached for him, brought its phantom mouth to his bleeding breast and kissed the wound. Enoch began to sing, as the sad pathetic remnants of his mortal frame dissolved as darkness that spilled into the mirror.

Beyond the Wakeful Senses

I beg your mercy, You, all that I love,
Deep in the dim gulf where my heart lies now.
It is a world of doom with leaden skies;
Horror and blasphemy float in its night.
—BAUDELAIRE

I took up the box of calamander wood and set it on my lap. The smooth wood, darkly striped, had an almost hypnotic effect as I stared and stared at its pattern. Finally I opened the lid and, pushing aside the dried rose petals, took out my third thumb. I had had the digit surgically removed at age seventeen, and after it was embalmed I kept it in the antique box, nestled in its bed of petrified petals. As I held it to the light its nail, buffed and polished, shimmered like some bit of dainty porcelain. I had had its stump fitted into a key-ring, and I wore it on my person for those occasions that I deemed especially significant—such as that afternoon, when I was scheduled to encounter my correspondent from India, Amos Capernaum.

It was a short trolley ride into town, to the old cathedral where we were scheduled to rendezvous. I ascended the pitted steps to the huge copper doors and entered in, walking past the archway that led into the nave. He stood just below the large round stained-glass window; he was so impossibly beautiful that he could have been one of the gorgeous saints depicted on that window, descended from the glass into shadow and incense smoke. I admired his black-clad body, which stood erect with weird rigidity as he scanned the decorative ceiling. I approached and knelt before him, unable to remove my eyes from his face, which was wan and hollow-cheeked yet still spectacularly lovely. The face was framed with wavy locks of sable hair, and his wide brow was marble-white. Beneath delicate nostrils was a fine mustache, impeccably groomed. Finally he lowered his head and peered at me, and I shivered at the sight of his purple-black eyes. His hand drifted to my chin, which he tugged so that I rose before him. Smiling, he spoke my name and then led me from the coiling smoke and shifting shadow into daylight. I had practiced my initial speeches of introduction, but when we linked arms and strolled to catch a trolley, I felt no need to prattle. We had no use for words—our eyes spoke volumes.

We stepped into my humble home, and he stood at my bookcase as I prepared our drinks. He carefully observed as I returned my third thumb to its wooden box, smiling slightly. "I'm so glad we have found each other, Samuel," he spoke. "I knew from your book of verse that you were the exceptional fellow with whom I could companion. We are the queer souls in this neoteric age, where the thoughts of men are commonplace, where they dream of dull contemporary things. You and I see beyond the modern world—into the magnificent past and its potent visions. We realize that there is nothing *but* the past." He shut his eyes for a moment, as if to conjure forth an added potency of language; and when he opened his eyes again, I was thunderstruck at the ebony luminosity with which they smoldered. "However," he continued, "there is a cosmic past that even you, my heart, have not tasted. It is a place that I have sensed in night-tide apparitions. Alas, my psychic energy is not vital enough to carry me to that Outside plain; but with you beside me, Samuel, there is nothing we cannot accomplish."

Tilting to me, he touched his fingers to my lips. My kiss upon those digits was gentle. His face was very near my own, and I felt as though I might drown in the ambiance of his black eyes. As I studied the quality of those orbs, I suffered a momentary vertigo and felt as if I might slip from present reality into some waiting dream. He took my hand and smoothed his thumb over the place where my third thumb had once protruded; then he gazed quizzically at the box that I had set onto the sofa. Guiding me to that piece of furniture, he motioned that we should sit with the box between us. His hand let go of mine and reached for the wooden object, which he moved onto his lap.

"Ah, calamander wood. Very old wood, I perceive. Oh, the old, old things—how they speak to us." Opening the container, he took my thumb from it and placed it on his palm as if it were some priceless relic. "I have learned many secrets from olden things, from books and scrolls and glyphs. My eyes have keenly penetrated the poetic mysteries of *Al Azif,* that tome that stole the light from out mine eyes. It taught me the signs by which its mad poet author crossed the threshold into Outside dimensions. We, too, are poets, Samuel—and we wear our taint of lunacy. But madness need not be linked to foolishness or debauchery. With it we may be able to smash beyond the mirrored wall of sleep into an antediluvian epoch unimaginable."

"The mirrored wall . . ." I muttered.

My companion shrugged. "What are the dreams of most men but the dreary reflections of their dull lives? But we are poets, and we have intuited the echoes from beyond, the antique cosmic reverberations." He closed his fingers over my third thumb and buzzed a strange old tune. Holding his fist to the sunlight that streamed into the room through the nearest window, he shook that fist at the sky, and then he lowered his hand and opened it so that sunbeams reflected on my severed digit's polished nail. I watched as he guided his hand to his forehead, clutched my petite appendage with the thumb and forefinger of his other hand, and pressed the severed thumb's smooth nail to his forehead, whereon he etched an elder sign. When he then brought that nail to my face and dug it into my brow, I did not move or utter sound. His free hand dipped into a pocket, from which he took a small square of dark cloth that was folded onto my hand.

"Push this against your wound so as to stop its tiny trickle of blood. No, I do not bleed as you do." He smiled at the drops of crimson that had slipped from my forehead onto his hand and the object that it held; and then he brought my third thumb to his mouth and kissed the blood away. Nodding, he dropped my digit into its box, the lid of which he shut. "Calamander. In Ceylon we call it *kalu-medhiriya*—'dark chamber.' The place that awaits us, Samuel, is a chamber of vaulted darkness the likes of which you have never imagined. It is a timeless audient void that listens as we weep its praises. Ah, Samuel—you will see it with me, now."

His hand took mine, and together we stood to face the light of the sun. Those radiant beams seemed to melt into his eyes, whereon they were weirdly reflected. A cosmic cadence filtered from above us as a kaleidoscope of impossible color sparkled from my cohort's eyes, tints that were of more than earthly hue. Tendrils of luminosity touched the sigil that had been etched into my temple, and we began to drift out of the mundane world, as if we were insubstantial matter. Onward—onward—through shimmering gulfs of embers that were stars. The daemon beside me clutched my hand, tightly as he whispered outland-ish language—potent idiom. My senses altered, and I could smell the dimension through which we drifted—the outré realm that carried an odor of agedness. It was as if we were water leaked into some hoary cellar. I was aware of something that listened to him as all color dimin-ished and we confronted a wall of shimmering obscurity. He did not shut his eyes, and neither did I, although I shuddered to realize that the reflective wall before us was of the same smoldering hue as the eyes of Amos Capernaum.

"We need to make one singular sign, and only you can do so. For know you, we have departed from your common reality and entered a place of dreaming; and it is here that you, my poet, are now as once you were. Only you can make the sign that will crack this galactic mir-ror and form the fissure through which I can filter. Your hand alone can accomplish the improbable task. You have performed the feat in dreaming, although you cannot recall it. Raise your hand, Samuel."

I did so, and spread my fingers before me, on the hand that wore twin thumbs. I moved those digits weirdly, remembering hazily how I had performed the sigil in deepest dreaming. The wall of reflection waved before us, and I heard it crack. The cleft manifested itself, be-yond which a blacker void apprehended us. I experienced a shiver of monstrous ecstasy as I prepared to sift through that fracture and frolic on the other side, hand in hand with my beautiful friend, for whom I felt an irrepressible adoration. I turned to gaze into his satanic eyes, wherein I saw my doom; for when I peered into his eyes, I saw that they were vacant of anything approaching human empathy. Whoever—whatever—he was, Amos Capernaum had no interest in me. He was replete with the void, in which he would find an eternal demesne, perhaps from which, millennia before, his essence had been formed, a quintessence that had lost its place. He did not smile as he released my hand and waved me away, and I screamed as, reaching for him, I hurled through gulfs of darkness, into light.

But I am not sad, for I am left with more than memory; for whatever thing he is, whatever force or dream, Amos was not a part of the human husk that had been his earthly host. He had told me himself, as we soared through starlight, that we would enter a realm of rich dreaming. My clumsy flesh had stayed earthbound, and only my psyche, or my dreaming mind, had soared with cosmic light into the eldritch dark, guided by the daemon that had need of me. His body was still seated beside me on the sofa when I awakened from the dream, his body that I have embalmed and placed inside a casket of calamander wood. And in that coffin, with my beauteous friend, I will one day be interred.

Ye Unkempt Thing

I.

I met my friend in front of the large green door of the Providence Art Club on Thomas Street, and she led me into the building and to its spacious exhibition room, where a new showing was being set up.

"We're just waiting for my other two acquaintances who will be joining us," said Candice. "They should be here—oh, they've arrived!"

I turned and greeted the ravishing black woman and her tall, handsome companion. "Do you two know each other?"

The black woman said, "No, we have just met out front. But I am acquainted with the work and reputation of this artist." The fellow stooped slightly in response and then winked at me, and I sensed that he might be a bit of a rogue. But as he was a friend of a friend, I would suspend judgment until I knew him better. The woman, whose tight yellow dress was really too low-cut and exposed her breasts rather alarmingly, held out a hand, which I took timidly. "And you are the Reverend Henry St. Clair, author of *Midnight Din and other Weird Stories?*"

I confessed that I was. The artist, as he was referred to, introduced himself, and then Candice bade us follow her out of the building and down the inclined street to #7, the Fleur-de-Lys Building, which I was especially interested in investigating, as an ancestor of mine had had a small studio there from 1930 until his suicide in 1951. We stopped to admire the fantastic façade of the old building, with its queer design and gargoyles and small-paned windows, and then we were let inside. I loved everything about it—its delicious evocation of the past, the

71

stairways and antique paneled doors. One spacious room was crowded with work tables and various paintings, mostly unframed, leaning here and there or hung carelessly on walls. We then followed our hostess to the upper regions and into smaller rooms, and I was certain that I recognized one of them from family photos of my poor deceased relation. As I entered the room, I fancied that the atmosphere became subtly chilled, and I hugged myself protectively while the beauteous black woman offered me her strange smile.

"The past is alive here, is it not? One can feel it on this air breathed in and see it reflected on the windows where modern light is oddly muted." Her words bewildered me, as they seemed meant to have significance especially for me—which was absurd, of course: none of these people knew of my family's past relationship with the building; it was not something I confided to others, nor had I expressed it in any of my fiction. I watched as the dark woman stepped to a window sill that was half in shadow and on which a cluster of dust had settled. She bent to that dust and shadow, pursed her lips, and exhaled. Her eyes, as I peered at the woman's face, darkened, as if suddenly overcast with storm clouds. The afternoon light dimmed on the other side of the room so that we stood in dusky gloom, but my attention was caught by the movement of the dust onto which the woman had blown—the dust that lifted and shaped itself weirdly as it seemed to conjoin with coils of shadow that rose with it. I watched the pygmy shape cavort in its corner on the sill, as if it were engaged in crazy dancing. And then the sun came out from behind clouds and light spilled into the room once more, and where I had imagined I had seen a fantastic shape there was nothing but some few particles of dust that fell to gather on the floor. I glanced at the Negress as she reached into the black leather bag that hung from its long two handles resting on the woman's shoulder. She removed a white cloth and dabbed at her moist mouth.

We were shown other sections of the building for another half hour, and then returned to the steep hilly street, where we bade Candice goodbye and climbed up to Benefit Street. "There's a great sandwich shop a few blocks down," the artist chimed. "My treat, if y'all are hungry. I have a hankering to visit the churchyard at St. John's, where

Poe used to court Sarah Helen Whitman, or so legend says. You two interested?"

I was rather hungry. "I have no appetite," the woman informed us, "but a visit to the churchyard would enchant me. I'm Marceline Dubois, of Sesqua Valley. You're from Florida, yes?" I replied that I was. "Then New England must seem almost a foreign land, yes? Such richness of history, such sensation of past things."

I turned to the artist. "And you?"

"Boston, so this is just like home, creepy burying grounds and all. Come on, I'm famished. This sandwich joint is good. I'm staying at an old bed-and-breakfast inn near it and had the best corned beef sandwich ever last night."

A ten-minute stroll took us to the café, and their corned beef sandwich was quite excellent. We walked, we gents, with Miss Dubois between us as we chomped on our food and sipped from our bottled juices. Eventually we came to the steps that took us to the long winding brick pathway that led into the hidden churchyard. We had our old cemeteries in Florida, dating to the early nineteenth century, but there was certainly a different feel to the one we entered at that moment. The walkway took us toward the back of the venerable church, to a spot of land where we approached some few tabletop tombs that were entirely black with age. The artist leaped onto one of the slabs and danced irreverently.

"You're a merry fellow, Mr. Coffin," the black woman addressed him. "Would you court a woman in such a place?"

He stopped his silly capering and looked around. "I'd bring her here on a moody moonlit night and tell her such a ghastly tale that she would flee in horror, that would be fun."

"I fear you are not a romantic soul, Mr. Coffin," the woman scolded.

"I'm a beast, m'lady," he rejoined, bowing to her and then leaping off the opposite side of the tomb, toward the church. "Pah, what the hell is this?" We walked to where he stood and saw the curious pile of soiled clothing and bits of bone and other less recognizable debris that lay bundled on the earth. "Gawd, it stinks. Somebody meant to bury their pet or mother and changed their mind. Look at that hat—it's been gnawed on by graveyard rats, by the look of it. Ever seen any-thing so filthy? Pah!"

"It certainly reeks," I said, as Miss Dubois left my side and knelt before the pile with the strangest smile on her enchanting face. I watched as she picked up the grimy hat and sniffed at it. "You don't want to touch that stuff, my dear," I warned. "It's coated with heaven knows what." Without answering me, she placed the hat onto the pile and leaned a little closer to the rubble. Subtly she blew upon the heap, and as she did so the sunset grew a little darker. I watched her eyes as they caught and reflected the gold and amethyst shades of sundown.

"Well, this has been an enchanting afternoon. I have enjoyed your company," the lady informed us, standing and obviously signifying that our exploit was at an end. "It was wonderful to meet you, Mr. St. Clair. I hope we may look forward to a new collection of tales soon?"

I bowed to her and shook her hand. "My publisher has been mak-ing encouraging noises in that direction."

She turned to the artist. "Good day, Mr. Coffin." The handsome man refused her outstretched hand, strode to her, and took her into his arms.

"The pleasure has been all mine," he sang as he lowered his head and pressed his mouth to her exposed bosom. "Let's come here alone some night before you leave and I'll spin you a macabre story."

"I think not, sirrah," she returned as she gently pushed him from her. What curious creatures, I thought, as I walked with them up the red brick path to Benefit Street. I followed Miss Dubois up some steps, and then stopped as, holding onto the black metal handrail, the woman turned to gaze one last time at the ancient church. I turned as well, and saw the impish figure that watched us from where it stood near one of the flat tombs. Was it a child, perhaps, dressed in outlandish garb? As I watched, it raised one arm and seemed to wave to us, but something about its appearance disconcerted me and I did not return its gesture. The lady standing just before me did, however, lifting her hand-some hand and moving it peculiarly, as twilight engulfed the sky.

II.

I accompanied the peculiar Enoch Coffin to his B&B on Benefit Street and accepted his invitation to his room, a spacious chamber on the first floor in which there was a large bed and choice pieces of good furniture. We sat in comfortable chairs before curtained windows and talked of Poe, weird literature, and other things. He asked why I had come to the city of seven hills.

"My publisher has sent me on a small book-signing tour of New England and New York, a short three-week affair. It's rather nice: I've never been one for doing much traveling. I'm anxious about New York—not much for crowds and such. Providence has been delightful, and the signing last night was well attended."

He asked the name of the bookstore where I had signed, and nodded when I told him. "Yes, a charming little shop. I'll go there tonight and pick up your book. Interesting idea, a religious fellow writing horror. Being Christian, you naturally believe in evil. Yes, I thought you would. Have you ever confronted it, Reverend?"

"I've seen its manifestations, in crime and debauchery, certainly."

"Manifestations, yes." His voice was very quiet. "Personification? No? That's something I try to evoke with my art, you see—the essence of malignant evil. Not an ordinary everyday iniquity, but the malevolence that one may detect, if one is keenly attuned, in secret places. *Old* places."

"But places of human habitation nonetheless, I think. Our conception of 'evil' is, these days, aligned with human crime, wouldn't you say?"

"That is a potent wickedness, certainly. But I was thinking of a different kind of—sin, let us say—that, although implemented by human corruption, has aspects of, um, *otherness,* something beyond mortality and—not quite human."

"Ah, yes, I try to suggest such things in my weird fiction. It's all fantasy, of course, but it can make for a powerful imaginative effect. It's a seeing beyond the veil, I tell my friends who criticize my penchant for writing horror. It's a lifting of shadow so as to peer, if one has the nerve, to that which lurks beyond."

Coffin clapped his hands together and nodded his head. "The great Outside, beyond the rim of time and dimension. The secrets of the grave, or beneath the grave. Gawd, how I adore it! How I love to conjure it with my art and give it aesthetic *life*. I love how it triggers things in the fools who react to my canvases and criticize them. They may not like what I paint, but they cannot deny its *effect*."

I had had enough of the fellow's ego and eccentricity, and so I made my excuses, explaining that the next day would be my last in Providence and I needed to prepare for my trek to Salem. I had forgotten that it was late, and the darkness outside rather disconcerted me. Something in Coffin's energetic enthusiasm for 'the secrets of the grave' had gotten to me, which was amusing given that I was, after all, a horror author. I was at first uncertain where to walk so as to reach my rooms on College Hill, and so I crossed the street and walked toward the sandwich shop, which was about one block from where Coffin was staying. Right next to the old building that housed the café and some ascending apartments there was what looked like a large vacant parking lot, which was empty of everything except a large dumpster. I was still carrying my plastic bottle of apple juice, which I drained as I stood before the lot, and I decided to pop the empty bottle into the dumpster. The night was very quiet, deadly still. Going to the dumpster, I lifted its lid and dropped the bottle inside. The bin reeked, and something in the rancid odor seemed disturbingly familiar. It was as I lowered the lid that I noticed the shadowed figure, the dwarf in darkness, that stood against the cement wall just beside the dumpster. I thought at first that the figure was merely some flat silhouette that had been spray-painted onto the high cement wall, but then I saw the thing shiver and lift the head that wore the large round hat. The nighted area was too obscure for me to see any semblance of face or concrete form—the thing was just a shape that shivered momentarily and then lifted an arm, as if requesting alms. Saying nothing, barely breathing, I backed away and hurried out of the lot.

I climbed a steep street that took me to a cement staircase, and grabbed onto its railing as I ascended to the area that took me to the neighborhood near Brown University where I was renting a room. Interestingly, I had felt a sudden itch to write, and so I walked to the bookshop where I had sat signing my collection the previous evening. The friendly proprietor smiled at me and indicated the table on which my book was being featured, and I was happy to see that there were far fewer copies than had been there when I finished signing. The book was selling well. I told the lady that I wanted to buy a couple of notebooks in which to scribble, and thus she led me to a section of the shop that featured a variety of types of notebooks and personal journals. I bought two thick notebooks of lined paper and this journal in which I am writing now. It occurred to me that I might be able to create an effective little tale concerning my experience in the parking lot, although I would have to expand on the horror. The idea came to me that my narrator could be a homeless hobo who had gone in search of food and found edible garbage in a dumpster, and so he climbed into the cozy den of compost and began to partake; and then he would fall asleep in the safety of the small confined area until awakened by *something else,* something ravenous, that came in search of sustenance. I played with an outline but was suddenly too weary to write, although it was not yet late enough to sleep. My room looked out on a busy street that was active with college nightlife, and I opened my window so as to let the sound of youthful chatter and distant rock music filter into my little world. I welcomed the din of humanity, the buzz of mortal activity; for I had been touched by an aura of implacable menace ever since my meeting with the strange dark woman and the weird fellow from Boston.

I must have fallen asleep in my chair, for I awakened with a start. The activity outside my window had ceased, but music sounded still. I thought at first that one of my neighbors was either playing some exotic recording or that some foreign chap in a neighboring room was experimenting inexpertly on some flute or horn—at least, I assumed it was the playing of an instrument, for I don't think that a human throat could produce such a peculiar high wail; and yet, the more I listened, there did seem to be a kind of *articulation* in the sound. My chair was near to the window I had opened, and I shifted my head a little so as to peer into the gulf of night, outside. That word—why did it send a tingle through my flesh? Outside. There, in night's gloom, where I saw no stars, I could but dimly discern one black globe that drifted ominously in an abyss of pitch. The midnight disc then opened two diamond-shaped stars in which sunset colors frolicked. Sparkling beams from those twin points of unearthly illumination drifted to me through the stillness of air and spilled into one corner of my room. It stood there, suddenly revealed—the dwarfish creature that wore its wretched rumpled clothing and from which a nauseating stench assailed. It lifted the malformed head that wore the tattered hat, and some void within what masqueraded as a face split so as to issue a high wailing that corresponded with the noise from the adjoining room. I saw the thin slits that served as nostrils and the pits that were vacant of eyes. The thing lifted an arm, as it had when I encountered it at the dumpster; but now I understood that it was not asking for alms but rather meant to *take* some kind of offering from me. I blinked as chilly exhalation froze my features, and I sensed the nearness of the black cosmic sphere that, having entered my little room, puffed upon my face. It brushed my countenance, an unholy gust, and my eyeball, inexplicably loosened, escaped its socket. The wretched imp, now very near me, caught my orb with its hand held out.

I awakened a second time, in my silent little room, with the wind of evening pouring to me from the opened window next to which I had slumbered.

III.

It was my last day in bewitching Providence, and I wanted to drink my fill of it before I boarded the late afternoon bus to Salem. I was rather annoyed, therefore, to run into Enoch Coffin soon after leaving my little room so as to walk the city lanes. He hadn't shaved and was dressed rather carelessly, I thought. He smiled at me in such a way that it seemed almost a condescending leer.

"Reverend St. Clair, how amazing of you to look so immaculate so early in the day. I have your little book and was hoping to run into you. Please, if you will." He proffered my book and a fountain pen, and I inscribed my name. "Excellent. I've read a few of the stories. You have a nice little style and a lively imagination. I like the one story set in Florida—it is a real achievement to evoke horror in such a dominion of sunshine."

"Evil may lurk during the brightest of days, Mr. Coffin," I rejoined.

"Indeed. Well, I don't want to abuse you if you're occupied. I was just on my way to Prospect Terrace on Congdon Street—such a wonderful view. You haven't seen it? Tag along if you like; the view of downtown and other westward regions is really spectacular. I've got some postcards in my valise, as I like to sit on one of the benches and jot wee notes to chums. You'll come? Delightful."

We walked together without speaking, and I grew suspicious when at last we entered the small park, as a familiar figure was seated on one of the benches and gazing toward the city spread below. Her bright red hair, which had been piled upon her head the previous day, now hung past her shoulders. She was attired in the same yellow dress, over which she wore a bright red coat that reached to her ankles. I almost wanted to make an excuse and depart, because I didn't want to be a part of any game they might have planned to play with me. It simply couldn't be coincidence, my being there with both of them. I decided I would be cordial for a little while and then be off. The woman stood as we approached her, and I tried not to gaze at her bosom, which seemed more exposed than it had been previously, shockingly so. Coffin leered brutishly and let an obscene whistle escape his lips.

"Gentlemen, good day," she said. "I was just about to make my way down to Benefit Street. There's a forlorn little plot of wooded land just there." She pointed to an area below us. "It has a charming path that turns into wooden steps adjacent to a shunned house of ill repute. It would make an excellent little scene for some eerie horror story." She smiled at me. "Will you let me show you?"

"Um, I actually have some things I need to do before I catch my bus to Salem."

"Ah, certainly. Mr. Coffin? You will find the spot exceedingly atmospheric. You may want to sketch it. I'll pose for you, if you like."

"I'm all yours, wench. Nice knowing you, Reverend."

He held to her his arm and they prepared to walk away; and I was suddenly angered at being so easily dismissed, and so I cleared my throat and muttered something about joining them for the briefest moment. We walked, the three of us, down an extremely steep hill, and then along a rather rough road until we came to a path that took us into a little wooded region. We walked down the inclined path into a patch of gloom from which the light of day was held in abeyance, stopping just before a rather stout tree.

"Oh, look—our familiar friend."

I did not understand what Miss Dubois was alluding to until I drew nearer to the tree and saw the heap of clothing next to the base of the tree, on top of which rested the squalid hat. My anger increased.

"I don't know what kind of game you two are playing, but I am not amused."

"I think this would be a perfect pose," the Negress laughed as she leaned against the tree and unbuttoned more of her dress, so that her breasts spilled out. "What say you, Reverend?"

"Most inappropriate," I scolded, not looking away from the alluring sight.

Coffin raised his head and scanned the area. "It's a delicious atmosphere, don't you think, St. Clair? Triggers the imagination, don't you find? Come on, don't be so stuffy. Good grief, you write weird fiction! This is the clime that you at times skillfully stir up with your delicate prose. You really have an engaging style. How wonderful to find the beauty of the beast, the wondrous secrets of the darkened realm. But you could see it more clearly, if you only tried. We can help you there, partner. Would you enjoy *really* seeing into the darkness, into the Outside? Would you?"

"I have no idea what you're babbling about."

"Let us conjure darkness for you, Henry," the woman sighed. "Let us show you what lurks therein and help you to retain the taste of terror so that you can transfer it to your text. You have a splendid talent already—you just need a little assistance." I watched as she bent down and picked up the ruined hat, and I protested as she placed the wretched thing upon my head. "Nay, don't resist, my pet. Enjoy one new sensation."

She bent again, so as to dig her black hand into the debris of dirt and ash and bits of bone; and as she did so, Coffin pressed his lips together and began to whistle, and my blood froze as the sound that issued from his pursed lips was exactly the tune I had heard, in dream or delirium I do not know, in my rented room the previous evening, that impish air, that fiendish melody. The Negress rose before me, her face a black sphere in which her eyes were fantastically transformed and took on a diamond hue. I lifted my hand, wanting so to touch her eyes, as she brought forth her own hand and the pile of death that sat upon her palm. She blew the stuff into my eyes, and I blinked and blinked again as my vision altered, as I was able to see the darkness as never before, and that which lurks therein, as the cosmos whistled and shrieked idiotically all around me, and something, some dark thing, kissed at last my eye.

Half Lost in Shadow

"I am half sick of shadows," said
The lady of Shalott."
—ALFRED, LORD TENNYSON

It was my fiftieth birthday, and I resolved to get drunk. So I left the cozy porch that was my refuge and strolled that afternoon to the liquor store, where I spent a fortune on a bottle of rum that had been distilled in 1952, in Martinique. Clutching the paper bag in which I carried my bottle of golden nectar, I strolled along the shoreline where most of the ancient wharves had been broken apart or fallen in rot into the water. On one dilapidated pier, however, a phantom danced. Her theatrical gown of black swayed about her and conjoined with the dark veils that hung about her figure. I was too far from her to make out her face, most of which was covered by her length of raven hair; but I thought that perhaps she wore a pall over her countenance. We had many zanies in Kingsport, among our poets and painters mostly; but their crazy antics rarely *disturbed* me in any real way, as this creature did. I watched for a few minutes, until she stopped moving as she faced my direction; and the way she was bent over, heaving and juddering, so reminded me of a bird of prey preparing for a kill that, nonplussed, I continued on my way to Water Street and the ancient cottage whose porch I called my home.

It was going on late afternoon by the time I reached the high iron gate that opened onto my place of residence, and I was happy to walk past the gnarled trees in the front yard, among which strange large stones had been oddly grouped and painted so that they resembled the queer alien idols of some obscure Asian or African temple. Those stones had been effective in keeping people away from the former occupant of the cottage, a tall lean centenarian known to most as the Terrible Old Man, an unsocial fellow who paid for groceries and household items with antique coins of minted silver and gold. It was my habit to camp out on the front porch of the centuried cottage, an area that held warmth no matter the time of year; but I didn't want to spend my birthday alone, and so I pushed open the narrow oak door of the dwelling and entered into a dusky room that was crowded with the bizarre items that its former sea captain occupant had collected during his decades of travel and plunder. Near one small-paned window I had set a table, which I had found in an otherwise empty room and on which a collection of peculiar bottles had been placed, in each of which a small piece of lead or stone was suspended pendulum-wise from a string attached to the cork stopper. When the Terrible Old Man lived, he would sit at the table in the small room, drink his booze, and talk to these bottles, and after the old captain's disappearance I continued this practice. But I didn't like the lonesomeness of the little room, and so I had moved the table and its bottles to the more spacious main room, next to a window that overlooked the yard and its suggestively painted stones.

I took the bottle of Rhum Clément Très Vieux X. O. from its paper bag and set it on the table, pulled up a high stool, and sat. "I drink to you, my hearties," I saluted the dusty containers before me, touched the bottle's mouth to my lips, and sipped. The liquor was dry, woody, with a hint of spice and fruit in its body. "Shall I drink to another fifty years? Am I doomed to exist here as did the captain, a lonely loon aged one hundred years, lingering on because extinction was of little import? Ah, but where are my manners?" Leaning toward the dusty old bottles, I poured a little of the precious liquid onto the stopper of each one, smiling as minute streams of rum trickled down the streaked sides of murky glass. "Imbibe, mates."

I drank until the light of day extinguished outside the small-paned window; and then I lit three stout candles near the table and drank some more. As flickering shadows danced about the cluttered room, I made up pirate ditties and serenaded the pendulums inside the bottles, those pendulums on which small indistinct faces had been chiseled. In a voice that grew slurred, I spoke to those pendulums of my easy life, of the poetry that I had written, of the poems I may yet compose; and as they harkened to my words, those pendulums seemed to vibrate in sympathy with the mutterings of a drunken fool. I laughed as eyesight blurred, as the dusty old bottles took on new shapes, and I gibbered at the shadow that pressed against the window from outside, the shadow that seemed to regard me and to which I raised my nearly empty bottle of nectar. "Come in, come in. Rest among our other shadows and dream the misty dreams of Kingsport. Come out of the cold wind and chilly moonlight. Have a sip as I celebrate this disease called 'Life.' Come on, no need to flitter beneath the gnarled trees, among the scheming stones. Enter!"

I laughed as I was answered by the wind that danced among the branches of the nearby trees, those branches that tapped against the antediluvian dwelling. A momentary movement of tempest rushed about me as the cottage door was opened, and I nodded at the shadow that spilled into the room. As my blurred eyesight took in the phantom, I thought I recognized it; and as I scrutinized the being it began to spin, so that its black dress and dark veils lifted to the room's low ceiling. I watched its danse, and my sodden head began to spin with it, until the wormy walls appeared to bend. The creature stopped to contemplate me, but how it could do so I could not comprehend, for it wore no face. Lifting my bottle to it, I proposed a toast, but then I noticed that my rum had been entirely consumed. However, I had a half-bottle of white wine among my stash on the porch where I slept, and so I struggled to my feet to fetch it; but before I could take more than a half-step, I fell and felt my face crash against the floorboard.

"A pale thing floating in a blur of fleecy jet, with eyes that watch as it twists to and fro. It sways like the small humming things inside the Terrible Old Man's bottles, those petite pendulums on which faces of a sort have been carved. Ancient eyes in a youthful face—penetrating gaze. Strings of lifeless hair, dull brown in hue, and the thin hungry mouth. Oh, the sad sad smile."

Soft laughter sighed from her as the phantom listened to my talk, my words that I had meant to be thought alone as I emerged from the shadow of my drunken blackout. The figure had removed the veil with which her thin and pretty face had been covered. Bending to me, she smoothed one hand against my forehead, where I felt a tender pain. I detected a scent of lilacs in her tangled hair, probably an ointment. Suddenly, she floating upward and perched onto the edge of the chair at the table, and I watched as she examined the dusty bottles. "I had a pirate ancestor who was engaged by an old sea captain." Turning her head, she looked on me with an expression I could not read. "Philippa Angelica Ellis, of Toronto." She returned her attention to the bottles and began to hum an eccentric tune, and I sensed the hanging pendulums beginning to vibrate in response. Crawling to the table, I elevated my hand to her mouth and stopped her noise. I could feel the delicate bones beneath her mask of flesh.

"When was your last meal?" She shrugged, but I caught a tinge of woe that darkened her eyes. Holding on to the table, I lifted myself to a standing position and stalked to a shelf that held a number of antique metal boxes. Opening one, I took some gold doubloons from it, returned to her, and pressed the coins to her palm.

She wiggled her fingers so that the coins danced in her hand. "Pirate's booty? How quaint."

"What brings you to New England?"

She hesitated before answering, and then sighed heavily. "I had been performing in an acting troupe, and we played in nearby Arkham."

"You speak in past tense. Are you no longer with the company?"

"I have grown sick of shadows," she recited, and then cocked her head in a curious way. "That's from Oscar Wilde. I saw that you have the novel on that small shelf of books outside."

I nodded. "What brings you to Kingsport, my lady?"

"The car I hitched a ride with is from here, so I pretended this was my destination. Once I saw the town I felt a kind of glow, a warmth within me. I think I've visited this place once, in a dream of mist and moonlight." She rose out of the chair and raised one hand to my breast, as if to take hold of my heart, and I saw that she was little more than a child. Some tragic element in her being filled me with sudden sorrow, and I wanted to protest when, suddenly and silently, she glided from the cottage, into outer darkness.

Becoming aware of a subtle pulse of pain on my forehead, I sat in the chair, placed my elbows on the table, and buried my head in my hands. This main room inside the cottage had always worn an uncanny air, but there was a new element of strangeness now, and the lingering fragrance of lilacs. I reached out to smooth a finger against the cool glass of the tallest bottle, the one that the Terrible Old Man had called "Long Tom." I smiled at the memory of my early years in Kingsport, when I had dropped out of the world and first began to camp on the comfortable porch of the obsolete cottage. The sea captain seemed to welcome my presence, and soon he began to invite me inside his cluttered home and spin yarns about his journeys around the globe. My memory of him was crystal clear: the blue eyes that sparkled in a deeply lined face, the long white hair and beard, his olden way of talk and queer vocabulary. We would sit together at the table in the otherwise vacant room, and he would include his bottles in our conversation, calling them by name—"Jack" and "Peters" and "Spanish Joe." I regarded those antique bottles and realized that the smallest, the one called "Mate Ellis," was missing. A kind of panic swept over me. After the old man's disappearance, I had felt a sense of duty, of watching over his habitation and keeping invaders at bay. Groaning, I stood and walked out onto the porch, grabbed my jacket and stepped briskly out of the yard. A bright moon illuminated my way to the wharves, and on one dilapidated pier a phantom danced.

The horn of some invisible boat moaned in the distance. It was low-tide, yet I could see that the water was quickly creeping toward shore. The water's rhythm oddly matched the movement of my blood, and I could discern its relentless motion in my ears. The young creature's ditty, too, seeped to my ears, the faint song of lunacy that blended with the baleful hooting of the distant horn. Reaching the wharf, I stepped onto its antique timber and felt the entire thing sway, coaxed by the movement of her dancing. Her scent of lilacs wafted to me. "Miss Ellis," I whispered.

She stopped spinning and studied me from behind the dark veil that concealed her countenance once more. Her hands were wrapped around the small bottle, which she pressed against her bosom. "He's called to me in dream, but I could never locate him. I was too young, too sane—not yet claimed by our heritage of wanton madness. Yet the dreams always tugged, especially beneath the shifting stars of Arkham, and I finally found my way." Holding the bottle up to lunar light, she studied its moving pendulum. "I've lost all my family, but I'm happy to have found him. He's danced with me in dream and kissed my eyes. What kind of wizardry was woven, I wonder, that spliced his soul to that small pendulum inside this bottle?" Looking upward to the moon, she sniffed. "Can you smell it, the rising mist over the water that washes toward us? Do you taste the water's antique memories, of sunken ships and drowned souls? How wonderful to feel such kinship with others who have lost their way." Her eyes regarded mine. "But maybe you cannot. Your mind isn't wayward enough, I think. You haven't dreamed deeply enough. Something inside you resists the marvelous things. And yet you insist on lingering here, in this realm of dark enchantment and spectral trance."

"I sense it keenly enough. I choose not to partake. My wizardry is language, the spinning of poetry."

"Poetry benefits from madness, good sir. Let's drink of lunacy together, now."

I could hear the waves of the encroaching sea. The sound of moving fabric filtered to me, as she began to dance once more, as one arm swung outward and hurled the bottle onto the rocks. She twirled and tittered, ignoring the murky shadow that formed over the place whereupon the bottle had smashed. I watched the thick wisps of blackness that coiled toward us, that enshrouded the entire pier. Her scent of lilacs was replaced with a stench of wretched death. I heard the disembodied moan that was not the horn of any vessel. The rotting wharf shuddered beneath our feet as ghostly tones vibrated in the helix of shadow, a masculine voice that uttered an old sea ditty that the Terrible Old Man and I used to croon to the bottles in times of happy drunkenness. I saw the pale and pretty face that moved toward me from the darkness, and so I called her name; but then I realized that, although it shared the young woman's features, this was the visage of a young man. Sickly, he sang to me and drifted to my face so as to kiss my eyes. I felt the wharf shudder more forcefully and heard it begin to break apart. Backing away, I raised my hands to the shadow in which I was sheathed and tried to find my way to land as waves began to sound more forcefully upon the rocks below us. The wood on which I staggered suddenly collapsed, and I fell a second time that night, onto a bed of rocks, the sharp edge of one cutting into my forehead. I blinked through the tiny stream of blood that trickled onto my eyes as the tide lapped at the legs that helped me creep to land.

Shadow lifted, melting into moonlight. Gasping, groaning, I twisted my head so as to look at where the ancient wharf had stood, and saw that it had entirely collapsed and dropped onto the rocks. I saw its remnants, and the various sharp-edged boulders, and the waves that washed over the debris of stones and timber. That was all. Then my attention was caught by some shining things that shimmered at one spot beneath the waves, and I saw that they were a handful of gold doubloons that caught the sheen of moonlight. A rising wind eddied to me from the water, on which I could detect a faint fragrance of lilacs.

Circular Bone

I.

My brain is thick with heavy ignorance
As weary dullness weighs my eyelids down,
And thus I struggle for one stupid glance
Of your bleached beams that dress me in a gown
Of gossamer; a ghastly raiment, aye,
A frock of filigree, a phantom robe.
Grimly, you grin to me from moving sky,
As white as bone, a wan and senseless globe.
Some say they see your face when you are full,
A wrinkled visage winking in the skies.
I see a somber disc, a rotund skull
With malformed mouth that aches to kiss mine eyes.
I shut my weighty lids and fall to place
My hand in earth as your lips touch my face.

II.

As your lips touch my face I strangle scream
And plummet hands into the filthy sod
And blindly claw the turf that I have trod
In crazy dance within your pallid beam.
My feet are still as my hands do their deed
And dig the place that I have seen in sleep,
And sink in earth that I may rightly reap

The booty that I know is here buried.
Blind and diseased, I plunder earth until
I press my touch unto your curve of bone.
I tremble on my knees, possessed, alone.
I tremble to a supernatural thrill.
I clutch the dainty object I have found
And free it from its pit of graveyard ground.

III.

I rise to standing stance and suck the air
That rushes to my mouth as midnight storm.
My eyelids open to your insane glare.
My clumsy feet take flight as I perform
The danse of alchemy that has been taught
By murdered witches twitching on their twine.
And tho' her face is now a thing of naught,
I speak rare language to your rich moonshine
And watch the web of light in which I'm clothed
Unwind and lift unto her slate of bone.
Death, the final phase, despised and loathed,
Is mocked by magick in the words I moan.
At last, one uttered sound makes my mind flame
As her new-fashioned maw bespeaks my name.

Jester of Yellow Day

I repeat to you, Madame, that I did not kill the clown, and further inquisition would be fruitless. Continue to confine me if you must, my story will not alter; truth has not been distorted in any way, and if at times I seem confused it is because the yellow cloud of that pernicious day still weighs upon my brain and poisons my dreams. At times I feel dizzy, and it would be kind if you would return my cane; walking is difficult without it. The hollow of my hand is so vacant. There is pain behind my eyes.

As I have repeatedly informed you, I have come to Providence on holiday, wanting to escape the crush of New York. I find Benefit Street charming, and I took a temporary residence in that bed and breakfast near the armory. Being excessively weary that first evening, I retired early and sank into the red nightmare of which I have spoken, in which I almost beheld the shapes of nameless things. I was not aware of sound; but I seemed to sense a vague movement of reverberation some place outside the dream, like an echo from another dimension. Madame, I cannot help but express myself as I do; I am a sensitive soul. I tell you again, I awakened from red nightmare into the haze of the Yellow Day. The curtains of my room had not been closed, for I enjoy looking at the night. Counting starlight helps me sleep. When my eyes finally close, I can still behold the stars as they swim through my brain. But that night the velvet shadow of night's abyss became tainted with a crimson hue, and I awakened to the taste of copper on my tongue. Outside my window there was a yellow haze, and it seemed strange that morning sunlight should look so abnormal.

It was not sunlight, as I discovered when I ventured out of doors—it was the sickly aura of the Yellow Day.

I crossed Benefit Street and gazed at the yellow house beside which a small memorial garden had been constructed. Something in the nature of the house disturbed me, and so I always walked on the other side of the street and thus had never investigated the garden; but the way the trees swayed in the jaundiced light of the Yellow Day intrigued me, and thus I crossed Benefit Street and stood before the small copse that rose before me as wooded hill. I saw the growth of bluebells just beyond the sidewalk, and I marveled at how ghastly their purple hue glowed in the radiance of the Yellow Day. Stepping over a low steel barrier, I moved onto a path of flagstones that took me past the brilliant flowers, to a series of ascending rough-hewn stone steps that led up into the copse. It was then that I became aware of the sound of weird music.

Balancing myself with my black cane, I climbed the eight steps of stone that took me to a short dirt path; and then I ascended twelve wooden steps to a small clearing where I beheld the clown. I call the creature clown because of the odd mask of motley that it wore, which seemed to be composed of metallic beads. A coxcomb of four spears pointing upward, with bells fastened to their tips. The upper portion of the jester's face was covered with a half-mask that resembled a toad's countenance composed of beads that were gold and black and green. The creature's stunted body looked distorted, but that may have been an effect of the mist of the Yellow Day, which seemed to distort vision. Experiencing minute dizziness, I clutched tightly to my sturdy cane of heavy wood. After some few unsteady moments, my vision cleared remarkably, and I was keenly aware of my surroundings.

The clown sat crossed-legged upon the earth, in a clearing near a towering tree, surrounded by pale money plants and nightshade. I studied the metallic box of peculiarly asymmetrical form resting on the figure's crossed legs. It was from the box that the peculiar music sounded, although I could see that the instrument was not a hurdy-gurdy or child's jack-in-the-box. The clown's dusky hand smoothed itself over the embossed hieroglyphics with which the box was decorated, as if it were reading Braille; and its thin lips moved as if in silent mouthing of the language that its fingers inspected. Wisps of flavescent mist rose all around, and I wondered if this place served as origin for the manifestation of the Yellow Day. There was, certainly, an uncanny aura, like some symptom of sickly dreaming. It was a dream in which aspects of Nature were distorted; for the leaves of the plants beneath us were unnaturally large, and the branches of the towering tree appeared sinister in shape. And the mouth of the creature sitting before me was too wide, and the void beneath the churning lips was as dark as nightmare. I fell to my knees before the fool and tried to follow the meaning of the words it mumbled. Perhaps—perhaps one needed to touch one's fingers to the box and thus be guided in enunciating the queer tongue.

I touched the box, and light darkened. Silently the lid to the box began to rise. Inside the cavity churned my red nightmare, and I was captivated. Bending low until my nostrils were almost touching the rim of the metallic box, I inhaled. Strings of my red nightmare were sucked into my nose, until I could taste them on my tongue. I was coaxed, tingling with a desire to bury my face inside the box and drown within the depths of nightmare; but then I heard the subtle cackle of the clown, and my blood ran cold within its veins. Shouting violently, I pushed myself away. Savagely I grabbed hold of my sturdy walking stick and smashed it, again and again, on the diabolic box, until I could see nothing but weird red nightmare. My mouth watered, and my tongue tickled. I extended that tongue until it touched the crimson madness. I supped.

You say you found me there, bent over the brutalized body of a murdered thing. You say my mouth was moist and red. But I tell you again, I did not kill the clown. My stick, of which you have robbed me, destroyed the fiendish box and its senseless sigils. And yet, how peculiar that I can feel the shape of those sigils on my liquid orbs, and when I gaze into your eyes, Madame, I see those sigils swim within a reflection of red nightmare. Bend to me, good woman, for I have appetite.

This Splendor of the Goat

The young woman knelt in the area halfway up the mountain and smoothed its surface of rock with pale hands. The mountain stone was as white as polished limestone, and its shiny façade reflected the bright afternoon light. Turning, she looked down into the valley and smiled. They would not follow her here, and so she could escape for a little while their queries and queer glances. Laughing, she lifted her hands to the sun and clapped, and then she rose onto her feet and looked above her at the magnificent arched peaks that resembled two wings on the back of some daemon. Playfully, she studied her shadow on the rocky surface and shaped her arms so that her silhouette resembled, however feebly, the appearance of Mount Selta. She glanced happily around her, until her sight fastened on the nearby bust that had been sculpted from a large rock. She went to it and admired the skill with which the face and torso had been fashioned. The sunlit features were as grotesque as any she had seen in Sesqua Town, except that here they wore a slight difference from that of the children of the valley; for their Sesquan faces were a bizarre combination of frog and wolf, whereas this sinister countenance was distinctly goat-like.

Perhaps this was meant to be a portrait of Pan, and that idea inspired the woman to begin to whistle a strange and lively tune. Once more, she raised her hands and clapped in rhythm to her song; and as she whistled she began to move her feet in dance. She was but vaguely aware of her peculiar tune, and when she stopped a moment to listen to it she could not recall where she had learned it. No matter; it fitted her mood precisely, and so she kept whistling it as she unbuttoned her blouse so that she could feel the delicious morning sun on her breasts. As she cavorted about the bust she examined it carefully and decided that there was something exquisitely sensual in its expression. Stopping her gyrations, she knelt before the bust and touched her breasts against its baleful countenance. She became vaguely aware of the one who observed her.

Playing over the sculpture's hair with pale hands, she bent to kiss the creature's brow. Without turning she shouted, "I came here to be alone!"

"Then you shouldn't be so pretty and so wanton. Good grief, prancing around with your tits hanging out! How could I resist watching? Anyway, you're invading my special haunt. This is where I come to think."

"What could possibly be on your mind, Arthur, that requires such a trek?" she asked as she turned and sat on the ground, not bothering to cover her nakedness.

"Memories, and expectations. What brings you here, Monique?"

"Oh, a momentary escape—from them. This is one of the few areas they seem to shun." She shrugged. "I get tired of the way they react to me, the way they're always watching me."

The young man laughed and knelt before her, glancing around. "So where's your friend?"

Monique frowned, confused. "What?"

"That dark naked guy who was dancing with you." Her frown deepened, and her eyes narrowed in annoyance. "He was right over there, by that outcropping of rock."

She tilted to him and smoothed his brow with a pallid hand. "Your eyes are playing tricks, Arthur. We are here alone. There are no dancing naked men." Her laughter bubbled from her as she buttoned her blouse and got to her feet. "It's getting hot. Did you drive from town? No? Excellent, walk back with me. You can protect me from any dark naked gentlemen we may encounter."

They descended the steep mountain path, and Monique wondered again at the utter lack of vegetation on Selta. When at last they reached the valley floor, she looked up at the twin-peaked titan and sighed.

"She does look amazing, doesn't she?" Arthur commented. "Almost like some slumbering daemon that is just awaiting that special spectral moment of wakefulness. Do you remember how Simon reacted when I found that large piece of rock that had rolled off Selta, and I took it home and sculpted a replication? 'Munroe, this is *not allowed*,' he barked, and then he took my piece and put it on display in Creighton's antique shop. Did I ever tell you about the outlandish dreams I had as I was making that sculpture?"

"Dreams of what?"

The young man sucked in air. "Can't tell you. Can't remember. When I try to recall them all I see is a blur of hazy shapes inside my mind, like formless shadows in a mist. But I remember the ecstasy and horror those dreams inspired. Ah, the air grows sweet again. Funny, on the mountain the air is fresh and ordinary, as it is outside the valley. But down here it regains a cloying sweetness that takes some getting used to. I like this little clump of woodland; there's something calming about it."

Yes, the woman thought, this was a restful place, and she was in no hurry to rush through it. But the woodland ended too soon, and they found themselves on barren, blighted ground. The air they breathed turned rank, and they tried not to inhale too vigorously as they stepped through tall patches of yellow grass, past trees that were twisted and diseased. "This reminds me of the Hungry Place," Arthur muttered, "only ten times worse. Ugh!" Finally they came to the end of poisoned ground and on to a rocky road that led toward Sesqua Town. The sun had risen higher and the day was warm. Arthur removed his shirt and used it to wipe the sweat from his taut torso. Smiling coquettishly at her friend, Monique removed her top as well, and then laughed as Arthur leaned to her and kissed one pert young breast. They wandered nonchalantly down the rocky road that took them to the main section of the small town, and the girl slipped on her blouse but did not bother to button it.

Monique looked at the old buildings, the wooden planks that formed the town's sidewalks, and the few denizens who shuffled on those planks. "Do you remember the first time you looked upon this scene? You came from city life, too, didn't you? I remember taking it all in and feeling that Sesqua Town was both charming and absurd. Somehow I knew that I belonged here, almost that I had been summoned by the valley itself because of my predilection for occult things; and yet, when I first arrived I thought my visions of the valley had been drug-induced delusions. How did you learn of Sesqua Valley?"

"From a little cult I dabbled with," Arthur answered. "Simon used to join us, and I was especially beguiled by his sorcery. He was impressed with my grasp of esoteric languages, so he brought me here and showed me some manuscripts in his tower library that he was pondering over. He's such a freak. I could tell that he was hesitant to bring me to the valley, and yet he couldn't contain a kind of enthralled pride in showing me some of its wonders. And then we had a little, um, erotic escapade, as part of a ritual, and I was hooked. The place haunted my dreams when I returned to the city, to such an extent that I sold my business and relocated here. Now I feel totally adopted."

Monique looked past the downtown section, to the mammoth mansion that stood on a low hill just beyond. "Let's go visit Leonidas. I want to look at your sculpture of Mount Selta. Oh, stop moaning, it'll be fun. Leonidas is such an oddity."

Arthur laughed. "That's what's said of you, sweet thing." He bent to kiss her cheek, and they walked past the storefronts and to the ascending road that took them to the enormous mansion. The upper rooms of the building were rented out to the few who were passing through the valley or staying for limited visits to Sesqua Town. The mansion's lower portion mainly housed the mad antique and curio shop of Leonidas Creighton, an occultist originally from London.

"Ah, he's burning dragon blood incense. I wonder if he has any tenants," Monique whispered as they climbed the steps that led to the wide porch and front door. "I haven't noticed any outsiders in town." A little bell sounded as she opened the door, and they strolled into a spacious smoky room. The room was arranged with rows of olden oak display tables on which fascinating items were carefully arranged, with taller cases filled with books or objets d'art. Wonderful paintings hung on the walls, the most magnificent of which was a large oil of Mount Selta and the valley at sunset. The young woman followed her friend to a low table against one wall on which what looked like a collection of religious icons had been gathered.

"I caught her, didn't I?" Arthur asked his friend as he examined the sculpture of white stone.

"You did indeed," Monique agreed as she examined the sculpted image of Mount Selta, "but you've—enhanced—her image as well, given her a more sentient aura."

"No," her friend countered, "I've caught her during one of her restless moments, that's all. Haven't you ever gazed at her and seen the twin peaks bend just ever so slightly? It happens most in moonlight." But his companion did not regard him; rather, she walked away, toward another table on which another artistic display had been assembled.

"Oh, look—it's the kindred of our acquaintance on the mountain."

A figure oozed toward them from one dusky corner in the room. "They are the work of Edith York." Leonidas, sans his tall hat, regarded them somberly. Monique had never known the man to smile and was rather glad of the fact; for this English gentleman seemed to have had his teeth filed into small, perfectly shaped pearls with pointed tips. "What acquaintance on the mountain were you referring to? Have you been ascending Selta?"

Arthur chortled roguishly. "Aye, Leonidas, we have trespassed the sacred rock. We found a bust there, rather similar in style to some of these here. Perhaps it is the work of this Edith York."

"Unlikely. Miss York is a child of the shadowland. She would never surmount that prohibited place. This bust of which you speak . . ."

"Is Edith York still among us, or has she returned to shadow?"

"She is entirely reclusive since the demise of her brother. I hope you're not thinking of disturbing her."

Arthur picked up one of the small sculpted satyrs and examined its countenance. "Are any of these for sale? This one could be one of the children; look at that ugly mug. No, for display only? Pity. But what the devil is *that* supposed to be?"

"That is called 'Shub-Niggurath,' one of her most complex works. As one gazes on it, one almost fancies that it moves, however subtly— that it expands and contracts like some sentient cloud."

Monique touched the thing with timid hand. "Are those faces etched within it? Damn, it's creepy, like a beast of vapor in which the visages of trapped souls cry out for mercy."

"No," Arthur countered, "not mercy. I mean, they are almost in-distinguishable as faces, but they suggest, somehow, *elation* more than woe. A twisted kind of ecstasy, perhaps, but ecstasy nonetheless."

"I believe they symbolize the thousand young of the black goat of the woods. Ah, you aren't familiar with that particular legend. A minor Outer God, so legend says, and curiously wedded to terrestrial regions. I know very little about it, actually. Simon could tell you all there is to know."

But Monique wasn't listening. She was utterly captivated by the outré object, and by her sudden desire to become acquainted with the woman who had created it.

II.

The bent, grotesque creature listened again to the timid knocking, and then used her cane to move through a corridor to the front door of her large old house, slightly alarmed that someone would be invading her privacy, which had never happened before. She opened the door slowly and observed the pretty girl who stood there, an outsider dressed in a gown of simple beige cotton, whose sleek black hair was tied with a ribbon of white cloth. And there, held in one hand—the violet chapbook.

"Hello. Please pardon the intrusion. Are you Victoria York?"

"I am not."

Monique paused, uncertain how to proceed, hoping that her real intention wasn't obvious. "Oh. I found a copy of her book of poetry and was hoping maybe I could get her to sign it."

"My sister has escaped mortality," came the woman's queer reply.

"Ah. Are you Edith York, the sculptress? Leonidas showed me your pieces at the curio shop a few weeks ago."

"Do you sculpt, Miss . . . ? Would you care to come inside? I am just having my afternoon tea."

"Oh! Thank you. I'm Monique Lambert. No, I'm not artistic at all."

She followed the hunched woman into a comfortable sitting room, where a pot of tea and tray of cake slices sat on a low table before a petite settee. Edith motioned for Monique to sit, and then went to a sideboard and fetched a second teacup. "What is it that you do, Miss Lambert?"

"I'm a daemonologist, studying with Simon," the young woman answered as she watched the other pour tea into a cup. "Mmm, that smells good. I was so impressed with your work on display. And I was struck with the goat-like features of some of your figurines. There's a bust with similar features on Mount Selta, chiseled from a boulder. Could that possibly be your work?"

"My kind do not trespass on mountain ground."

Monique observed her new acquaintance as she sipped from her teacup. "But you're different from the others. Your features are more caprine than wolf-like. And your eyes, although silver, are tainted with a yellow element that the others lack."

"You are very observant. Yes, I have issued from a different pocket of shadow from most of the other children. They enter mortality in adult form after having followed Simon out of the shadowed realm. I, however, was a child when I arrived, and was adopted by the York household. I think Simon set it all up, although I have never inquired. I tend to avoid that unpleasant beast."

Monique laughed politely, and then quickly changed the subject. "There was one piece of your work that particularly intrigued me. Leonidas said it represented an entity called Shub-Niggurath. It has piqued my curiosity."

Edith raised her eyebrows in surprise. "Certainly one who studies unclean sprites with the beast of Sesqua Valley is aware of the Outer Gods. No? Has he never mentioned his passion for Nyarlathotep? Remarkable. What then is the nature of your studies with Simon?"

Monique set down her empty cup and leaned back onto the comfortable settee, placing the chapbook beside her on the cushion. "We study the elementals that are especial to the valley, and he has conjured some of the local imps to partake in our rituals—the strange dark folk and the frogs with human infant faces. He feels that my art has a rare potency that may enable me to summon creatures from secret pockets in the valley, fiends with which Simon is unfamiliar."

"And have you?"

"I felt a presence in the woodland that affected me curiously. Strangely, I experienced the exact same sensation when I was studying your sculpture."

"Ah, that is splendid. You have tasted the aura of the Black Goat of the Woods with a Thousand Young that lurks within our woodland. My sister experienced that eidolon as well." Edith motioned to a corner of the room where a life-size statue stood, the quality of which was so stunning that Monique could not resist rising and going to inspect the figure's workmanship. "Of course, you know of Victoria's passion for that particular Outer God from having read her poems. If, indeed, you have acquainted yourself with her work."

There was a pregnant pause, and then Monique couldn't help but snicker. "Damn, you've found me out. But of course you would. I'm not here because of Victoria. I spent the past few weeks learning more about you from the locals, and then an acquaintance gave me her extra copy of the chapbook. I'm here because of your sculpture of Shub-Niggurath and its spell over me. It has triggered some uncanny instinct inside my soul."

"Then you *are* here because of Victoria, in ways you may be unable to ascertain. There are no accidents in Sesqua Valley, Miss Lambert. I advise you to read my sister's poetry and let it instruct your dreaming."

The young woman gazed at the statue. "She had an almost regal beauty."

Edith nodded. "She was majestic in every way."

Monique turned to her. "Are you entirely reclusive? I could come and visit, if you like, and help alleviate loneliness."

For the first time, the ancient woman smiled. "One is never alone in Sesqua Valley, child. Especially my kind. I am visited by evening mist, wherein I hear the pleas of my shadow kindred to return to the realm of origin. I shall probably be returning before long. Not that I have much to do with those of the common swirl, being the fruit of unconventional pocket."

"It's so captivating when your kind speaks of the realm from which you came to our mortal clime, although none of you seem to have any clear memory of that other region."

"Oh, I remember it—every bit."

"Is it entirely different—from here?"

"As dream differs from the waking world. Don't forget to take your chapbook, dear. You are quite lovely. Perhaps you'll come again and sit for me."

"I'd be honored, Miss York." She went and took the chapbook from the elder creature's hand and quietly exited the house. The day was mildly warm and bright, with a slight breeze that felt comforting as it played with her strands of glossy hair. Removing her shoes, Monique walked past the center of Sesqua Town and stopped to lean against the mammoth sculpture of a sphinx, the stone of which was comfortably warm against her bare arms. Opening the chapbook, she squinted as the bright light of day was reflecting from its pages onto her eyes. Blinking, she began to consume poetry.

"What do you have there, Lambert?" asked a familiar voice.

"The poetry of Victoria Elizabeth York."

"Ah, yes, a very curious case," Simon Gregory Williams replied. "She vanished from the valley after an intriguing supernatural manifestation. Quite curious indeed. Her brother died a few years ago. Edith—now she's rather intriguing. She slipped into this mortal realm from an infant pocket of shadow and came to us in the form of a child. She's not like others."

"Her eyes are different—slightly."

Simon raised an eyebrow. "You've encountered her?"

Monique nodded. "I've just come from visiting her. She wants me to sit for her—for a work of sculpture, I think."

"You little nymph, how quite remarkable. Well, you're as much an oddity as she is, thus it shouldn't surprise one that you would find common ground." He looked at the chapbook and frowned. "I lack that in my collection at the tower. You will donate it, of course."

"Perhaps. What is this part here, these two lines in Greek?"

"Let me see," he demanded, holding out his hand and clutching the offered booklet. "Hmm, yes; it's an antique chant to the Black Goat of the Woods with a Thousand Young." Monique jumped at the sudden sound of Simon's loud voice declaiming old Greek, and the sun lit his silver eyes with greater intensity. It was always thus when he participated in some arcane rite, when his malformed mouth spoke magick. There was such vibrancy in his tone, and authority. It was at moments such as this that Monique knew she was dealing with a wizard of monumental potency. How strange that the sun seemed to darken at the continued sound of his chanting. A bestial thing howled from some distant place, and she detected an edge of cruelty in the sound—malice laced with unwholesome appetite. Simon, soaking it all in, grinned wickedly as he came to the end of his chanting. "Oh, that was fun. Whatever did we evoke, I wonder?"

"We evoked poetry—sublime poetry. Did you know her?"

"Victoria York? Not well. She and her brother were brought to the valley by mistake, by their foolish parents. They were very young, the children, and the boy was pathetic and spineless. He was an outsider to his very last day. They planted him yonder, in the Hungry Place. The mother was a child of shadow who had a sickening desire to remain mortal, and so she left the valley and married. But she could not stay away, and eventually they came here to live. He lasted longer than any of us expected he would, but eventually he went mad and deserted the family."

"And the mother?"

"Returned to shadow long ago. As for her eldest daughter—Victoria's fate has remained an enigma, and little hunchbacked Edith has stayed entirely reclusive." He smiled impishly and nodded to her. "Until touched by your seductive allure."

The young woman pushed away from the sphinx and shielded her eyes. "I'm in need of shade. Wander the woodland with me, Simon, and help me to memorize those Greek lines from Miss York's poem. I like the way they sound. I like their energy."

"Yes, they shimmer with influence, those words. How charming to see them work on you. You have disappointed me by being so unadventurous. Daemonology is a fascinating study, but a study of animism is mere theology unless put into some kind of practice. The best way to research and analyze devils is to evoke them, to feel their presence on one's eyes, to drink their poison with one's nostrils. That is the path toward which I have guided you."

"Yes, you have, and your seduction has had its effect. Come on, I need to get out of this sunlight."

She moved away, without looking to see if Simon followed, and walked the distance until coming to a woodland path, onto which she stepped. The effect was instantaneous: the light that filtered through the trees and touched her eyes felt softer, and the air lost some of its cloying sweetness.

"You needn't tramp so vigorously. One would think you were applying for some military position, the way you march."

"I've always liked this," she said, stopping to touch a three-foot-tall sculpture of a night-gaunt. "Is it true, Simon, what I've heard hinted—that the night-gaunts cross a hidden threshold in Sesqua's woodland that is somehow joined to another world? I have a feeling there are so many things you've yet to teach me about this valley and your real reason for bringing me here."

"The woodland here is pregnant with pockets to other realms, with which the wise do not tamper. I live in such a zone, which is why it is impossible for others to locate my residence."

"You lived there with the poet, Manly, until his strange disappearance. Take me there."

"Don't be absurd. I never allow mortals into my home."

Monique leaned toward him and smoothed his cheek with the back of her hand. "I am no ordinary mortal."

"Nay, do not touch me, nymph."

"It's what I do, Simon. It is my one trait of alchemy. I touch—and seduce."

"You will remove your hand this instant. No, do not cover my eyes, Monique."

Her laughter was a gay sound. "Ha, that's the first time you've called me that. You see, you are already under my spell. Show me your abode, beast of the valley."

Simon spat air, and then he smiled diabolically. "Come then, and follow me."

She watched him walk a narrower path than the trail she had been following, and she wondered at the sudden sense of uncanny fear that gave her pause. Then he vanished from sight, and the idea of being alone where she stood aroused mild panic, and so she rushed after the beast, through the weird woods. When again she saw him, Simon had stopped to fondle the yellow flowers of the spreading branches of a tree.

"What a lovely laburnum," Monique said as she joined Simon and stroked one of the hanging blooms. "Oh dear, the fragrance is rather heady—quite similar to the air of the valley. It catches in one's throat."

"So beautiful," Simon intoned as he held the yellow flowers, "and so poisonous. I have a recorder made of laburnum wood, beautifully carved and with an amazing tone. I use it when I want to summon something particularly noxious."

Monique blinked as she gazed about them. "The light is different here, weirdly diffused."

"Everything is different here, nymph; we are near to the vicinity of the shadowed realm, to its barrier of dream. Manly wanted to remain close to home, and so he built his cabin in close proximity to the wraith-like rim. Come along, we're almost there."

They followed the narrow pathway together, side by side, and then she saw the little cabin in its charming setting. Monique could not suppress a gasp of joy as her eyes drank in the beauty of the scene, the remarkable loveliness of the tall trees that hung their branches high above the small residence, the gorgeous beds of unfamiliar and fragrant flowers that surrounded the wooden structure.

"Welcome to my demesne," the beast uttered.

The young woman fell onto the soft ground and sighed at how warm and wonderful the earth felt upon which she knelt. Like one intoxicated, she clawed into the soil and brought handfuls of it to her face and hair, rubbing the substance onto her flesh. She looked around and espied an object near to her, the sight of which made her cry out in amazement. Crawling on hands and knees to the bust, she embraced it, kissed it. "You have an amazing talent. There is a weird kind of sentience to your work, as if this were not a creation of stone at all but rather the fossilization of a once-living thing."

"That is none of mine. My brother had the artistic hand."

"Your brother? William Davis Manly? What a remarkable fellow he must have been. And I've seen the brother to this bust, on the mountain."

"Whatever are you talking about?"

"There's an identical replication of this work halfway up the mountain. Surely you've seen it."

"We children of shadow never trespass onto the surface of Khroyd'hon." She stared at him, confused. "That is the dream name for Selta," he went on. "No, I've never seen this other thing. But whatever it is, it's not the work of William."

"I tell you they're identical, in every way. Obviously the work of the same artist. Manly visited Mount Selta, undoubtedly. Why can't you walk on the mountain?"

"We do not. There are zones in the valley that disturb us if we enter them. I've walked on the mountain twice, in aid of magick, and twice I have severely regretted it. I'll not repeat that error." He watched as she petted the sculpted work, and something in the way she touched it annoyed him. "But come, you wanted to see inside our home. Rise and follow me."

The woman did as she was commanded and entered the cabin with her host. The rooms were small and cluttered with fabulous debris. One wall was completely covered with over a hundred flutes, all of curious design, which rested on fittings that had been fastened to the wall. Stepping into the bedroom, Monique sensed a powerful and morbid sorrow in the atmosphere, and using her arcane inclinations she deciphered that this was the place where the beast wept. She could smell his spilled tears of the pillow as she sat on the bed. "More than brother."

"What's that you say?" Simon sat next to her, and his face wore an expression she had never seen it bear before. He did not protest as Monique took his hand and touched it to the pillow.

"Manly was more than brother to you. Your sorrow, your aching loneliness—my god, how you work to conceal that aspect of your psyche from everyone! You play at being cruel and monstrous, a masquerade that you have mastered. But it's mostly nothing more than a fiendish mask, a toy of personality with which you torment others. So as to shield the torture in your soul."

"I have no soul, nymph."

"Oh, Simon," she answered, placing one hand on his brow and the other at his chest, "you have more than most."

"Nay, do not touch . . ." But he could not continue, for she *had* discovered his secret, and now she touched it with her witchery, which he had enhanced through his instructing her in alchemy. Simon shuddered and shut his eyes, and soon the hands that touched him became, in fantasy, the hands of another, of one whom he had loved and lost.

Hours passed, and the wan moon lifted itself over the twin peaks of the white mountain. A nude figure emerged from the cabin and stretched in the pallid beams that filtered through branches onto ground. The young woman saw how one beam fell directly onto the goatish bust, the sight of which entranced her. She saw the small creatures that had surrounded that bust and were singing to it, the small frogs with faces of human infants. Going to them, she knelt before the sculpture, allowing the wee creatures to kiss her hands as she joined in their song. There came, from beneath the ground on which she knelt, a growing pounding, as if some gigantic heart beneath her had awakened with preternatural life. Monique listened as the freakish amphibians began to chant, in thin high voices, to something in the woodland, some *thing* with which Monique had become subconsciously linked. She listened to the strange and potent ululations that issued from the infant faces, listened until she had learned their language enough so that she could clearly speak it. Her voice, strong and clear, sang to the deity of woodland.

III.

The small dark man emerged from the woodland and walked the road that led to Sesqua Town. Dressed in a suit of simple design, he held an undersized suitcase in one hand and a tote bag in the other. The morning sun shone on his black eyes, those eyes that twinkled with humor as they glanced at the surrounding sights. He smiled at the quaintness of the little business area, with its old establishments and sidewalks of wooden planks, and then turned to walk up a rising road that took him to a stately mansion of mammoth proportions. Climbing the steps of the porch, he found one of the two front doors open; and so he stepped through the threshold and entered a broad hallway, where interesting figures sat on antique walnut hall tables, and where fascinating paintings hung on the walls. He stopped before one large painting and drank in its curious scene.

"Fantastic, isn't it?" The dark man turned to acknowledge the youthful figure at his side. "It's an original Pickman. There's no signature, but the style is unmistakable, and he did other renditions of the same scene. Are you here to see the shop?"

"No, I've come to rent a room."

"Ah, then I'll introduce you to Leonidas. He's just here in the showroom." The lad walked toward the double doors that, when opened, revealed a very large room crammed with antiques and curios. Two figures sat on an antique English oak settee made in 1780 and examined a large tome that rested on a beautiful hand-carved mahogany coffee table with white marble top. The taller of the two wrinkled his nose as if at an unpleasant odor as they took their eyes from the volume and regarded the dark man. "This gentleman desires a room."

Leonidas Creighton, arising and stepping to the stranger, was in his usual attire of black suit and caped black overcoat. His smooth white hair fell past his ears and stopped just above his shoulders. Had he smiled, he would have revealed twin rows of serrated teeth; but Leonidas did not smile, for something in the nature of the outsider disconcerted him. "How long will you be staying?"

"That is undetermined." The dark man's voice was low and contained an undertone of buzzing that was quite peculiar; but the sound of it reminded Simon Gregory Williams of something he had encountered while investigating the mythic woodlands of Vermont, and he rose from the sofa and joined the others.

"I am Simon Williams," he said, bowing slightly, "and I welcome you to Sesqua Valley. Pray, what brings you to our little outpost?"

The dark man returned Simon's courteous bow. "Basil Scratch, your servant. I've come to dream visions of Khroyd'hon and enter, psychically, the valley's shadowed realm. Merely as an experiment, of course."

"You are quite informed about our realm," Simon responded, in a low voice that was laced with menace.

"I am a keen occultist. I know that you prefer to keep the valley's secrets to yourselves, and the mountain is indeed potent in shielding your dominion from most of the outside world; but there is another Outside realm, between the stars and beyond dimension, and in that place the valley is well known indeed."

Leonidas stepped a little nearer to the dark man and peered into the fellow's black eyes. "Ah, you are from Outside. Quite so. Yes, I see the void reflected in your orbs. This is a singular visitation. Cyrus, show Mr. Scratch to the Yellow Room. Your privacy, sir, is assured."

"My humble thanks." Basil bowed once more and then followed Cyrus out of the room.

Simon's mouth curled into a snarl. "Pah! That fellow smells like a goat den. Most curious, this. We shall keep a sharp eye on this researcher of our homeland. Penetrate the shadowed realm? Preposterous!"

"Calm yourself. His trick is obvious."

"What trick is that?"

"Mr. Scratch was far too bold and outrageous in explaining his visit here. It was naught but theatrics, overly dramatic so as to conceal his authentic reason for invading Sesqua Valley. Oh, he is without doubt an occultist of some kind—but he is much more than he lets on. We shall go along with his charade, and we will study his every move until we blast his mystery. Don't scowl so. This may prove quite entertaining."

"Were you one of us, you would not find it so. You like to see me squirm, Creighton. The idea of my authority being thwarted pleases your sick and fiendish mind."

The other fellow bowed. "Coming from the valley's supreme fiend, that is a delicious compliment. But you're mistaken. I have always supported you, however playful I may be at times, however wanton. True enough, I am and shall always be an outsider. But that is my lot wherever I have settled. I am quite singular, and my unnatural existence has had many dark moments. I have been condemned and hunted, thrown into prisons and pits, reviled and repulsed. It is only here that I have found the facility to exist as I am, in all my vileness; and that is why I have stayed here for eight decades, and will stay for eight more. The valley is now my home."

But Simon was too distracted to listen, abruptly turning from Leonidas and marching out of the mansion, into the light. The sky was clear except for some few beds of flocculent clouds that drifted over the valley. The beast raised his face to the sun and wondered why the day was already so hot; usually the weather in his valley was pleasant, not something one would be aware of because of extremities of coolness or warmth. He walked into town, stopping at the first building he came to and listening to the sound of laughter that came from inside. His curiosity aroused, Simon entered the artists' studio and observed a small group of women and men who were at work on various projects. Sneering, Simon approached a shirtless fellow who was seated at a tall table and working on a sculpture.

"What is this, Munroe?"

The young man did not bother to look at Simon as he spoke, but continued his labors. "Amun Ra, in his ram personification. I've succeeded in making the horns especially wicked, don't you think?"

Simon scrutinized the sinister goat-like countenance that the sculpture wore. "What a curious physiognomy you've given it. However did you envision such a visage?"

"Oh, I copied it from the bust on the mountain. I made a lot of sketches, of course, but the real inspiration came from my dreams of the thing."

"Is this your sketchbook? Let me just glance through it." Arthur aped nonchalance and returned to touching up his figurine as the beast studied pages on which the bust on Mount Selta had been sketched.

Simon's blood tickled in his inhuman veins. The sketched image was identical in every way to Manly's goatish model. "Most peculiar." He had not meant to speak the words aloud.

"Why is that?"

Simon shut the sketchbook and narrowed his eyes at the young artist. "I find it most peculiar that you outsiders invade the mountain's exterior when you clearly understand that the area is proscribed. Your wanton behavior will not be tolerated."

"Sod you, Simon. You have no power over me."

Ah, what cruelty curled the beast's malformed mouth! "Do I not?" Arthur watched as Simon's eyes darkened with menace, and he felt his flesh prickle as the beast began to whisper phrases in a most peculiar language. The atmosphere in the room grew chilly and creepy, and the other artists stopped in their labors and observed the valley's first-born shadow-spawn in fascination and fear. They watched, unmoving, as Arthur picked up a mallet from his table and began to smash his work of art violently, until it was merely a small pile of wreckage. Simon smiled at the rubble and then gently took the mallet from Arthur's hand, kissed the implement, and playfully tapped its leaden head against the young man's brow. Then he tossed the tool onto the table and made his exit from the studio.

IV.

Their bodies were intertwined within the circle of stones, their ritual of sex magick just reaching its climax. Together they screamed, and then they laughed and rested on their backs. Monique's hand played through the mass of hair that decorated Arthur's chest. "Is your beast soothed, my dear?" she queried.

The young man sneered. "Don't use that word. Damn him and his arrogance. It was one of my finest pieces. He knows that art is sacred here. I've never seen him so nasty." He paused and studied the girl's expression. "What?" She frowned at him, as if to say she did not understand his implication. "You have a knowing look in your eyes."

She shook her head. "It's nothing. I think, perhaps, his fury is linked to the enigma of another local artist—the enigmatic William Davis Manly."

"Manly was a poet. There's a statue of him in the cemetery where outsiders are buried."

"He sculpted as well. I think he did the bust that we found on Selta."

Arthur shook his head. "The shadow-spawn don't go near the mountain."

"Simon's been there, twice; and William Davis Manly was no ordinary child of shadow. Maybe that's why so few people mention him. Perhaps he was banned in some way, banished from the valley."

"They'd hardly pay tribute to him with a statue, if that were so. Why do you laugh like that?"

"This is Sesqua Valley. Its denizens aren't going to make sense, Arthur."

But he wasn't listening to her, and she saw his face grow stern as he gazed past her, into the woodland. Monique turned to look into the moonlit timberland, and she saw the suggestion of a figure that was studying them, the silver eyes of whom caught moonbeams. The humans did not move as the shadowed one stepped toward them.

"Your magick is ripe. I could scent the sex far off, and it inspired a pang of sorrow in the fact that I have never partaken of such primitive pleasure. I've come to sketch you, Monique." Edith showed them the sketchbook that she carried in one hand, and they observed the bulky shoulder bag that had been packed with artistic implements. "No, don't hunt for your clothes—you are charming just as you are." Without hesitation, the Sesquan set her things on the ground and began to remove her clothing. The humans watched, entranced, never having seen a child of shadow nude. "I am not, as I suggested to you, my dear, like others of the shadowed realm. I have more in common with the strange dark folk. You will notice that my feet are partially hoofed, and the fur covering my breasts and loins is sleek and black. My kind almost never follow Simon into this mortal realm when he tempts us with his reed and sorcery. We prefer the mountain in her primitive dream-state, as majestic Khroyd'hon. We mingle with the dreams of slumbering Cthulhu and howl in mockery with Nyarlathotep. We inhale the airy exhalation of that which is worshipped as Shub-Niggurath. Iä! The Black Goat of the Woods with a Thousand Young!"

As she spoke the ground beneath them began to pulse, and some dweller on the mountain bayed at moonlight. The entranced couple saw the mauve mist that began to issue from distant trees and collected as a miasmal entity that oozed toward them. They listened to Edith's murmured song, to the language of her litany, and watched as she picked up her sketchbook and drew a pencil from her bag. Edith's strange song turned coarse and became a cackle as she seemed to welcome the nude prancing figure who danced toward them out of the mist. The small dusky man with goatish facial features clapped his petite hands as he continued the song that Edith had been warbling. His voice was high and contained a quality of buzzing, and the frenzy of his clapping was so infectious that the mortals could not resist the urge to rise and join him in satanic frolic.

The beast of Sesqua Valley brought the weighty mug to his mouth and drank, while in that liquid that corresponded to mortal blood he could feel the uncanny rhythm that was the valley's heartbeat. The lounge in which he lingered was not overfull, yet each of its few inhabitants could not help but study Simon with surreptitious glances, each of them alert to the sensations in the air and underfoot. The valley came alive, eerily, when potent alchemy was practiced within its confines; and this kind of activity strangely affected those shadow children who had escape the realm of their origin so as to dwell for one slight season among mortals. A youngish creature who had been sitting in a dusky corner got to his feet and sauntered to Simon's table, then sat down opposite the beast.

"You've been looking so pensive for weeks. What ails you, Simon?"

"Enigmas that should not subsist," the beast replied before he was fully aware of speaking. Something had indeed affected him. He took another sip of brew and licked his twisted mouth. "The valley is pregnant with ritual, Cyrus. I should locate the source and join in the lunacy—and yet I am lethargic."

Cyrus grinned as the bartender brought him a glass of Sesqua brew, from which he drank heartily. "There's something unique about whatever's happening tonight. The air smells as it never has before, and the moonlight is peculiar. Do you understand any of it?"

"I am apathetic."

Cyrus blew air out of his mouth in frustration. "What the hell is wrong with you?"

The beast shut his eyes and raised his head a little higher, in an aspect of listening. "I hear the shadow summoning my return. My stay has been overlong."

Some figures arose to their feet in shock. Not knowing what to do, the younger creature took Simon's hand and petted it. "You are the first-born spawn of shadow. You were the first to awaken when the outsiders initially invaded this valley, and you were responsible for their disposal. You are our diabolic lord and master. You can't abandon us now."

Something in the beast seemed to awaken. He removed his hand from kinship's grasp and sneered. "Can I not?" He glared at the other onlookers. "Do you think I would never leave you and return to the realm of origin?"

"But you *do* return to it. We've seen you dance into the mist and watched it swallow you."

The beast squinted his evil eyes and sneered at Cyrus. "Ah, ye've been spying on me. Yes, I have returned to mist and shadow, but in my mortal frame. To fully return and be as once we were one must completely discard this husk of mortality and its contents. Pah, how little you perceive."

Cyrus banged the table with an angry fist. "Because you have drawn a mental veil over us, so that we cannot recall our homeland. We see glimpses of it merely, ghosts of memories." His sudden anger cooled when he noticed the look of sorrow that re-entered Simon's fantastic eyes. "What's wrong, beast?"

Simon's voice, when at last he spoke, was barely a whisper. "I thought if I waited long enough he would return to me, from wherever it is he has vanished to. More and more, however, I am reminded that I know too little, that I have no answers. Did he go away at all, or is he here in some form, in some secret plain of which we are ignorant? He understood the valley far better than anyone. He was keenly attuned to her magick, her mystery and madness. Perhaps he hasn't left us at all—not really. Simply, he no longer needs us—me."

With that, Simon stopped speaking. Despondently, he reached into his jacket pocket and produced a lean black flute. His music, when he played, was so heart-wrenching that the others could not abide it, and thus they departed. Cyrus stayed at the table for as long as he could endure the sound; but the noise was so wretchedly poignant that he, too, had to rise and leave. Simon played on and on, and Sesqua Valley's heart, far beneath the earth and shaking the valley floor with her daemonic pounding, seemed almost to break in pity of the beast.

V.

She climbed up the winding stone steps, her hands outstretched and running their fingers over the dry brick with which the Cyclopean tower had been constructed; and it amazed her, as it always did, how the atmosphere altered the nearer she got to the circular room at top in which Simon Gregory Williams kept his collection of arcane tomes, esoteric scrolls, and other occult matter. The air changed its fragrance as her eyes saw the glow of reflected light that began to hit the walls that surrounded her, and then she stepped into that light and thought that Simon had lit three hundred candles, the room was so illuminated. Monique looked around for the room's occupant, hearing his voice before locating where he sat beneath a long table.

"Begone. I've no appetite for your abusive mortality this day."

"I have never maltreated you," the young outsider answered.

"Your very existence is an assault. I am sick of humanity. Begone."

She knelt beside the table and reached out to him. "What ails thee, beast?"

"Nay, do not touch me with your healing trickery. Save that for your fellow humans. You were up to something last night. The valley reeked of your flesh, your liquid and your marrow."

"We were engaged in ritual with the black goat of the woods."

"We?"

"I name no names."

"You've been cavorting with that Scratch creature, have you? Charming. And does he designate himself the Black Goat of the Woods with a Thousand Young? And have you any comprehension what that means?"

"He's an avatar of Shub-Niggurath. Edith says his being here is a fabulous portent." She paused, studied him, and scowled. "Must you be such a pouty little infant? You lured me to this vale to teach me wonders. You should be happy that such marvelous episodes are re-curring and instructing me. Is it the idea of Manly that has you so mis-erable? Come, then, let's engage in ceremony and summon him. I'll bet you've never actually tried."

Simon backed away from her, out from under the table and to his throne. Reaching for his seat of power, he hauled himself up and climbed into it. "You are woefully ignorant if you think I would engage in such a ritual with an interloper who has yet to comprehend the ways of Sesqua Valley. I thought, when I encountered you, that you had possibilities and would aid the valley with your properties, which are still so in embryo; but now I see that you are quite dull-witted, and I discharge you as my pupil. Begone."

Standing, Monique pushed a pile of books on the table so as to make a place where she could sit with her back to the beast. Graceful-ly, she raised her arms and began to make strange shadows on the wall. "You were inspired to bring me here, beast, by the valley, and by the Outer God."

"Outer God? Is this the rot that Scratch has fed you? Do you fan-cy that your fate is wed to this demesne? I brought you here, and now I dismiss you. What, you'll not leave? Then I shall. Good day, wench." He waited and watched, and then he stomped the ground. "Is my au-thority completely invalid? Have I lost my rule as Supreme Beast of this valley? I will not tolerate this disrespect another instant. I am the first-born of shadow. I am the one who lures the children from mist and shadow into the light of mortal day. Do you sit there and smile at me and defy my authority? Begone!"

He grimaced at her as she sat unmoving on the table, and then his frown deepened as he saw the expression in her alchemical eyes; for she was a being of power, a seductress not only of mortal desire but of Outside influences. She had possessed her power from infancy, and her time spent under the tutorage of Simon Gregory Williams had merely enhanced her abilities. Pursing her lips, Monique subtly whistled an enchanting song, one that the beast had performed for her on his flute. It was a whisper of sound, barely audible, and yet at the sound of it the room's candlelight dimmed. She pushed herself tenderly off the table and drifted to the beast. Bending, she removed his shoes and kissed his grotesque feet. Monique kept her head bowed low as she spoke. "You found me in my lonesome place and lured me to this uncanny realm. You saw something within me that I could never have discovered on my own. Together we located a talent, which you have helped to nurture. But there is more to my being here than you initially realized, a fate that I have half embraced although I don't know what it is or what it means. The valley has worked through you to bring me to my destiny. Sesqua has bequeathed its awesome power and authority to you, its first-born son. I do not understand my affinity with the Outer God, but I will kiss that providence because you were supernaturally guided to lure me here. Defy you? I adore you!"

The beast narrowed his eyes at the crouched figure before him; and then he tilted forward and placed a warm hand onto her head. "Arise, mortal, and tell me of this avatar, this black goat of the woods."

She sighed onto the floor and kept her head bent low. " I don't understand much of what he told me, such as his being aware of Sesqua Valley because its woodland is conjoined at one point to the forest of the dreamlands. I sense that you fathom what that indicates. Perhaps one day you will explain it to me, as you have explained so much, as you have molded the way I think, even the way I speak, as though I am your puppet. He did not explain the nature of the Outer Gods or of them whom he calls the Great Old Ones. At one point he hinted that these gods and Old Ones know of this valley because of you, because you have studied the arcane tomes and spoken their formulae aloud. If I understood him correctly, you have memorized each extant edition of something he pronounced oddly—it was like he was buzzing the title instead of articulating it."

"*Al Azif.*"

"Yes—you say it exactly as he did, as if there is more than one voice proclaiming it. The vibrations of your chanting from the book have transcended dimension. The scent of your language has been picked up by Outer Gods such as Shub-Niggurath and Nyarlathotep, and brought this valley and its mysteries to their notice. They dwell at times, these outer ones, in pockets of shadowed dimension in the woodland that even you cannot detect, and they watch you. At times their influence is seduced by your power as a wizard, and they leak into the dreaming of those of us who dwell here—mortals and shadow-kindred. Your bringing me here was not chance, not accident; you were guided by an Outer God, to whom you will offer me with all your majestic potency. I am to be a vessel for one of the thousand young."

"How glorious! And what is Edith York's connection to your fate? I know that she has an interest in Shub-Niggurath. Leonidas has her sculpture of its representation in his curio shop. Does she speak to you of her elder sister? No? That is an enigma I have yet to grasp." Simon stretched. One hand made curious signals to the air, and Monique could hear the electric sparks that frolicked between Simon's moving fingers. He moved out of the chair, onto his feet, and walked past the woman without saying another word.

Exiting the round tower, Simon walked the woodland until he came to the ring of stones wherein the young couple had performed their ritual of sex and enchantment. The place still smelled of magick, and Simon saw that he was not alone. The dark man danced within the circle, but stopped when he realized that he was being observed. Gracefully he genuflected to the beast.

"Do not fawn before me, Scratch. Explain your presence here."

"Ah, first-born seed of shadow—favored above the million-favored ones, sorcerer extraordinaire! You are like some fallen angel, dwelling on paltry sorrow. Mortality has tainted you, you who have existed in this realm too long a time. Did you think that you could subsist among humanity for more than a century and not be infected? They bequeath you their diseases; why, even your blood has altered in chemistry, and the heart to which it rushes has grown mellow and affectionate. You were once such an exquisite fiend, protecting your valley from measly humanity; and now you bring this child from outside, to study with you and become skilled at your magnificent art. We weep for thee."

"We?"

"We from Outside."

"The girl has purpose here?"

"Aye, we shall make use of her. But what of you, Simon Gregory Williams? How often must the shadowed sphere cry out to thee before you return unto it absolutely?"

"Not long, perhaps." The beast raised his snout and sniffed. "I smell providence—potent and compelling. Whatever has brought you here is soon to pass. Why do you smile like that?"

"It is you who have caught our attention, beast. Just as the outsiders initially settled in this place and awakened you in your realm of shadow and mist, so you have drawn us from Outside with your fervid chanting, your demented deviltry. You cannot bend dimension and not be a focus for our questing appetite. You have tugged, subconsciously perhaps, and we have responded."

Simon clasped his hands together and rubbed them over his monstrous face. "So be it. I don't want the girl harmed in any way."

"She will be glorified."

Simon nodded at the avatar of Shub-Niggurath, and then turned away as the goatish figure began again to dance.

VI.

Edith York held the folded gown before her, an offering to the girl. "It was an eccentricity of my siblings to dress oftimes for dinner. Victoria was partial to this frock. You're as tall as she was, I think. Wear this tonight." Monique took the dress and embraced it to her breast. She then set the gown upon the bed and removed her clothing. Naked, she sat before a bureau and closed her eyes as Edith brushed and anointed her hair. The oils used smelled of frankincense and myrrh. Edith paused in her grooming of the young woman, and when Monique opened again her eyes she caught the elder woman's momentary emotion.

"Oh dear, how poignant and friendless are the valley's offspring this night. You ache to see Victoria again. And yet—I sense she isn't far. It's odd, I feel that way about the other poet as well. William Davis Manly."

"You're wiser than you know," Edith told her, going to the bed and lifting the gown so that it fell open. The naked girl stepped to it and allowed Edith to help her into the dress. "We're off, then—to the circle."

"I'll meet you there. I have one small errand to perform." So saying, the young lass left the house and entered the woodland. She walked some distance and then stopped, perplexed, leaning against one tree and wrapping her arms around it. "Assist me, Sesqua Valley—guide me to his lair. The hour has come for his return." The trees moved above her in the growing wind that pushed her farther along the path. Extending her arms, Monique clutched at the air that guided her, until she came at last to the hidden bungalow. She entered and found Simon, fully dressed, sitting within a circle of extinguished candles.

"How dare you infiltrate my lair. Begone." He tried to snarl the words, but they were empty of emotion, spoken as a form of habit that lacked vitality.

Kneeling before him, the girl offered him her hand. "Come with me. Please, stand with me as I meet my fate."

"I can perceive the sensation of whatever happens to you here. The valley tells me everything."

"Oh, venture with me, Simon," she sang. "You've taught me to embrace the madness of magick. Join with me now in its rich lunacy. Come, daemonic and demented beast, and we shall howl as one." She watched as his sneer became an ugly smile, as his paw lifted so as to seize her proffered hand. Monique winced a little, for his hold was tight and cruel. She could almost smell the depths of his emotional turmoil as he stepped out of his ring of scented candles. Tenderly, coaxingly, she sang an esoteric song that he had taught her as she escorted him from the bungalow. Playfully, she gently pranced about him on the path that took them to the place of ceremony.

Simon gazed at the sight before him, surprised that there were only two other participants. Edith was crouched within the circle of stone, while the one who called himself Basil Scratch moved around the stones in danse, a garland on his dome. Watching his movement seemed to enliven the lethargic beast, and Simon reached into an inner pocket of his jacket and produced a pipe. His music was an eldritch sound, and it delighted the goatish man. Nodding his head in time to his tune, Simon reached into the pocket again and produced a second flute, which he tossed to Scratch; and then moved into the danse, leaping and stomping on the ground as Edith's silver eyes sparkled with excitement. The small woman reached out to Monique, who joined her within the circle as the valley's floor began to pulse to the influence of song and transforming alchemy. And then song and movement stopped, replaced by the noise of Edith's harsh voice raised in chanting. Monique peered into the darkness of the woodland as she sensed the approaching mist, the swirling brume that crept toward them like some unique sentient entity. The young girl watched, entranced, as an outline formed within the mist, a figure that caused Edith to cry out. The being floated there, in the whirling miasma—an eidolon that was, in every way, a replication of the statue that Edith York had sculpted of her transformed sister, she who had been strangely wed to an essence of Shub-Niggurath. Monique did not move as Basil Scratch reached into the circle and offered Edith his hand, which the child of the valley grasped. The black goat tugged the elder woman to the mist, and that which had been Victoria York enfolded her shadow-sister within her arms.

The dark man turned and tossed his flute to Simon; and then he raised his hands above his head and made strange signs to aether. Opening his devilish mouth, the fiend began to utter an alien litany, and as his droning voice buzzed he began to shed his human façade, transmuting into a thing of black vileness, a gelatinous patch of ichor that stained the valley's air, the stench of which caused Monique to gag. It stretched, this noisome blasphemy, and became gigantic; and then it split open and released a gas-like monster that spread over the place of ritual. Monique gawked at the shapeless mass, in which she could discern globes that were half-formed faces grimacing as if they ached to cry out to her. An atrocious wisp of the horrific Outer God unwrapped itself from its bulk and filtered to the circle in which the young outsider knelt. Monique beheld the ghost-like visage therein, the mouth of which called her name. Lifting her head to the spectral tissue, Monique pushed her face into its hazy substance and kissed the ethereal countenance. The filmy thing thrust itself into the human tissue and sank into pores, nostrils, gasping mouth. Monique felt this aspect of the thousand young plant itself as seed within her. The obsidian patch of poison that was the black goat of the woods, no longer immense but shrunken and resembling a spillage of shimmering tar, oozed toward the gas-like entity and embedded itself into it, where it pulsed like some filthy heart. The others watched as the Outer God folded into itself and vanished above the valley's brumal bank.

Sesqua pulsed as never before, its buried heart grown wild. Snouted things atop Mount Selta howled awfully, joined by Edith and Simon. The elder woman reached out to the beast, and he stepped toward her and partially into the mauve mist.

"Come with us now, first-born beast. It is the time for your perpetual return. Come dwell with us forever in our home of mist and shadow, beneath the crimson peaks of Khroyd'hon. You often visit there for brief seasons, so as to lure our kindred who ache to taste a time of mortality; but they can do that now without your guidance, so come and follow us. Escape this husk of semi-human hide. Cease to conjure alchemical fiends and *be* the beast that you were destined to be."

Simon reached beyond Edith, deeper into the mist, with both hands and mind. He scanned, supernaturally, the realm of shadow; but the one he sought did not dwell there. Ruefully, he winked at Edith; then, turning away from mist and shadow, Simon Gregory Williams stepped toward the circle of stones, holding out his hand to the young woman who wept there.

"It's gone, and I am unaltered. How is this possible? I was to be transformed, transferred. I was to exist as one of the nameless spawn of Shub-Niggurath."

"Tut," the beast replied. "That trickster who calls himself the Black Goat of the Woods has played you. And, really, what a dreary existence it would have been to be numbered among so many. Nah, child, your fate is unique, and you have found your home. Come, follow me."

Monique took Simon's proffered hand. She gazed into his eyes and saw his still-wounded expression, his loneliness and pain. Lifting his paw to her mouth, she touched her lips unto it, and then she pressed her head against his shoulder as he guided her back to Sesqua Town.

Monstrous Aftermath

The antique woman led him up the ancient flight of wooden steps, and he felt a frisson of enthrallment at being in this place of which he had so often dreamt. It had not been easy, saving the money that enabled his flight to Paris—but he knew, at that moment, that the effort had been entirely worthwhile. They reached the top landing and stood before the door to the infamous garret room, where the withered beldame hesitated before pushing the key into its lock.

"It is strange, Monsieur. I always feel—I don't like disturbing the quiet of this room. It's silly, I know, but I always expect it to be occupied—by him. You would think that his suicide would have given the room an aura of death and gloom, but instead one feels—his youthfulness. They portrayed him horrendously in that silly film. I'm originally from England, and had no idea of the man's legend when I married my French husband, may he rest in peace. The artist's legend began to grow in your own country, when Hollywood decided to film its fabricated story of Honoré Radin. And now you tell me that you are writing a biography of the painter."

"A novel, Madame Dupin. The success of the recent horror film related to his notorious painting and its supposed curse has generated a lot of interest in the artist himself. I'm unqualified to write an authentic biography, fiction being my métier; and, in truth, so little is known about Radin that an actual account of his life would be a very short book."

"And so you've come to his garret room in Paris to help you in creating its—quality?"

"It's *ambiance,* just so."

The elderly woman nodded, and then she shrugged slightly and turned the key in its lock. She did not walk into the room herself, but rather motioned to it with one frail hand. "Entrez, Monsieur Blake." The young man moved past her, into the room, and in so doing he imagined that he had stepped into another world, an elder realm. The woman at the doorway continued talking. "When the people from Hollywood came to film the opening sequence they spent a fortune restoring the apartment to how it might have looked on that evening of 1848. They succeeded rather well, as you can see—the gaslights, the faux antique furnishings. I've removed the hangman's noose they fastened to the beam—that was a bit much. Oh, yes, it was in our contract that they would leave the room exactly as they restored it—it was the only payment we required, knowing as we did that we could then charge the curious to visit the chamber."

But he could not heed her, for he was absolutely focused on the painting above the mantelpiece.

"This is the replication they had painted?"

She nodded. "You know, of course, that they acquired the original for when they filmed the sequence of Radin's suicide. That was a wild day. They actually invited me to portray the original propriétaire in the film, but I simply *couldn't* be in the same room with that—thing in oil! This imitation doesn't capture the *aura* of the original. We had steep security that day—the museum would let us have the oil for one day only—because of the painting's reputation. Of course you know of the lunatics who sense that the picture is evil, and of their attempts to destroy it at the museum where it is now kept locked away in some secret chamber. I stood here as they were installing the original in its place—and I felt such foreboding. The room took on a different atmosphere. I have never believed in foolish superstition, and I thought of evil as something that existed in humankind alone. But when I looked at that original painting—I knew that it had been the work of a macabre soul, an artist who had knowledge of secret things; and although he took his life, the evil that he conjured with his oils did not die, but continues to cast its shadow on any who glimpse too keenly the secret on the canvas. A mental shadow, evoked by a diseased artist; and the shadow casts an aftermath of malevolence."

Although his back was to her, the young writer could sense the shudder that convulsed her petite frame. Turning to face her, he said, "How dramatically you express it, good woman." Her haunted eyes held him for a few moments, and although he had been moved by her queer language, he conjured a smile and laughed a little. Her eyes then returned to the painting, as did his.

Her voice, when she spoke, was a low whisper. "I will leave you, then, with your grim reaper."

He turned to wave to her and saw that he was alone, and suddenly he was seized with an absurd sense of panic. He did not want to be alone in the room, that garret of silence and shadow and memory. Some of the artist's original belongings, so it was rumored, were still in the room, which his queer old landlady had locked up and refused to rent after the painter's suicide. Looking up, the novelist gazed at the ceiling beam on which the rope had been secured that had helped the artist extinguish his mortality—an act that, now, had ushered the painter into a kind of immortality, because of the lurid legend of his painting and its curse. An element of that legend lingered in the room, centering on the replica of the notorious oil.

The writer walked to a tall bookcase and studied the titles of its books, most of which were in French. Surely these could not be the actual books belonging to Radin, who had been rumored to traffic in sorcery and black magick. The novelist had studied languages at Miskatonic University, where he had become engrossed in the library's assemblage of arcane lore. Thus the titles on the shelves before him were familiar. He touched the spine of the Comte d'Erlette's *Cultes des Goules* and did not like how slick he found the binding, as if its boards had been soaked in sweat. He whispered other titles: Gaspard du Nord's thirteenth-century translation of the *Book of Eibon,* and the strange *Sorcerie de Démonologie.* Pulling out a sheaf of bound foolscap he trembled in discovering it to be the highly obscure French translation of the *Necronomicon,* a copy of which had disappeared from a thir- teenth-century monastery in southern France. No, these titles could not be authentic, they must be clever props manufactured by the movie people.

And yet it was not unlikely that the painter had indeed owned such a library, for he had boasted in correspondence to his father of having trafficked with the dread god Thanatos, and one of the legends surrounding the artist was that his suicide had been his final sacrifice to that dark deity. This part of the legend had been magnificently if luridly portrayed in a dream sequence in the Hollywood film; but as he stood in that room the writer knew that the movie had not explored the depths to which Radin had been a connoisseur of the daemonic arts, and this realization caused him to turn now so as to contemplate the *pièce de résistance* of Honoré Radin's celebrity.

The infamous painting had been entitled "The Grim Reaper," and it was whispered that whoever owned the painting met with violent death, and that their demise was preceded by a warning from the painting itself, in the form of stigmata that appeared on the Reaper's blade. He stepped closer to the canvas and touched his hand to the scythe's curved blade, and as he did so he felt a genuine chill of terror evoked by the mastery of Death's portrayal. He then noticed, scrawled in russet French script, a line of verse at the bottom of the painting, which he recognized as belonging to one of Shakespeare's sonnets. His brain quickly translated:

"And nothing 'gainst Time's scythe can make defense . . ."

Was this transcription part of the original painting? There had been no reference to it in the American horror film based on the legend of the painting's curse. Was this the key to Radin's maniacal occult quest—immortality?

Blake turned to peer into one murky corner of the room, where a tall object had been enshrouded with a sheet of black cloth. He guessed what the thing was from having seen the film so many times. This, too, would figure in his novel based on Radin's mad life and secret death. Going to it, he clutched the cloth and dramatically yanked it to the floor. Before him stood the framed full-length mirror that had, he knew, been in the room since that drear evening in 1848, when the artist had tied one end of his hangman's rope to the ceiling beam. Blake stared at the figure that had been painted onto the mirror's surface, and the chilly room grew colder. Before him, in muted colors and hazy detail, the mad artist had painted his self-portrait. The thing was almost complete, except for the very lowest portion of the trouser legs and shoes, which were missing. It gave Blake the curious impression that the life-size figure had stepped into and beyond the surface of silver glass. How uncanny to stand before this image, which added a peculiar feeling of *presence* to the room. It was as if the painter's frozen reflection had been caught into the chemistry by which the mirror had been constructed.

The painter had been a handsome fellow. The American film had portrayed Radin as a man of early middle age; but if this mirror-image was exact, the artist had been as young as Blake himself. Only the eyes seemed aged, like those of one who had gained, through nefarious study, a world of rare knowledge, if not wisdom. The young man's face, as it had been painted, was very pale; and Blake noticed a place at the forehead where the mirror's surface had been slightly scratched, forming a kind of weird webbed symbol in the middle of Radin's brow. Blake studied the hands held down at the artist's sides, palms outward, and it perplexed him to see, in the middle of one palm, the selfsame symbol that had been scratched onto the mirror; but the symbol on the palm was a part of the painted image.

Blake stared into the beauty of the artist's eyes. The portrayal's lips were parted slightly, as if about to whisper some rare words. From somewhere in the room a breeze began to stir, which drifted to the novelist and sighed into his ear. Blake knelt upon his knees and studied the image on the palm, as shadows began to shift behind the painted figure. Not understanding what motivated him, Blake closed his eyes and pressed his mouth against the painted palm.

Wind rustled at his ear. It kissed him. The palm moved away from his mouth and wove its fingers into his hair. He could sense moving shadows on his eyelids. The hand in his hair tightened its hold and lifted him to a standing position. Was it the velvet wind that kissed his eyes so softly, that chuckled so lowly? Blake opened his burning eyes and could not comprehend the whirling void in which he found himself. It was a place outside of time and space, a realm between stars and bedlam. It was not untenanted. All about him Blake could sense an all-observant incorporeal presence. It brooded before him, blasphemously, haunting the darkness. It mocked him with its mirthless laughter. It took form as an unholy silhouette that crept near to him like some disordered flaw, a spectre wrapped in a robe of obsidian degeneracy.

He shook with fear yet could not turn away. The strange dark one smiled with a cynicism that scorned mortality; and when it raised one hand Blake shivered as the void decayed, as time degenerated. Nothing escaped the crawling chaos. Blake watched and understood immortality. An essence of the soul would linger always, rootless and ruined, in the deterioration of everything. The novelist wanted to clamp shut his eyes, but could not; and thus he watched as the phantom before him reached into the void and brought forth two pale orbs. Blake somehow knew that they were the last dying stars of ruptured heaven, and he wept to see how feebly they sparkled. He gasped as the Outer One struck the stars together so that a bolt streaked from them, shooting toward the thing of clay and bone and blood. He felt the symbol that was burned upon his brow and, finally, was able to turn away from nightmare and scream for mercy. Before him he beheld a sheet of glass. He gaped through that glass, into a gaslit chamber that was untenanted. He saw, vaguely, his reflection and the symbol that pulsed with light on his forehead. With lunatic force, he smashed that forehead against the sheet of glass.

Madame Dupin heard the crash from within the shunned room. She paused before the door, wondering why it had been closed. At last she pushed at the door and grimaced at the smell that wafted to her, the smell of some vile burning thing. She hesitated again before creeping cautiously into the chamber. How faintly the gaslight flickered, as if it cowered from some ghastly manifestation. There was no one within the room, and yet the elderly woman was certain that the young man had not vacated it. Her first shock came when her eyes rested upon the replication of Honoré Radin's noxious canvas—for there, spread on the image of the Reaper's blade, was a thick smear of ichor, a stinking mess that might have been Night's bloodstain. The room's stench emanated from that smear. Turning from the hideous sight, she saw where the mirror's glass had shattered, littering the floor with shards. How could this happen to a relic that had endured for so many decades? What had the American done inside the room, and where was he concealed? She bent to pick up one piece of glass, on which there was the painted image of a hand. She held it tenderly until she noticed the trickle of blood that moved down her finger. How odd to see the way her blood, slipping toward and onto the portion of mirror that she held, was somehow *absorbed* into the property of the glass. She threw the piece of mirror from her.

The ancient creature then noticed movement on the floor, a dark image that seemed to flex itself on the largest shard that lay among the detritus of shattered mirror. Bending low, her bloodstained hand picked up the weighty shard and stared at the face that shuddered in its depths. She did not understand why the painted image, which she knew should have been that of the suicidal artist who had hanged himself inside the room so long ago, was now that of the room's recent visitor, the novelist Blake. When that visage flapped open its bruised lips and uttered a wounded howl, Madame Dupin fled the room forever as the large shard of enchanted mirror, dropping from her shaking hand, shattered into bits.

An Element of Nightmare

And in this muted heart of mine
Something awakens ever after—
From lips half-drunken with her wine,
An echo of her pagan laughter.
—SAMUEL LOVEMAN

You came to us with storm clouds, rushing into our demesne on your frail bicycle. Because we love the sound of rain, we paid no attention as you flew into our inn and dripped upon its floorboards. You approached the bar and asked Selma if a room was available, and it was then that I turned to look at your pathetic form in its disheveled state. The long gabardine that encased you shone wetly in the inn's pale light; and when you removed its hood your damp hair hung like sodden weeds over your large ears.

"The Amber Room is available," Selma informed you as she offered you a cup of coffee. You leaned against the bar and held the hot cup with both hands.

"I can show you the way, sirrah," I uttered. You turned to regard me, and I noticed the momentary look of surprise and vague unease in your eyes. It was almost as if you had recognized me, although I knew that we had never met. Thus I, too, experienced a sense of disquiet as, rising from my chair, I reached for my hat and placed it on my dome. Clutching tightly to your red leather briefcase, you followed me out of the dining area, into the dusky hallway and up one flight of carpeted stairs, to the second landing. Entering the Amber Room, I went to the small table and turned on the lamp, which filled the room with soft golden light.

You looked around the room and nodded, and then you studied me again with your peculiar gaze. "This is Sesqua Valley, isn't it? I wasn't certain, I thought there was a huge mountain."

"She has been draped by storm clouds and thus hidden from view. Is it the mountain that has drawn you to our land?"

"No, it was poetry. My name is Ezra Klum, from Tacoma. My grandmother lived here for a few years when she was a girl in the 1940s. Hilda Young, the poet?" I pretended that the name meant nothing to me. "Long before your time, no doubt." You removed your raincoat and draped it over the room's one wooden chair.

"Have you no dry clothing?"

"In my duffel bag, tied to my bike. I parked in-between this building and the next, beneath the eaves and out of the rain. I'll fetch the bag in a moment. I wanted to ask you—" You paused and looked at me beseechingly.

"Simon Gregory Williams, your servant."

"Mr. Williams, are you familiar with a local poet, Davis somebody? You see, my grandmother used to read to me when I was a kid, and one of my favorite books was this slim purple volume of poems by this Davis guy. It was a long time ago, and I can't remember the author's full name; but Davis stuck in my memory for some reason. My mother has recently been admitted to a nursing facility, and I've been in charge of going through her things. I was hoping to find my grandmother's books, but apparently they've been given away or misplaced. You see, and this will sound weird, but I often dream of my grandmother reading me those poems, and of the tone in her voice at those few times she spoke of Sesqua Valley. Kids are impressionable, and it really affected me, the way her voice would alter, the peculiar light that brightened her eyes when she read those poems. Sometimes, when she reminisced about this place, she would hold a photo in her hand and stroke its image." You set your briefcase on the bed and unclasped it, and when you turned to me again I saw what you held. "I was able to find this," you said as you handed me the small framed snap. "That's my grandmother—isn't she young!—and that fellow is the poet Davis. The image is kind of faded, and some of his face is in shadow. Are you related to him, Mr. Williams? You resemble him."

"We are kindred. His name was William Davis Manly."

"And is that his house they're standing in front of? God, I'd love to see it. I've become a bit obsessed with finding a copy of his poems, and I figured the best way to do that would be to try and find this town."

"And find us you did, how clever. I doubt you'll discover anyone willing to part with their edition of Manly's poems. It's a rare book."

"Wasn't there a pirated second edition, published in Boston in the 1960s? I'd settle for one of those."

"You are very well informed," I answered, trying to keep mischief from my voice. "The majority of those were destroyed in a warehouse fire—or so the story goes. They're probably rarer than the original edition." You bit your lip and nodded sadly, and then you stepped to the small window and pushed aside its lace curtain. We listened to the rain.

"I hope this storm is temporary. I wasn't planning on staying long, but I did want to find that cabin and have my photo taken in front of it, holding my grandmother's photo. Do you know the place?"

I sighed. "It's sequestered within the woodland and is little visited. Yes, I can show it to you. But for now you'll want to fetch your bag and get into dry clothing. There is kindling and wood in the stove there. You'll be quite cozy."

"Damn, that thing's ornate! Must be an antique." You walked to the wood stove and placed your hand upon its cool metal.

"You must be exhausted after your long ride, despite your youth. Your limbs are full of aches. You'll find the bed extremely comfortable. This is a good room to dream in." I spoke in my lowest tone, and you began to yawn as you listened to my words. We walked together out of the room, and I laughed as you hopped down the stairs and rushed out into the storm.

The others studied me as I re-entered the inn and strolled behind the bar, and they remained silent as I took up a glass and began to pour certain liquids into it. I then examined a series of small bottles that were filled with powders of different hues, and choosing one I pulled off its stopper and sprinkled some of its contents into the liquid. Turning to Selma, I smiled.

"He'll return to ask you questions, and you will offer him this. It will make him dream."

I exited at a side door and stepped into the rainfall, raised my face, and let the water slip into my mouth so that I could taste the sky. With smooth language, I spoke to the storm and listened to it melt away. Laughter came from inside the inn as I lifted my face to the small window of your room, which was lit with lamplight. Welcoming the purple shadows of evening, I scanned the skies, where cosmic wind pushed clouds away so that I could feel cold starlight on my eyes. Time passed, and then the light in your window went out. Reaching into my jacket's inner pocket, I produced a lean black flute and played a melody that would coax the cosmic wind. As I performed, that upper gust descended and deteriorated the clouds that had clothed Mount Selta. The white mountain stretched her twin peaks as something that lurked among them howled to heaven. I could almost see, with my wizard eyes, the particles of mutated windstorm that shook the building before me and crept through crevices at the window of your little room, where it would dream-toss your mortal mind.

The morning broke in brilliant light. Feeling reckless and restless, I entered the Hungry Place, a spacious burying ground where the first white people who came to Sesqua Town buried their dead. The ground in certain places of the valley is unwholesome, tainted by unearthly subterranean forces that rise and clutch at psyches. To dwell too long on such ground is to be despoiled by rich dementia. Being rather fond of temporary lunacy, I sometimes visit these spots of infected soil. I strolled to where the statue stood on its rough-hewn stone dais, studied its countenance, and remembered days of yore; and then I felt your shadow on the ground beside me and heard your quiet voice.

"He visited me last night." I moved so that my eyes pierced yours, and thus you beheld my bestial visage clearly for the first time. You could not conceal your shocked confusion. To your kind I look monstrously grotesque, and some human instinct within you seems to understand that I am not of your nature, but outside it. "The poet," you continued. "He recited one of his poems, one that I sort of remembered from when I was a kid. It was weird, because sometimes his voice was his own as he recited, and sometimes it sounded like grandmother's; and then sometimes it didn't sound like a human voice at all, but like a wind that mocked human speech. Dreams are crazy." You turned to study the statue of William Davis Manly that had been erected in the Hungry Place after the poet's disappearance. "He looks so much like you, although more refined." You smiled crookedly. "No offense meant, of course."

"Of course," I answered; and then I took your arm and guided you from the place. "Do you remember the poem?"

"No, I don't have any memory for words. The poem expresses a kind of yearning for far-off travel, I think; something about visiting moonlit towers of the North, and sunken secret catacombs in the East. But I remember the effect it had on me when I was young, because I've always suffered from an intense sense of loneliness. Maybe that comes from being raised by a single parent, I don't know. I've had a difficult time fitting in. What was it Oscar Wilde said, that other people are a mistake and that the best 'society' is oneself? I've always felt that, and hearing Davis speak the poem in my dream reminded me of how emotionally I feel those sentiments; for I could sense the poet's outsider nature, his feeling of being an alien among humanity." You stopped moving and stood staring at the sparkling white stone of our majestic mountain. "Funny, I feel different since my arrival here. Something in me feels—found."

I grinned and led you into the woodland, and I knew beyond doubt that your coming to us was no accident. The seed had been sewn long ago, when in childhood you had listened to the poetic lore of Sesqua Valley, from a woman who had once lingered here and whose memories colored your dreaming. To dream of Sesqua Valley is to trigger her interest and her appetite; and thus she lures you to her, in time.

You could not help but notice the uncanny nature of our woodland, the way in which the trees are bent, the shape of low branches that rake the pathways, the phosphorescent patches of moss that compel to be kissed.

"This place is rather creepy," you muttered.

"It owns a fantastic aura," I agreed. "Why do you smile?"

"I'm just remembering the times when my grandmother's voice would take on a mysterious tone when she was reading me poems from the Davis book. There was an odd light that sometimes darkened her eyes—it spooked me. I loved it because it confused me. I mean, it's nonsense—how can light be dark? I remember the creepy sensations of those times when I visit strange haunts like the old Granary Burying Ground in Boston. Oh, the first sight of that place gave me a thrill! I'd never seen anything like it, the slates so black with age. Standing among those antique slabs reminded me of the queer sensations I experienced as I listened to my grandmother read the bizarre poems of that purple book."

"I understand the charm of such realms," I told you, "and have searched for them in far places. There are hidden pockets on this globe, sinister and uninhabited. How one thrills to find them, to listen to their sinister secrets whispered to one's imagination. Ah—here is one before us, which few mortal eyes have beheld."

It had squatted there for two hundred years and more, protected from the elements by the wizardry that occupied it. The unpainted timber with which the cottage had been constructed was beautifully aged, and its exterior cast a spell on all who looked on it. Dappled sunlight fell through thickly tangled branches, feebly illuminating some few of the patches of moss that covered the building's slanted roof. You stared in amazement at the structure, and at the two huge leafless elms on either side of the bungalow.

"Damn, I should have brought my camera." I looked at you as you motioned to the cabin. "It's his home, where he stood with my grandmother when they posed for that photograph. God, look at it! It's like something out of a spooky fairy tale, so old and—odd. It looks like it rose out of the earth, doesn't it? Isn't it strange, the way some houses can affect your sense of fear? Ha, my imagination's working overtime! The very air seems bewitched."

I walked to the cottage and pushed open its door. "You must cross the threshold of your own volition," I informed you, as your eyes revealed that you were becoming more and more aware of the spectral elements that wove into your psyche. I have often mocked the inadequacy of the human brain; and yet, it has the power to mold one's personal actuality, potently. It was, after all, this mortal energy that awakened us children of shadow and mist, in our realm outside your reality, and helped us to locate a pathway to your sphere. It was now our turn to show you another path—to the Outside, that place that has so touched your imagination through the mystic poetry read to you as a child.

Stealthily, you advanced toward the cottage and stepped onto the rough, mossy rock that served as doorstep. You looked, for one moment, as if you would not enter in; but then the perfume of the inner air wafted to you, caught you, entranced you. You crossed into the low-ceiled chamber that was illuminated by numerous candles, the scented wax of which helped to perfume the place. Your sense of wonder ignited and succumbed to the sovereign influence of Sesqua Valley. You then noticed the figure who sat, unmoving, in one dusky corner of the room, like some figure from a book of fairy tales. The shadows of the place at which she sat seemed almost to weave into the texture of her black skin, and when she began at last to move and work her spinning wheel you saw that she was unclothed from the waist upward. You listened to the faint sound of her moving wheel and tried to comprehend the garment on which she worked. I could almost hear your heartbeat quicken when she rose off her stool and floated to where you stood.

"Will you help me into this?" she asked, as one breast brushed against your arm. You clasped the thing she held to you with fingertips, and marveled that a woven garment could feel so light as to seem almost nonexistent, as though it were spun of web and shadow. Something in its quality made you feel so wonderful that you wanted to press it against your face and meld it into your flesh; instead, you watched as the black woman, her back pressed against you, wound her hands into sleeves and then used those hands to lift her length of red hair, into which you buried your face. Wasn't it fantastic, when you closed your eyes, that an optical illusion whirled before you, bright particles that might have been stars dancing in some heaving heaven? We could not help but chuckle at how you whimpered when Marceline moved out of your embrace. She turned to smile at you, and you admired the perfection of the breasts that remained uncovered. Rank human lust polluted the atmosphere as your teeth began to grind.

I raised my hand so that a glimmer of light flickered momentarily at one place, and your noise transmuted as your eyes fell upon an item that was on a nearby table. Moving like a dreamer, you approached the table and took up the purple volume. When you brought the book to your nostrils and drank in its old aroma you almost purred. Your eyes had adjusted to the dim lighting of the room, and thus you were able to read when you opened the volume to a middle page.

> "You wheel above me in some haunted space
> And plot to pull my eyes into your dance.
> I feel your cosmic cyclone on my face.
> I lose myself within some phantom trance
> That would disintegrate my firm foothold
> With which I am cemented to this sod,
> And transport me unto that region told
> Of in the tomes that speak of Elder God.
> I see the Elder God within my mind,
> That Beast that dances in-between the stars.
> I'm drawn to secret path on which I find
> The Revelation that mutates and mars.
> It is a ruin into which I ride
> In celebration of the bleak Outside."

A feminine voice quietly joined your speech as you breathed the poem, and you raised your eyes to glance at Marceline as you quoted the final lines. It perplexed you to see her mouth unmoving while still some lovely voice accompanied your own, and it came to you that this voice was more like memory than actual articulation.

I said, "You seem quite familiar with that sonnet."

"Yes," you answered, "my grandmother read it to me often. I asked her once about this thing, 'the bleak Outside,' and she would tell me the most outlandish things, in a voice that trembled as fever burned her eyes. I think that was when I knew I wanted to write poetry myself, although I've never had the nerve to show my stuff to anyone. I love poetry—it's transporting." You stopped and thought. "Transporting—that was a word I learned from grandmother, when she whispered of the Outside. You'd think the description of it would arouse a sense of horror or fear, but I found it alluring, far more enticing than dull reality." You then removed your jacket and hung it over a wooden chair. "Not much circulation in here, is there?" you said, smiling as you strolled to one small window, at which you frowned. Instead of window pane you found what appeared to be a surface of highly polished obsidian. We watched as you raised one hand toward the black surface, as you shuddered at the chilliness that your hand encountered there. Marceline moved to you and placed her hand over your own. She guided your hand to the window, and through it, and laughed at your yelps as you touched the bleak Outside. She reached through the window with her other hand and then pulled out, in your conjoined hold, an ebony substance that simulated the texture of Marceline's skin of jet.

"Let me take that, Ezra, and place it in my lap as I ready my wheel. Yes, the instrument is antique. We like olden things here, and drink their aura of past eras. You are a soul who cherishes the olden realms, we know. Let us clothe you, now, so as to enter the eldest of all realms."

"You have been nourished," I spoke, "by the spell of wonderment that spills from the spoken poetry of a child of Sesqua Valley. That magick has rooted in your soul, and thus you sought and found us. We understand how delicious it is, to be kissed by the Outside, and how provocatively that passion plays within mortal blood and pumps audaciousness into the human heart. Oh, the longing—the dark elements that bloom in solitude and form a perfect approval of what to those who lack imagination is hideous." I moved to you as I spoke and wound my talons in your hair. I breathed upon your eyes as I began to undress you. Nude, you watched the witch rise from her wheel and hold to you the newly fashioned robe as I backed into a shadowed place and brought forth my flute. You seemed to understand Marceline's twinship with the cosmic void and with them that howl within it, and you tilted back your head so as to wail as she draped her fabric around you. As you bayed, you reached with one trembling hand for the book of Manly's poetry, which you pressed to your heaving chest. Bringing the reed to my mouth, I filled the room with enchantment. Bending to you, Marceline kissed your mouth, and then guided your lips to her perfect breasts, which you worshipped with your tongue. And as your mouth tasted her sorcerous essence, your ears reverberated with the woman's impious laughter. Your eyes became lost in the black texture of her necromantic hide, that husk of darkness in which she kneaded you, until you felt like some lunatic god, passing through an element of nightmare wherein you stalked among the stars, the book of unholy poesy in your eternal hand.

Some Unknown Gulf
of Night

A prose-poem sequence inspir'd by
H. P. Lovecraft's *Fungi from Yuggoth*

I.

It was a place that smelled of olden days, time-swept into some distant era of night, haunted by an age-old odor of dust, of darkness and dead dreams. It was like some obscured realm half-lost in time, disjointed from the dull modern age, with ancient alleyways into which one feared to walk lest one would be beguiled by secret things. The stench of rotting quays built over stagnant tides washed to me on the chilly wind and made me anxious to find the hidden place I sought. It was a place that had been marked upon a curious map found in a ghastly book and accompanied by a faded photograph. I thought I had been familiar with the antique town, but with the aid of this map I now explored a pocket of the place that had lain unexpected and unsought. I staggered through queer curls of fog and followed the spray of mist that was my frosty breath, then stopped beneath one historic curved lamp post to study the photograph again beneath feeble electric light; and then I looked up and saw it huddled before me, like something stumbled upon in dream. I approached the window with small panes and peered into the dusky place beyond, not comprehending the twisted pillars that rose from various places of the floor and almost reached the room's low ceiling. I gazed a little while, until my cloud of breath fogged the pane and thus concealed the cluttered room.

I backed away from the blackened building, then spilled toward the narrow plank that was its door, a threshold that did not hesitate to let me in and closed behind me without sound or force. I could not ascertain the source of dim illumination that filled the crowded room, the soft old light that was easy on my eyes and charmed my beating heart toward calm. The twisted pillars that I had detected from peering through the window proved to be piles of books stacked impossibly high and draped with filigree of spiderweb. A drowsy odor of wormy age wafted to me from the books thus piled, and for some moments I shut my eyes and listened to the silence of the place where I was its single tenant of blood and breath. Yet even with my eyelids closed I saw those twisted trees that were the piles of books, those balusters that seemed to hold the blanket of shadow that loomed above them; and as I watched them through closed eyes I saw them lean and twist still more, beguilingly, so that their movement coaxed my limbs to bend until one thumb pressed against the floor as the other touched a thing of smooth cool leather. I opened my eyes and beheld the book next to my hand, and when I allowed my hand to open the book I was confronted with curious symbols that might have been words. I tried to speak one alien word aloud, although my lips protested the effort; and yet my whisper seemed to float into the air, which echoed it beneath the wind that laughed against the outside window.

I turned another leaf and found a second photograph that revealed the dim reflection of a woman who was attired in a gown that seemed familiar, a figure that disturbed me for reasons I did not understand. Placing the photograph inside my coat's inner pocket, I stood and peered about me. I was alone in the room, no seller in sight, and yet my imagination fancied that it could detect another presence in the room, someone whose low and subtle laughter sounded beneath the moaning wind outside the window. I grew afraid, for in my fevered imagination I thought I saw the dark blanket above me sink a little lower and begin to churn. Perhaps the blackness meant to take the book away, and so I wrapped it inside my coat as laughter sounded once again, within or without I could not tell; and a burst of devilish wind thrust open the narrow plank that was the door toward which I flew until I found myself outside. I stood beneath the feeble light of an antique lamp post—under the sky of a calm, a windless night.

II.

I kept the book beneath my coat and stepped into the quiet harbor street, walking through heavy coils of diseased fog that rose to meet the tendrils of black cloud with which they intertwined. I could not understand the curious shapes I seemed to see within the yellow fog, the flimsy faces lacking strength or substance that filtered toward me as if to kiss my visage with their melting mouths. A melancholy wail rose from the hidden harbor, perhaps the forlorn howling of some horn, perhaps the weeping of some lonesome beast. How curious that the faces in the fog curled their mouths as if in jollity. I could not comprehend the cruel laughter that echoed in the sickly yellow air. Staggering through evaporating things, I saw the outlines of tall and lean habitations that rose above and tilted o'er the lanes. I knew that this strange town was very old, and yet these habitations seemed to represent a fantastic past that did not wish to perish, of which these structures were an eidolon. Were they real and solid, the high and leaning things of brick and plank; or were they some freakish growth of elder memory that one may behold with eyes of lunacy? The hazy sight of them haunted my eyes and teased my buzzing brain with crazy hints, and I felt as though they watched me on my way with keen attention. Perhaps they knew that I had looked into the book, and thus my mind had been infected with occult residue. Perhaps if I placed my soft eyes against their planks and brick they would cool my buzzing brain with their cold surface, and I could rise, with them, above the harbor lane with tranquil peace of mind and watch the world in silence.

Thus compelled to kiss one antique wall, I crept toward the nearest dwelling and placed my mouth against a window pane. The vapor that was my mortal breath touched the glass as adhering cloud through which I peered into the place before me. I seemed to gaze into a haberdashery in which nebulous mannequins stood as still as stone, figures attired in unfathomable fashion that clung unwholesomely to their indefinite forms. Nearest to the pane through which I peered was a thing wrapped in yellow, tall and dominant and masked with a silken sheet that sheathed its dummy head. I breathed onto the glass as I looked in and hugged the secret book closer to my chest; and I wondered at the heavy beating of my heart, at how its palpitations echoed in the filthy air. When finally I brought forth the book from underneath my coat, I fancied that my pulse sounded within it, as if my throbbing organ had been coaxed inside. I opened the vibrating pages before the window and showed them to the yellow mannequin as quiet laughter sounded in some obscure place (within me or without I could not tell). The figure behind the window raised a yellow talon and pressed it to the patch of my mortal vapor that still fogged the glass. A golden emblem formed beneath the moving finger, and I frowned as I tried to recollect where I had previously encountered the insignia. Something in its liquid shape disconcerted me, and thus repulsed I backed away as the yellow sign displaced itself from the window's surface and floated to the ground, where it floundered like some aquatic thing that had escaped its bowl.

I fled the place and flew down darkened lanes through fog and shadow and harbor stench. The buildings watched my flight as I rushed past them, and I could almost detect the furtive faces that smiled at me behind the curtained windows. What kind of creatures hid within such dwellings? What secrets did they whisper in the dark? I sensed those rare whisperings pursue me, as if they hungered to nestle in my ear. Stumbling once, I dropped the arcane book, that tome that had captured the beating of my heart. It opened and heaved my heartbeat into the lightless aether. I bent and picked up the tome and clutched it to my quiet chest, as I—a heartless mutant—escaped the haunted harbor lanes.

III.

I staggered through the yellow fog, following the vibration of my heartbeat in the air, until I saw the house that my grandfather had built when he was young, the place that I had inherited after father's death. It was there that I lived my little life in silence and solitude, where some few nights would find me in the dusky attic wherein grandfather's library had been stored. I was happy to see the clean black sky above my house, no fog or amber moonlight or winking stars. I gulped in air that was no longer tainted with necromancy or nightmare as I pushed open the little gate and advanced to the steps that I climbed to the solid porch. I paused for one small moment and listened for any sound that might have followed me from the unwholesome elder realm; but all that could be detected was the faint pulsing of my lonely heartbeat, a sound that seemed to bend the air nearest my mouth. Whispering a weird little song, I removed the book from underneath my coat and opened it, and I laughed as my heartbeat fell again onto the pages that, quickly closing, trapped my mortal vibration once more inside the book. Pressing the book against my chest I said a little prayer, and as the words were whispered I sensed my heartbeat pass through the book and return once more inside my breast, where it frolicked with my blood.

My eyes were enchanted by the soft pale light behind the door's small rectangular window, and I leaned against that door so that my eyes touched the window's cool glass. Before me were the muted and familiar shadows of my home, the silhouettes of grandfather's antique furnishings. I saw the double doors that led into my library, the place where I often slept on a comfortable couch with the book that I had been reading on my chest. Ah, what dreams had been inspired in that place by the books that lined its shelves—and what dreams might blossom in my brain now, woven by the heavy book found in a foreboding shop! Contemplating this, I pressed against the door with that portal, the heavy book, in folded arms; and as I leaned forward the door opened against my weight. As I stumbled forward, my large foot caught upon the doorframe, and in my attempt to catch my balance my arms flew outward and dropped the book, which opened as it fell before me and landed gently on the ground, caught by adoring shadow. I gazed onto the pages before me, at the ancient script and bewildering symbols, and ached to understand the esoteric lore revealed. Clutching the book, I carried it to the library doors, but when I looked inside the room it seemed too sane, its atmosphere too modern. Thus I climbed the steps that led upstairs and passed through the door that took me to the other steps that ushered me into the attic where grandfather had kept his library of ancient lore. I did not often enter this attic space because of the way in which it had been built. The walls and roof slanted slightly in curious ways, giving the room a queer irregular shape; and the air, inhaled, tasted dry and vaguely sour, so affecting my senses that I breathed in an unnatural manner. Electric light had not been installed in this portion of the house, and family tradition dictated that candles were to be the one source of illumination. I did not instantly light a candle because of the vintage tailor dummies that stood among the furniture and trunks and shelves of ancient books. The purpose of these mannequins was never explained to me, but something my father once said suggested that the feminine garb with which they were attired had belong to my grandmother, a woman I had never known. Thus they stood like forlorn eidolons, silent speakers of an unknown, unknowable relationship; and they seemed so intimately conjoined with the gloom of the dusky room that I did not immediately care to debauch their aura with living firelight. I stood as still as they and did not breathe, until the red glare of suffocation burned into my wide eyes, choking me so that I coughed and spat ungraciously. No, I could never ape the perfect stillness of these phantoms of the past. I was too human.

Sitting at a centuried desk, I lit a candle and placed my hands on the weird old book that I had pilfered from the curious shop. It was fabulous, in an uncanny way, how the candleglow caressed the leather binding of the book, causing it to lighten from dim brown to dark yellow. Gazing at the thing I became aware again of the beating of my heart. I placed a protective hand inside my coat and pressed it against my chest, an action that reminded me of the photograph I had discovered between the leaves of the archaic tome. Slipping it out, I studied the faded creature pictured thereon, a woman whose face was a feminine copy of mine own, whose sensual body wore a gown that I had seen before. Lifting my head, I scanned the room and beheld the tailor's dummy attired in an amber evening dress, and I marveled at the way the attic room's flickering light played upon the golden broach pinned to the gown. I floated to the mannequin and touched my hand to the smooth antique fabric of its attire as an aura of pale shadow encased both the thing and me. Lifting the hem, I pushed myself beneath its yellow folds and kissed the sleek black wood of one of the three supporting legs of the dummy. Raising myself higher, I ran my tongue along the rough surface of the feminine trunk as my hands scrambled to the twin mounds that were its imitation breasts. I stood and turned around as the gown fitted over and embraced my body.

The ancient book was before me. Touching it, I pressed the pages to my heaving bosom as some outside thing shook the attic window with faint fumbling. I watched the small window open and tasted the different air that rushed toward us and played with the frocks of my sisters. A breath of wind took hold of my photograph and lured it to and out of the attic window, and reaching for my flat and latent image my hand became elastic and spread toward outer darkness. Holding my book tightly, I drifted through the window, into night.

IV.

We rise as smoke, we sisters of all flesh. We curl around the altar that has called. We relish the weird old language, however inadequately it has been spoken by your mortal tongue. Newly reawakened, we teach your tongue correct enunciation in time of dreaming. We whirl around the dank stone of an altar that rises from some small pool of unclean water; we whisper at the thirsty things that flow to feast upon the pool's squalid nourishment, those beasts that ape the shapes of men as they spit madness into your mortal realm. The day has come at last, when the child-like thing that huddles in the hollow of an olden oak will dig its claws into the rank herbage on which it grazes and wrap it-self in moist and filthy roots as it whispers predictions into the starlit vault of sky. Aching to feed upon its apocalyptic murmuring, we con-join (we siblings of all flesh) as one entity and filter to the hollow of an elder oak. We twine the moist vines and leaves that cling to bark into our phantom hair and blend our spectral blood with pus and pulp. We chortle as the child-like thing speaks the name of a strange, grey world with such precision that the air nearest its mouth thickens with chilly darkness. We love the cold dead world past the starry void, Yuggoth and its fungi. We ache to settle within its pockets and its pits, to flow beneath antediluvian bridges as substance in the swift black rivers on which the ghastly light of a daemonic moon sneers.

And now the child-like thing seeps from its hollow in the primordial oak, to stretch its pale white body toward the altar that rises from a stagnant pool. We creep below it as its black shadow while a ground-mist, rising, chokes your mortal mouth. We weep with pleasure as the child-like thing dips its lips into the pool of distasteful water and, rising, turns its coy countenance to you. We love the fear reflected in your mortal eye, the fear that wears a taint of beguilement as the child-like thing seeps toward you, to your mouth, and drools its monstrous language into your maw. And now it is our turn. We rise as smoke and becloud your eyes; your nostrils suck us in so that we may frolic with your brain. We teach you how to shut your eyes and dream, and in your dream we teach you how to utter our rare language to the audient void. We swim to your roots of hair and flow out of your dome as strands of fungi that wave in rising wind. We teach you new appetite as the child-like thing spreads itself on dank altar stone and welcomes the ravishing of your mortal mouth.

V.

Your mortal mouth is pale and undernourished, famished for a taste of nasty keep; and yet you still refuse to acknowledge this, as if such a disclosure would confess mental or emotional disability. So I remain silent as you read my newest tale in winter moonlight, as we sit on this tabletop tomb in an ancient burying ground where once Poe walked. How nervously you laugh when once my tale is perused, and I laugh as well, but my mirth is evoked by the nervousness reflected in your eyes.

"You have outdone yourself," is your feeble commentary on my work.

I exhale a cloud of breath into the frosty air. "Really? Do you mean you find it more outlandish than my last? That other one gave you such macabre dreams—such a wonderful compliment. To make you dream is my most earnest intent."

"Oh, you've inspired innumerable dreams," you sigh, bending to my bosom and kissing the flesh just above the bodice of my yellow evening gown. You keep your face near my flesh and drink in my musky perfume. I lift my head and eye the myriad stars. "Let me take you home," you whisper, a daemon of desire. You lift your head and would gaze into my eyes, but I ignore you as I continue counting stars. "I would take you home and transport you to a place of which you have never dreamed," you promise.

I watch the black clouds that gather above us and, one by one, blot out the stars. I feel the sky-winds that spawn within those clouds fall to earth and comb my hair. You shiver at their kiss. "Your mortal dreams are so safe and sane," I mock. "But the dreams that I have sewn within your skull—ah, they are something novel."

You laugh, a paltry noise. "I couldn't understand them, your gift of dreams. They made no sense. They showed me a pale and shadowy place that I thought was familiar, although I knew when waking it was a place I had never seen in reality. I walked its roads, past domes and towers. I heard the distant pounding of some sea, the sound of which seemed to herald an impending fate. I entered a cemetery above the sea not unlike this one we haunt, and sat on a chilly slab, as we sit now. I could feel the age of that stone slab rise into my flesh and claim a portion of my essence. As I sat I saw a multitude of fireflies that congregated near the ancient church—that congregated and transformed into one solid form, a figure in a yellow gown, masked, who filtered to me through midnight air. She wore a yellow mask, and something in its features enthralled me, so that I hungered to kiss its silken surface. Just as, now, I hunger to kiss your face."

Your mouth is near my own, and I can smell your rancid mortal breath. I have had enough of this charade. I take your face into my hands and gaze into your eyes so that you can at last behold the stars that wink within mine own. I exhale a black cloud of uncanny breath that encases your startled visage, and then I remove my hands from your face and bring them to my own. I lift my mortal mask and thus reveal the black gulf that is my nature—and your destiny. "Let me take you home," I tease, as, full of jest, I suck you into my unfathomable void.

VI.

The wrack had been washed upon the rocks during the dark hours, and they were puzzled by its dilapidated state, for the night had been serene. It was not uncommon for vessels to wash ashore near northern Kingsport, but they sensed that this was different; for it was unlike any craft they had seen, exuding an aura of strangeness and decrepitude. The thing was a small three-mast schooner, such as had been used in carrying cargo from distant lands; but something in its configuration was all wrong, its angles and contours did not, in places, make sense. And when they advanced to climb on it, something in its reek of rotted wood caused unsettling sickness to churn stomachs and cloud minds. They did not like the way the shredded remnants of the sail moved in the gentle sea-breeze, or the way the disintegrating ropes twined around black and splintered poles. They did not like the way the shadows of the hollow northern cliffs played on the undulating waves that pushed against the structure like greedy things that would devour all.

It was the poet among the watchers who stepped below and searched the cramped cabin for any written log, for poets are not afraid to dream the dark dreams or taste the kiss of uncanny fear; but everything that he looked on was deteriorated—except the small black galley-table lantern with plain glass sides and a metal top that was decorated with star-shaped holes. The remnant of a squat black candle was still inside the thing, and the poet thought it might be useful on the dark cold nights he spent reading in his attic room, and so he lifted the lamp and carried it out into the upper air. The soft daylight revealed the curious scratches on the glass sides that looked like esoteric signals that might have been formed by etching with knife or diamond. The others to whom he showed the lantern did not like the way the daylight played on the surface of the thing's black iron, but he dismissed their discomfort to the effect of the mysterious craft and its aura of weirdness. This was Kingsport, and they who lived here had become attuned to extraordinary things and curious ways. And so he took the lantern home and found a place for it on a stand near his reading chair in the attic room to which he escaped at close of day. He sat in his comfortable chair and did a bit of work on a poem that had proven difficult, scribbling by candlelight as night wind whispered at the attic window. In time he set aside his pen and pad and extinguished the candles in their crystal holders. The darkness in which he sat was comfortable, and yet he could not quite relax because his eyes kept returning to the lantern on the table at his side; and so at last he struck a tapered match to his antique oriental flint box in which he kept opium and put its tiny flame to the candle inside the small black lantern. The little light that spread on the candle's wick played with shapes and shadows on the attic walls, and the poet frowned in incomprehension—for what contents within his little room could cast such outré forms on wooden surface, silhouettes of domes and towers and malformed bridges that crossed deep caverns? Why did the walls of his attic chamber seem to tilt and slant, and of what did that remind him?

The poet shut his eyes and began to sing impromptu verse that gave form to the outlandish phantasy in which he found himself. And wasn't it odd how he could suddenly hear the solemn bells of buoys from the distant harbor; and wasn't it weird how near they sounded? He stopped his song and opened his eyes, and did not understand why the room looked so utterly unfamiliar; and then he realized that he was not in his attic chamber at all, but had somehow returned to the small dark cabin of the wrack, the vintage lantern sitting on a crate beside him and casting a diagram of stars on the slanting walls. He noticed the small Oriental metal box on the floor, similar in style to his antique flint box, and he reached for it and unclasped the lid. Inside was the withered debris of age-old tea; and dry as the stuff appeared, still the poet could detect a slight aroma. Closing the lid and pocketing the container, he reached for the lantern and vacated the cabin with its crazy walls and slanted ceiling. Sharp moonlight mingled its dead illumination with the lantern's living flame. The ruined craft was still nestled on an outcropping of rocks, and yet one portion of it was in water that gently rocked it. Cautiously stepping to that portion still in water, the poet held his lantern outward and peered into the place below the surface; and he could not understand why the water seemed so deep so near to shore, nor could he comprehend the yellow thing that watched him beneath black water. Gazing at it steadfastly, he determined that it was a large figurehead that had fallen from some ship's prow. How its contours seemed to flow below the surface, so that the gigantic breasts encased in their yellow bodice seemed to heave! And the massive hand of one uplifted arm seemed to turn in circles; and as it circulated, the stars reflected on black water moved with it, churning before his captivated eyes and summoning him to join in their danse.

He backed away and, holding the old lantern before him, found his way off the craft onto the slippery rocks, and then to the road that took him homeward. When once more he climbed the steps that reached into his attic room, the poet was comforted to see that it had regained its regular shape. Sighing, he placed the lantern onto its table, closed his eyes, and sang himself to sleep. It was some slight sound that reawakened him, one that he could not identify. The squat candle in the lantern had burned low and was nearly gone. Aware of a weight in his coat pocket, the poet brought forth the Oriental container he had found aboard the craft. The wee nap had reinvigorated him, and he felt a keen desire to return to working on his ode. Rising, he went to one corner of the room where he had a single electric burner with which he heated water for his tea. There was water in the kettle still, and so he switched on the burner and prepared his cup and strainer. Opening the antique container he had found, he spooned out a small amount of the desiccated substance and spilled it into the strainer as the kettle sounded its banshee wail. Switching off the burner, he carefully lifted the kettle and poured hot liquid into the strainer. Clean water darkened as it filtered through the alien tea leaves. An aroma rose with the steam that sought his nostrils, pungent and full of promise. Resisting his natural inclination to pour sugar into the brew, he set the strainer onto a small dish and brought the china cup to his mouth.

He gasped and gagged. He dropped the cup and saw it shatter on the wooden floor, and then he watched the dark steaming liquid spread upon the planks and creep toward him like rapacious shadow. He gasped again and could not understand why the aether seemed so heavy and bitter. Again there came the noise that had pulled him out of dreamless slumber, the sound of wind fumbling at the attic window. Gazing again at the pool of spilled liquid, he watched the wisp of smoke that rose from it and shaped itself outlandishly as its tendrils wound to him through the air. His eyesight began to blur. There came again the sound of windstorm shaking the attic window, and the idea of gulping in that breath of nature so enticed him that he rushed to the small window, opened it, and pushed his head and torso into night.

There was no wind, but there was night certainly. Indeed, there was naught else but blackness illimitable. He could not see the walls of his house, could not view the silhouettes of trees that moved weirdly in daemonic darkness. There was no moon, no countless winking stars. There was no earth. And then the poet detected movement in some distant place deep below, and as he peered into the void a shape formed and lifted itself to him. She was encased in a tattered yellow gown that was decorated with filigree of seaweed, and he marveled at the splendor of her gigantic breasts that moved as she heaved a siren's song. She rose to him, through churning shadow, and the splintered lips of her chiseled countenance curled with sardonic ecstasy as, pressed to living flesh, they claimed the poet with their kiss.

VII.

No, do not offer me your white hand and try to hold me back. I do not feel your paltry fear. I am a poet, and poets relish velvet shadow and its secret kiss. Why else would I live in this old valley town, haunted as it is by mystic history? No, take away your hand and let me walk down the road that hies me to the great hill. Ah, you follow, do you? Then make no mortal sound, for I relish the supernatural hush of this spectral hour. Look at the late afternoon sky and the scene before us, looking so like that painting by the American Modernist, Albert Bloch, his 1938 piece entitled "Rutted Road." Look, there is the stone wall at our left, and the forlorn farmhouse with its spiral of smoke reaching for the misty grey-blue sky. Here and there stand the isolated trees naked of foliage, some living and some deceased. Another wall begins on our right-hand side, an ancient thing composed of rough-hewn stone much darker than the bleached rocks with which the farmer's wall has been constructed. It contains a curious . . . aura . . . doesn't it, this centuried wall that stretches before us into the place where mist thickens into fog? And there, half-hidden by the fog: Zaman's Hill, the forbidden place, with its dome rising to meet the gathering darkness of early nightfall. Listen, do you hear it, the cry of crow? There it flies, over us and toward the blanketed hilltop, our psychopomp escorting us to another realm, where we will dine on occult things. Ah, there is your white hand again; but this time it seeks comfort of companionship, so as to alleviate your fear. Let me wrap my black fingers around it as, together, we tread across this esplanade toward the haunted hill.

There, the clean white steeple of your god. Do you wish to step inside and grovel on your knees? Or shall we continue on our way, through this blanket of fog and up the tall and wooded hill, where perhaps we can encounter another deity to whom one can whisper lamentations? Come then, and climb, and thus approach the level where wind begins to whisper two centuries of secrets. Look there, our psychopomp the crow, dead and mangled on this green and wooded plot; but still it guides, with the wing that is unbroken and points upward to the place that has summoned. How like a lost boy you look, with your wide eyes and pale mouth. I shall tighten my hold on your white hand and lure you upward, to the place that awaits your mortal foot. The path grows steep and the fog begins to thin as we reach the end of woodland and emerge into a time of newborn twilight. Look there, my child, below us—see the muted lights of human habitation through the churning mist. How far away humanity seems now from this place that we have reached near the crest of a great hill. Forget that paltry light of human habitation, for there beyond us is another illumination, phosphorescent and unearthly, kissed by lunar radiance that shines down upon the ruins before us. Your hand is in my own, do not hold back; turn your eyes away from that vale of mortal memory. Press your foot upon the path that leads us to the place of buried lore and ghastly ceremony.

Smell the wind that brings the stench of Dunwich, two miles hence, and watch that wind frolic with my abundance of red hair. Smell the rot of some madness out of time that would split dimension and spill onto our eyes. What wonders would our eyes then perceive! Feel the cold moonlight that would drown us with keen lunacy! Help me free myself from this bodice of my yellow gown, rip it with your hot white hands. Allow my manumitted tits, no longer slaves of modesty, to point their nipples to the moon. Nestle your white face between my breasts as your savage hands continue their destruction of my dress, then sink onto your knees and worship the moist aroma of my sex. Kiss me there with your prosaic mouth, but do not work your phallus yet—you must remain a virgin one moment more.

Take my black hand, child, do not hold back. Let me lead you to the altar stone where dull dead stains remember when they were new and damp and darkly crimson. Kneel here, with me, before this altar on Zaman's Hill, in this place of ruin and remorse. Let me embrace you with my black arms as my dark mouth sighs whispers into that cavity, your ear. The wind continues to move and moan and pitch my length of hair so as to blanket your frail white mortality. Rise and moan with me, upon this altar stone; let me straddle you and rip my nails into your pale white flesh. Ah, how your wet red liquid fuels my appetite as it coats this altar stone. Yes, let it lift, my child, your aching phallus, plunge it deep within me as we ride the night-wind with ghoulish delight. Let my rich red hair blanket you as I ravage what remains of your soul. Pump and pant, my pet. Part your paltry human lips and gasp in pain as the hill explodes with wondrous sound. Watch with gluttonous eyes the blood that floods the lunatic moon, the moon that illuminates my charnel hunger—my jaws stretched wide.

VIII.

He had climbed the hill from which he could look down and study the ghostly seaport that had such a strange underground legend. One could well understand the whispers told of shadowed Innsmouth, for from this high point it looked like a huddled haunt in which nothing had dwelt for decades. The sunset had been spectacular, but as twilight approached he saw that there were no lights twinkling in the old town, which spread below like some lightless necropolis. The only movement was that of waves, of the sea that shook what remained of the rotting wharves, and the movement of thickened shadow as daylight died. At last he picked up his bicycle and rode down the trail that took him to the harbor, where the ancient winds brought evil smells from the sea and mingled with the sickening stench of Innsmouth town. The rain, when it began to fall, chilled his flesh but did nothing to dissipate the

odor of sea and dilapidation, and so he continued his trek to the center
of town, where he found, at last, the darkened shop that was his destination. Leaning his bike beside the weathered wall, he wiped away the
rain that streamed into his eyes and peered through the murky glass;
but all that he could discern was a tenebrous realm filled with curious
forms, with here and there twisting columns that threatened to tilt and
collapse. Bending away from the window, he raised his face to the rainfall and drank an effluvium of tainted sky, and then he stepped to the
narrow door and entered the shop, instantly beguiled by how the air
was altered, how his nostrils were pleased with age-old fragrance that
dispelled the grotesque stench he had encountered outside. It was subtle, this new aroma, but he thought he could detect a variety of spices,
plus the distinct smell of olden books. It was the smell of books that
reminded him of his mission.

An abstruse source of illumination came from one corner of the
room, and when he walked toward it he saw what looked like a very
old lantern that sat on a glass case, its circle of easy light not filtering
beyond that particular corner of the place. He walked past the twisted
pillars that proved to be columns of piled books reaching to the low
ceiling, from which decorative webs descended so as to cover antique
lamps and items brought in from alien shores. His hands pushed away
a tracery of dusty web from the glass of the case in which he beheld
the book of whose existence had been whispered to him in Arkham.
He then heard something that fumbled in one darkened corner, and
looking up he saw the creature that stalked toward the circle of light.
She entered the radiance, the tall black woman with lengthy coils of
burnished red hair that hung to the waistline of her yellow gown. He
was astounded at her handsomeness and wondered that a woman with
skin so black was devoid of any sign of negroid features. She seemed
to him like some supernal goddess of Arabia who, although in mortal
disguise, could not dissemble her cosmic sovereignty. There was something haughty and proud in her magnificent face, and he felt flattered
when she deigned to smile at him and speak.

"What is your desire?"

"To look upon the sign."

Her smile altered, strangely, and her breath, as she pushed it to him, was filled with the intoxicating fragrance he had detected upon entering the shop. "And what is the gift that will then be exposed?"

"I will know the satanic glory of what it means to be a god." His voice was calm, but his hands, as they pressed the glass of the display case, trembled. Bewitched, his eyes watched her reach into the case and bring forth the large book, from which another scent arose, one that he could not comprehend. Perhaps it was the effluvium of antediluvian sorcery, decayed yet potent still. He backed away a little as the smell reached into his nostrils and crept toward his brain, and then he blinked as his eyesight dimmed. Vaguely, he could see her delicate hands open the book. The blurred golden symbol took on solid form as he blinked his burning eyes. He beheld the yellow sign, and it possessed him utterly. He watched with eyes on fire as the goddess curled her black fingers around the sentient glyph and raised it over her amazing face. He watched, enchanted, as the symbol's three tails mutated with shaping, until the thing became a triple crown composed of gold-white lava. He saw how its liquid light spilled over the place where the goddess had worn a magnificent face, but where there was now naught but a featureless mask of obsidian blankness.

Her hands, unaltered and amazing, reached for his face and tugged it to the triple crown. As he peered into its potency, he knew for one brief moment what it meant to be a god, a creature bereft of heart and soul, merciless and mighty. The beautiful hands brought his face nearer to one spire of the sign until one eye was pressed against it. Ah, how that eye boiled and turned black as his flesh began to flake and he was transformed into a column of ash. From some place within the void that was her awful face an orifice opened, and the goddess blew his dust away.

IX.

Returning to the place that smelled of olden days, I staggered through the mortal throngs and sought the lonesome site, until I came to the leprous wharves that so infected my imagination. It was not only the coils of mist rising from water that haunted me, but also the sound of waves that slapped the rotted wood of dilapidated piers, a ghostly sound. It was a noise that felt like liquid footfalls on my brain, the tread of some dead thing trying to infiltrate my fevered fancy. From some distant indiscernible place I heard the baying of a vessel's horn, a noise so mutated that it sounded like some monstrous chanting to strange gods, and it was accompanied by the unhallowed gongs that were the clanging of moored buoys floating in some shoal. I walked away from the wharves and past the foreboding shop wherein I had found the ancient book, continuing to a network of alleys through which I hobbled, seeking the lonesome place that had been indicated on the curious map that I had found. Windowless walls tilted over me, their roofs almost touching, and I felt covered by a canopy of rotted wood and displaced time. I kept my hands in pockets so as not to be tempted to touch the stagnant walls, walls wet with slime that caught and reflected darkness.

I saw it then, before me in a secret plot of land, the black courtyard that I sought. Edging through filthy shadow, I touched the cold metal of the gate, and then I pushed the gate and passed through the threshold. How queer that I expected someone to be awaiting me, from whose lips would be uttered the mysteries of the worm; but I was alone, and the one whispered sound was the weird low song of wind in trees, and that was such a lonesome noise that, pursing my lips, I whistled in uneasy accompaniment. It was then that a dim light illuminated the vicinity before me, the moldy house of another era, where in one window I could discern an eerie glow. And from that window I heard a whistled sound that seemed to be an answer to my own, a noise that beckoned me forward, past a little pond in which glazed eyeballs studied me. I approached the black wall and slanting roof from which diseased vegetation grew, and as I peered into the window I saw the dancing swarm of headless things that moved in time to song of wind and distant rhythmic buoys. I watched them raise their handless arms and slap their wrists together as they danced, and then I perceived the thing around which they moved, the gigantic yellow mask that fumbled on the floor, inching its way like some diseased worm as its black lips puckered and exhaled a ghastly chirrup of airy lamentation.

I tilted as I fell to weakened knees upon soft ground and cried out a call that seemed to inspire the dancing things to more feverish movement. The lifeless light behind them cast their horrid shadows on my brow, and I fancied I could feel their fantastic forms melt into my eyes and find my brain, into which they capered as arcane beasts eager to endow my mind with ceremonial task. I wept for the headless things because I knew that I would never taste their diabolic kisses, would never feel the trembling of their missing hands upon my face and in my hair. However, I felt the vibration of the yellow mask that had won their veneration, and I sensed its hunger to suck my boiling brain from out its dungeon, my smooth skull, to feast upon my head and hands so that I could join its throng of revelers.

But I *will not* limp into that realm where human hope is démodé; for I have lips with which to breathe the arcane song that frolics in my mind, the tune that coaxes the yellow mask to lift itself into the air and float before my face, which it would eat. I still have hands, with fingers that are ripe for ripping and nails with which to shred a yellow mask and plant its tattered remnants into the necks where heads have been mercilessly severed. I watch the surrounding silent figures move as, now, the moon reveals her pallid mask within the window of the room, and with language learned from arcane books I blend that lunar light with sentient shadow so as to construct artificial hands onto the severed wrists that writhe around me. They watch me, my adoring horde, with new-made faces as I move my hands in symbolic fashion to the dead lunar light, and they lift their dummy hands so as to impersonate mine own with movement that is reflecting on the surface of the moon. We howl with wonder as the jaundiced moon assumes an expression that delights our morbid souls. I heave my whistled song into the air, accompanied by the things that shrill around me with those objects that have replaced their mortal mouths. They trill their puppet song into the cosmic darkness and move beneath the yellow lunar mask, remembering when they were living things. Nourished by mad necromancy, I step in their danse.

X.

You lift your moody eyes toward the moon and watch her sepia half-mask slip askance and fall through cosmic aether to your face, to which, sensuously, it adheres. The sphere's dead antique light consumes your visage and is your only apparel. I guide our little boat to the middle of the black lake and drop my triple hook into its depths as your windswept wig conceals your derrière and laces the loins from which your phallus hangs. Your mask stops just beneath your nostrils and thus your cruel smile is evident as you whistle a song to which we once had waltzed. My triple hook grows weighty with its catch and I drag the long-buried item from the depths until its heavy fabric floats into my embrace as, clutching it, I pull it onto wood. Excited now, you point your prick toward shore, and I work the oars of our little boat until we are secured next to the landing. Whistling still, you waltz onto dry land and lift your heavy arms unto the moon; and then you bend those arms to me and take the soggy yellow gown from out my hands. I plant my faun-like hooves into the ground and allow my hands to nestle 'round hermaphroditic loins as you slip into the soggy yellow gown and call to daemon wind to dry your dress. It comes, in answer to your call, yet it is not alone. I cannot see the flowers at my feet, for smoke and shadow cloud my dull eyes; yet I can feel the soft flesh of a rose and smell the wilted lily's rank decay, and I can taste the realm from which humanity dreams and weeps, the place to which you lead me in the blithe motion of continued dance.

We reach the neglected area of town and enter the dusky theatre. We push through double doors and glide into the crimson auditorium, where rows of ruined pews reek of shredded leather and stale tears beneath the candlelight of chandelier. I peer toward the raised platform that serves as stage and observe the twisted faces of embalmed clowns whose marble eyes wink secrets to the rafters where bedraggled birds mutter to themselves. I watch you run and leap onto the stage and stretch your yellow gown with naked hands. I watch you curtsy to the zany stiffs as if to teach them some new skill by which they could reanimate their limbs and blow you kisses from their dummy mouths. Your lips, delicately pursed, exhale an airy song, to which the birds above respond. I hear the beating of their tattered wings and watch their molted feathers drift onto the stage. I see them wing their way to you and plant their beaks into the fabric of your mask, and I smell the streams of blood that slip through the places where your mask is ripped. Your whistling assumes a liquid sound as bubbles of blood float from your lips toward the zanies that would admire you; and as those bubbles splash onto the charnel mouths the music you exhale is subtly accompanied with other whispered warbling, a pleasing sound from reanimated apertures of flesh to which the crazy birds flutter. I watch the dry flesh of the clownish faces fall away in pieces to the floor, yet still the whistling sounds through grinning jaws stretched wide on physiognomies of bone.

I cannot stand as passive observer any longer, and so I leap onto the platform and frolic on the floor, rolling into mounds of molted down that clings to that which answers for my flesh. And you, majestic master, finally appear, to hover over me with your strange smile as devil birds crown the air above you and laugh with beaks that are wet and red. At last you fall onto your knees above my loins and let your liquid mouth bleed into my womb.

XI.

We could hear the music, faint as it was, from our porch, and I confess I took a fancy to the sound. Thus I got on my bicycle and pedaled toward the meadow just off the Aylesbury pike where the road leads to Kingsport. This meadow has long been a place I like to visit because of the rugged megaliths that stand there—I like the way the wind sounds as it passes through their upper holes and hollows. You experience rare dreaming when you recline against those megaliths at dusk and watch the gulf of night deepen over you, like some abyss you might fall into as you step from star to star. It felt sweet to ride beneath those stars that night, nice and easy, no need to hurry, curious as I was concerning the muted music. The sky wasn't its usual black but rather a deep dark blue bruised with hints of purple, and the wind smelled especially aged as it pushed me on my way. I could just see the hazy silhouettes of the megaliths before me on the spread of meadow where nothing grew except tall dry grass, and although there was no moon that night the starlight seemed especially bright and so I could easily make out the yellow caravan and dilapidated pickup truck parked some distance from the groupings of pillars. The music had stopped for just a while, but then it started up again, and I knew that it was someone playing an accordion, although no person was in view. My bicycle glided to where the caravan had been parked, and I wondered how its yellow paint could look so bright in such dim light. Here and there someone had painted black stars on the yellow surface; at least I think they were meant to be stars, even though my eyes had trouble focusing on their forms, which seemed to shift and change in a way you wouldn't notice unless you stared at them with steady eyes like mine. Staring at stars was a favorite pastime of my kin—we liked the way their bodies stretched pointed extensions in such a way as to suggest living creatures in the sky. These black stars on the yellow caravan had a similar effect, never seeming still but always expanding and contracting, as if they were breathing.

I parked my bicycle and sauntered to the half-open door of the caravan, which looked as if it had once been part of a traveling carnival. The person inside, seated in a tilting chair, added to this impression, for he was a lean fellow dressed as a clown, with gigantic hands and cars and red rubber nose. Strands of hair escaped from underneath a bowler hat, and I thought it strange that the hair was identical in every way to the tall dry grass that sprouted in the meadow. The fellow's queerest features, his eyes, were sunken inside black hollows in his head—you could just see something shining inside those pits, something that gleamed like polished coal. An antique accordion was in his huge hands, its keyboard all shining silver with patterns of embossed design, and the music that he played from it, although rhythmic, had a quality of sadness in its sound, rather like the music played by a group of Jewish musicians who had given a recital at Miskatonic University when I was a student there. The clown fellow bobbed his head in time to music, and then he began to stamp one foot so that the entire caravan began to shake. I watched the puppets that were hanging inside large glass jars on a table near him, puppets with their rainbow-hued

strings attached in some weird way to the lids of the jars so that the funny figures hung in midair inside their cells. I wondered at the fabric with which those puppets had been constructed, there was something disturbing in the way the light of the place reflected on their sickly bleached simulation of skin. Maybe that was just the way the light played on and through the texture of the glass with which the large jars had been manufactured.

Clown-man stopped his noise and lowered his accordion onto his lap, and then he tilted his head and shut his eyes as if he were listening. I looked away from him, knelt upon my knees, and listened to the low haunting rush of the wind that whispered through the cavities of the standing stones. It was a sound with which I was familiar and one that I enjoyed. Indeed, when I was away for all those years, attending college in Arkham, I would sometimes hear this song of wind through ruins in my dreams, like a kind of summons that persuaded my return to Dunwich. I stayed away for eight years and obtained the finest education that I could, because it was my plan to leave Dunwich eventually and try to establish life in some city, as was common for most elder sons of this wasted pocket of the globe who have tasted life outside the village by attending Miskatonic or Harvard. Once I returned home, however, I knew that I would never leave. I felt too close a kinship to the domed hills and their secret sounds, to the dismal sky and those who dwelt beyond its dimensions. I relished the occult history of two centuries, fantastic legends of sacrifice on Sentinel Hill and of strange forest presences that laughed mockingly beneath the ground. That forest has a kind of enchanting beauty that I have never seen anywhere else, a beauty that soothes the eyes that behold it as powerfully as it disturbs the mind. So I returned home with a fine education and many books, and I worked my parents' farm and wrote poetry in my quiet hours. I was treated, almost, as a kind of outsider because of my education, because of the way I spoke, because I was able to write and think in a manner that was unusual to the ignorant lot that makes up the village. This backward kind of mockery reached its height when a small collection of my poetry was published by a small outfit in Boston. No wonder so many of those young men who had earned an education found it necessary to leave the land. I would never do so—the elements of Dunwich flowed within my streams of blood. But I understood too well the desire to flee ignorance and scorn, especially from fools who had never accomplished anything in life. But there were others in Dunwich village who subtly understood my ways and with whom I exchanged unspoken communication. I felt a similar kind of communion in that meadow and its quiet carnival caravan, where Clown-man and I listened to the song of wind that sighed through the crevices of pillars and chuckled inside hollows that wind and elemental time had formed.

The zany spoke. "I like the way yon wind sounds. You don't get wind like that in the city. Cursed city corrupts everything, including nature. There the wind is just another noise competing with man-made squeals and bangs and groans. Here, the wind sounds as it has for most of time, a wonderful primordial lullaby. Come, lad—let's go outdoors and taste the ageless effluvium."

There was a lilt to his voice that sounded foreign, although I couldn't place it. I didn't look at him again because of his lack of eyes, which affected my imagination to the point where I felt that if I peered into those pits too deeply I would get sucked into their black light. So instead I watched his shadow on the wooden floor next to the discarded accordion as he stood and stretched and hopped out of the doorway into the dry tall grass. I listened to his tread as he slithered through that grass like some cunning serpent, and I heard his hissing into the subtle wind. Not liking the way his puppets in their jars looked at me, with their sad appealing eyes, I rose calmly and stepped outside to where Clown-man was gazing at the midnight sky and pretending to shoot at a star with finger and thumb poised as pistol. How peculiar that the star, as I watched it, was suddenly extinguished. I felt my flesh grow cold as, laughing in a low manner, he stepped near me and pointed his finger to my heart and wiggled his thumb.

"I like your wee village," he whispered, "despite its smell. Actually, that stench is a part of its allure for me—such an old, forgotten taint, like rank prehistoric alchemy." His large nose touched my hair and sniffed. "Aye, I smell it on you too, a hereditary thing, no doubt, that reaches into a place of deep old time and those who pulse within it. I can smell the abyss of another dimension and the daemonic concavities of ancient earth, those places that have captivated your kind, those realms that have caught your imagination and keep you home. How rare, such loyalty. Come nigh, let's dance and reawaken dreaming things!"

He looked so comical as he raised his large malformed red shoes and began to tread on the ground to some music in his mind that I began to laugh and tap my toe to imagined song. Then, winking at me, he produced an ancient-looking Pan pipe, slim and double-columned and bound with black twine, with a length of cord with which one could slip the instrument over one's head and wear it near the heart. Pressing the columns to his mouth, he began to play the tune that I had heard inside my mind, an ancestral tune that I seemed to remember from another era. He played a little while and then he stopped beside me and, removing the pipe from his lips, offered the instrument to me. One heavy arm caressed my shoulder.

"'Tis easily done, laddie. Here, take it in your small white hands— there ye go. Listen to this lovely foehn that wafts to us from the surrounding hills and let it teach you how to blow. There you be—press those pipes to your lips and call the ones who dream in death. What a scintillating sound, like sparks of noise bursting into air!"

There was such persuasion in his voice that I couldn't help but play the role of Daphnis to his Greek god, and then something very odd happened. In my imagination the world around me blurred and altered and the distant atmosphere all around me became reflective, as if I were encircled by a wall of glass. Clown-man's gloved hands, suddenly larger than before, frolicked over me, wiggling their fat fingers in time to my piped song, and my dancing limbs seemed to answer to the movement of his hands, as if I were the creature's animated mannikin. As I danced, the wind among the standing stones became a howling mistral—at least I thought it was the wind that bellowed and pushed hot breath upon my eyes.

"Tell me, son of Dunwich, of the secrets you have dreamed. I've journeyed far to ascertain such knowledge."

His phrase, the title he bequeathed me, reminded me of my heritage and brought to mind my place. Whatever kind of creature this may have been, it was now in my familiar realm, with which I was intimate. "I can do better than merely tell you," I sang as I capered beneath his gigantic hands. "I can show you." My saying so subdued his alchemy that his proportions returned to normal size and whatever of his essence had leached onto my mind was gone. I slipped the pipe's cord around my neck and let the instrument nestle at my breast.

Sneering condescendingly, he replied, "You can show me a madness out of time, the pulsing shadow of unearthly dimension? I have sought such things around this paltry globe, aye, and the things that I have peered upon have stolen sanity and sight—but, oh, their rich reward!"

Finding my feet, I ceased my jolly cavorting and stood quite still. "I can dip you into other realms, into an abysm of old time, the place where secrets mutter underneath the hills of Dunwich. I can give you that, if such you require."

He turned his head toward his dilapidated pickup truck and thought. "I have misplaced my mortal eyes by peering into arcane darkness, and now darkness dwells within these hollow holes that once looked so innocently at the world. My shadows have appetites that I must satisfy. They itch to graze on occult things, to seep into the places where such revelation may be found. Take me, then, young lad, to this environ of mystic revelation. Let me fathom, if I may, its timeworn tale."

Easily escaped from his strange spell, I walked beside him to the vehicle and shut my eyes as he followed spoken directions to my abode. My kinfolk had retired, and so no one followed as I led Clownman into the depths of earth that composed our secret cellar. His malformed feet stalked that sod as his bulbous nostrils sucked the rancid air until he found the place of buried sorcery that held ancestral secrets of murder and mayhem. Excitedly, he leapt upon the circular timber that covered the ancient well, that plank that was still discolored by my uncle's blood from when he was young and foolish and moved the covering so as to sniff the tarnished drafts that siphoned sanity and sucked him into suicide. I was but a child at the time of his death and have no strong recollection of my uncle, but there have been times when, dreaming near the well, I have heard his hungry cry—or whatever it was that spoke to me from the depths. I heard as well the hacking of his ax with which he had tried to splinter the wooden slab, that slab that still contained deep slits caused by heavy blade. I smiled and laughed out loud as Clown-man capered on the covering as his comical nostrils sensed the beast below. Prancing to him, I indicated that we might, together, remove the cover and thus expose the banished foetor of a concealed place. He was strong, the zany at my side, and easily lifted the heavy circular plank and pushed it from us. I had never had the strength or inclination to try and remove the covering on my own, and it beguiled me that the nauseating stench that lifted to us was exactly as I had dreamed it at those times when, disturbed with loneliness, I had come to nap beside the centuried well.

"Alas," I whispered, looking down into the well. "There are no rungs on which to climb into the depths. I thought there would be. Too bad—it would have been wonderful to let you down there, to let you listen intimately to the earth-noises that have kept Dunwich slumber so uneasy. What revelations that dark place would reward your senses! Oh, well."

"Nay, laddie," was my companion's gleeful reply. "I have tricks yet!" So saying, he reached into the wide pocket of his ridiculous garb and pulled forth rainbow-hued lengths of rope, and how he could have kept such a lot of it in that pocket defied sane reason. Truly, he was a clever clown. "Now then, wee boy, wrap these ropes around my wrists and tie them snug. Good. Now, tangle these others around my ankles—there you go! Hold them securely, sirrah, as I climb into the well and work my way into its aperture. Nay, don't fret. I know a way to make myself as weightless as whispered sin. Here we go!"

He stood on the brick ridge and waved goodbye with comic exaggeration, and then he jumped into the tainted air. As he drifted downward his body seemed to shrink in size and lighten in weight, so that he seemed no more than a marionette for me to play with. Down he drifted, out of sight, but I could yet heed his ecstatic voice.

"Gawd! If you could see what I am seeing with what is left of my ember-eyes! It's terrible—monstrous—beyond anything! So this is the secret of decayed and poi-

soned Dunwich! How can I describe it? Not with mundane language. It's too utter-ly beyond thought—and yet I ache to name it so that you too can feast upon its hor-ror. But—but I think it knows you, for I seem to see your resemblance in the contours of its half-face! Is this the thing that calls to you in vision, the thing that stalks the stars? I have had visions of nameless horror, but I never dreamed of THIS!"

"Wait!" I called down. "Let me teach you ritual danse, so that you can adore it as it so demands. There, see how I pull your strings and move your limbs. What? It has suddenly noticed you, the thing that murmurs and has appetite? You're afraid? What's that? The noises of the earth are like needles in your stretched ears? How jolly! Wait, I'll pull you up a little, so that you dangle in the malignant air, just like your puppets in their jars. What will happen when I return to your car-avan and smash those jars with my uncle's ax? It will be a spectacle, I'm sure! Quick! Let me reach for the slab, which I pretended was too heavy for me, but look! I move it easily. Here, let me slip these ropes through the crevices in the wood, those crevices borne of madman's ax through which, just now, your howls echo like the wind that whis-pers through those standing stones. Hang there, in mirthless solitude, and let your companion feast. *Bon appétit!*" So saying, I hurled myself onto the slab of circular wood and imitated the jester's dance, laughing at his tormented howls. And then I took hold of the pipes that still hung around my neck, brought them to my mouth, and performed a paean to the horrors of Dunwich.

XII.

"Take my black hand, child. No, do not hold back," you cooed. It was strange to place my hand in yours and not to experience any sensation of heat or chill or sensuality. Your hand was as dry as any stick of wood, as smooth as any implement of marble. You tugged and guided me along the Brigg's Hill path, past the cemetery where witches once were hanged, until we reached the cottage by the rocky slope. It was then that I experienced a chill, for an element of dread had crept into the air.

"I'm having trouble breathing, Marceline. The climb has exhausted me. Why is the sky so yellow, like the skin around the eyes of a dying friend? There was an archbishop in Peru, I think, who said that the eyes are the door to the soul. When I look into eyes I see death only—except for yours. In your eyes I see bright darkness, a queer contradiction. Why do you hold my hand so tightly? I don't care to enter into the cottage. I'm going to sit here on this large flat stone. Look, some negligent child has lost its doll."

You paid no attention to my muttering but looked out over the hillside view. Sitting, I reached for the doll, which lay face down in the dirt. The thing's red dress had been faded by sunlight and its material was stiff with filth. Something about holding the creature increased my sense of isolation and panic. You looked down on me when I began to moan, standing just before the sun, and when I lifted my eyes to glance at you all I could see was your ebony silhouette against a sky of white fire.

"Poor neglected wretch," you sighed, reaching for the doll and taking it from me. I watched as you moved one slim and perfect finger through the soil with which the doll's face was covered, and pondered the sigil that you had etched thereon. You then bent as if to kiss the doll, pursed your lips, and blew Earth's dust away.

"The thing has no face!" I hooted.

How curious, the way you curled your lips. A strange low humming vibrated your mouth as you reached into a pocket of your amber gown and pulled forth a small piece of charcoal. I watched, as you pressed the implement onto the blank surface where once the doll had worn a face; and then I shouted when I saw that you had given the thing an imitation of my own visage. There was cruelty in your laughter as you brought the thing's face to your mouth and kissed it, as you then hurled it high into the air. It paused, airborne, for one moment, looking like a dry red wound in the sky, and then it plummeted beyond the slope and out of view. I felt a shadow on my face—the shadow of your midnight hand that beckoned my own. Clutching you, I stood. Together, we walked to the vine-hung cottage and through its threshold.

I think the cottage must have been very old, for its walls were riddled with wormholes, and there was an overwhelming aura of neglect or abandonment. The atmosphere of decrepitude was that, I think, which made me feel a forlorn sense of kinship with the place; for I had reached an age where life had been emptied of any illusion of hope, where the future was a bleak idea that filled me with a dull dreadfulness. It was this wretched idea concerning the future that inspired me to sit in darkness with a pistol in my hand as I endeavored to find the courage to place that pistol to my temple. You came to me in that darkness and forbade me to ruin what you called my magnificent face. You took the pistol from my hand and whispered of how you had admired my face from afar, and you cradled me in your arms and whispered dreams into my ear. Charmed, I followed you this morning along the rutted road that took us to the Briggs' Hill path, I held your black hand as you lured me into this cottage with its wormy walls. Together, we ascended the crooked stairway to a second floor, where we found the little room where the floor was covered with dust and ashes. I gawked at the multitude of masks with which the walls were decorated—those fleshy masks that hummed as the outside wind penetrated through the wormholes in the walls and sang through petrified mouths.

"Does it make you sad, this music of the spheres?" you asked. "Be cheerful, for you will never be alone again. Give me your sallow hands and dance with me." I lifted my hands to you, but I could not curl my palsied fingers through your own, nor move my stiff legs to your diabolic music. Inanimate, I stood there as you moved about me like some playful shadow. Your flexible fingers, such agile apparatus, smoothed the rough fabric of my face, and with one finger you etched an emblem onto my brow. How wonderful, when you took your hands away, to feel my face detach itself and fall onto your palms. How nimble was your movement as you danced my visage to the wall and pushed me against its surface, to which my countenance held fast.

The outside air, warm and perfumed, pushed through wormholes and filled my mouth. I expelled its music as I watched you dance with my faceless figure. I warbled music when you removed a bit of charcoal from your pocket and etched a sigil onto the blank surface where once my humanity had worn a face, and I could have laughed as you tilted to that surface so as to kiss it. At the touch of your beauteous mouth, my human form exploded into a mess of dust and ash, which drifted to the companionable filth upon the floor, through which you capered.

XIII.

I raised my fevered eyes to sunset flame that rose beyond the chimneys
of the hospital and waved at my mother's emaciated face as it peered at
me from behind the barred window. Smiling at her, I raised the golden
apple that she had given me as a gift, and then I turned my back to her
and strode past the fragrant growths of pale roses and purple hya-
cinths, to the great gates that opened beneath a darkening sky. No, I
would not catch the evening trolley to town; for I am a dreamer on the
nightside who loves to walk beneath the winking stars that began to
flourish above me in the gulf of night. After folding my large white
handkerchief around my apple and placing it within my coat's spacious
pocket, I followed an arrow formed of starlight that pointed into the
wooded place; cautiously, I climbed down its sloping shadowland, toward the river and its murmured summons. Other things, unseen and
unimaginable, muttered in the spread of tree limbs overhead; and although I knew it was impossible, I thought that I could comprehend
some of what they wanted to communicate, their dreams of forgotten
years, their secrets half-detached from dull reality. I could almost taste
the elder splendors of which they whispered to the leaves, the exquisite
desires that were nourished by roots and sinews in the soil. Creeping
silently upon that soil, I found a favorite outcropping of rocks that
stretched a little over the river's dark moving water. Climbing onto the
rocks, I sat and listened to night's sounds and silences. And as I listened my lids grew weighty, and so I shut them for some few moments
and smiled at the phantom shapes, red and black, that moved before
the folds of flesh. I watched, and knew a tinge of fear as those shapes
congealed to form a spectral façade, a noble black face with crimson
eyes that burned into my brain. I opened my eyes in an effort to banish
the phantom from me.

    I looked, and wondered why the place that I have often visited
seemed altered and unfamiliar. Pushing off the rocks, I floated to the
ground and walked beside the river, stepping over thick roots and half-
buried stones, as a daemon moon rose above the river and spread
ghastly light upon the place. Great gates, black with age, rose before
me, a thing that I had never encountered in other times when I had

trespassed upon this land. Pushing through the gates, I followed an ascending pathway that took me to a tall and ancient house that tilted toward me. From one high window a famished face wailed at lunar light, and then that white thin face looked down on me with inky eyes. What misery I felt as those eyes examined me, what desolation churned within the pit of my being as I saw the ruined lips that had been chewed upon by dull square teeth. Although the creature made no sound, my heart seemed to break as it lifted one emaciated claw and waved to me, as if I might have been a friend. I reached into my pocket and brought forth the handkerchief and its apple. Moving nearer to the ancient edifice, I hurled the apple through the dark air, and almost wept as the creature's claw caught the apple and clutched it to a caved-in chest.

The moon turned orange, as if it were an aged thing of rust, and in its debris of light I continued to follow the upward path through thick woodland. I felt the wind arise and touch me with its breath as it moved among the prisms that had been attached to upper boughs, and I smiled at the tinkling sound that issued from those objects of glass through which the tainted moonlight beamed and was transformed as spectrums of alien illumination. I stepped over the displays of multi-colored radiance, toward the white bulk that revealed itself at the place where the pathway ended. I marveled at her Grecian splendor as I approached and placed one hand onto her surface of sculpted bone, at the place where her wings were folded on her back; and I wondered what kind of skeletal remains could supply so mammoth a piece of porous bone with which to construct this thing of hazardous magnificence. Her beauteous face drank in the bloodstained moonlight as she regarded me with obsidian eyes. Kneeling, I pressed one ear to her mouth, so as to catch the whisper of her riddle; but I felt nothing except her hot scented breath, which may have been the wind. I stood and gazed beyond her, to the earthy plot of desolate land where I beheld the seven caskets. As I looked, the beast of chiseled bone queried in a strangled voice:

> "Where does one find the unplaced realm of Dreams
>   That has been loosened from the skull of Time,
>   That is the source of all that is sublime,
> That one may whirl within through starlit streams?"

I replied:

> "One finds it deep within an audient void
> Unsoiled by mortal tread, by mortal ache,
> A realm of tenebrous darkness, opaque,
> Where mortal hope is ruthlessly destroyed."

A tongue of fur stretched forth to lick my palm, but I did not heed it, for I was mesmerized by the moving of the coffin lids, by the famished revenants that rose within those caskets. I floated from the sphinx, toward the six phantoms that hungered for my living breath, for the luster of my liquid eyes. I moved into their danse, silently, and longed to open the seventh coffin on which the lid remained unmoving, sealed. I moved with them across the plot of earth, toward the silver tree from which seven golden apples dangled. I marveled at the fluctuating form, the cloud of black and red and yellow hue that separated as three nymphs of light and darkness. Dazzled, I disengaged from the famished fiends that would devour me and swam into the offered arms of the three sisters. I felt the yellow kiss upon my eyes, the crimson kiss upon my mouth, the shadow kiss upon my soul. I saw the three hands that conjoined as one and reached for one golden globe. The apple was placed beneath my nose so that I could drink in its fantastic bouquet. My teeth clamped into its flesh as its nectar stained my lips. I felt that fluid expand into a river of shadow and starlight, through which I swam to a cosmic place beyond all elder splendors, past all paltry mortal desires, into a realm of dream.

XIV.

I entered the city of mists on a day when the yellow sky was cool and clear, on an autumn day when dead leaves rushed around me and rose in whirling wind. Curls of chimney smoke mingled gracefully with autumn mist as I stepped down hilltop streets into the winding lanes of what seemed the main section of Kingsport. Stopping at one shop, I purchased a warm green scarf, for it was my fancy to sleep beneath the abyss of night. My walking tour of New England had been a wonderful experience, and although I had been a wayfarer for many hours I was not yet worn out. Studying the streets, I followed the winding lane that took me to the hillside burying ground. I climbed the steps that led to a sturdy bench, where I could sit and watch the yellow sky grow pale, then purple. I looked down the sloping hill, past tombstones black with age, over the rooftops, to the harbor. I knew that somewhere below was the haunted place that I sought and, taking the book out of my knapsack, I opened it to where I had placed a hand-made map given me by an acquaintance who had lingered in this town for three years. It was the book, actually, that had brought me to this mist-shrouded seaport—the slim volume of macabre verse by Winfield Scot. I came to Kingsport because I was obsessed with my dark dreams, and Scot's book of poetry was a collection of his cosmic nightmares put to rhyme—and some of them seemed damnably familiar. The bloke who had introduced me to the poet's work had been a part of Kingsport's transient community of artists, mostly students who had heard beguiling tales of the old town and came to seek mystic inspiration. His stories regarding the mysterious poet did not make Scot sound very interesting; rather, my acquaintance described the poet as a burned-out failure who lived like a street urchin and was overfond of alcohol. I listened to his tales with more interest than was evident— for he lacked the intimate connection of shared nightmare and was himself a rather blasé soul. My acquaintance had loved the old seaport, however, and was intimate with its lanes, and so I thanked him when he made me an impromptu map that indicated where I might find the antique house that the poet claimed as home.

I descended steps that took me to the road below, book and map in hand, and followed the handwritten directions as the sky darkened over me. A chill crept into the air, and so I wrapped my new scarf tighter around my neck as I approached the lonesome place that was the residence I sought. Moving past the queer-looking iron fence, I stepped onto a walkway of wooden planks that led past tall yellow grass in which a series of painted stones had been curiously grouped, reminding me of pictures I had seen of mysterious megaliths, although the things I passed as I tramped beneath the spreading limbs of gnarled trees were diminutive in size compared to the massive tombs in Ireland or other famous standing stones. There was something in the way the stones were grouped that made me think of secret things, and this inspired me to quiet my tread and walk as silently as possible toward the crazily slumped and tilted house ahead. Hearing a night bird's cry, I turned to look behind me, at the darkening sea from which a mist continued to rise. Then I made my way to the porch, where a figure sat reading by lantern light.

"Are you lost?" a slurred voice asked as I noticed the bottle of whiskey beside the fellow. The antique lantern's light was bright enough to illuminate his face, and I was surprised to find the chap so young-looking. I judged him to be around thirty-three years of age. I was disappointed in his dullard face, which seemed completely lacking in intelligence of any kind. Could this be the visage of the poet whom I sought, this tramp with dark disordered hair and dim expression in his slightly slanted eyes? His dusky flesh suggested a mixture of foreign blood, and his large Kafkaesque ears made me suspect he was, in part, Semitic. Something in the intoxicated bleary eyes disturbed me—I sensed that they might be some kind of camouflage concealing a persona that was not as dim-witted as at first appeared. They contained, those eyes, a kind of surreptitious knowing that only an intelligence as keen as my own might detect. Uncertain what to say, I merely mumbled some lines of verse that I had memorized from his book. His eyes darkened as he listened to my chanting of his poesy, and then he laughed and lifted the bottle to his lips.

I brought forth my hand that held his book. "I admire your work," I mumbled. "I want to ask about your dreams."

He clapped his hands once and held them to me. "Toss it here. Damn, I haven't seen a copy since I don't know when. I don't remember it being so slim."

"It's captivating work," I said, not moving as he thumbed through the book that I had thrown to him.

"Is it? I was very young when I wrote this stuff, a mere child. People reacted as if I were some kind of prodigy, those who weren't freaked out by the nature of the work." He smiled reminiscently. "I preferred the ones who were disturbed—that seemed the more genuine tribute to my art. The queer thing is that as soon as the book was published my dreaming ceased—poof, gone. I was a ten-day wonder, and then the sun had set on my talent and temporary fame. So I left home and began to wander, trying to find those places that might inspire new dementia. Hell, the world is a prosaic place overflowing with dull souls. One has to look far and wide to find the really special localities, those pockets of the earth that taint our dreaming and whisper to our souls of Outside things. Luckily, I drifted into Kingsport and found another dreamer, an ancient sea captain who could spin a tale that would set my imagination on fire. Damn, he inspired me, and the poetry poured forth once more." He must have noticed the excitement in my eyes, for he shook his head and laughed again. "Nope, never published. It's all in there, on yellowing sheets that have never seen the light of day." He jerked his thumb toward the door of the dilapidated cottage, and then his voice became a whispered sound. *"But you don't want to go in there.* Catch." He tossed the book to me. "Why do you seek me? You're not a poet."

"No—I'm a dreamer." A distant church bell tolled, and Winfield Scot sighed. "I've seen things that reminded me of your poems," I went on. "I've heard strange music piped by amorphous *things* that squatted before a throne of fire, music that was accompanied by the groaning of cosmic wind that fell from starlight. You've heard this too, if your poetry is any indication. Tell me what it means."

He suddenly stood and staggered drunkenly down the wooden walkway and onto the grassy place where the weird stones stood. Turning to gaze at me, he placed one hand onto the tallest stone, an oddly painted thing that resembled the Eye Idols excavated by Agatha Christie's husband in Tell Brak in 1937. Joining him, I touched my finger to the idol and found its stone peculiarly soft. Scot ignored me and scanned the sky with sober eyes. "Don't you get it, friend? There is no meaning. Nothing matters. We stumble with our paltry illusions on this tiny sphere of dust and then we die." He shrugged. "We are things of no significance. We come screaming into this sphere of mortality and experience the hideous thing called Life, which is its own hellish reward. The safest existence is the one that's impotent. I am a beast of nothingness. I do nothing except read and dream, and sometimes I sing to starlight. It suits me fine. Hell, don't look so dashed."

Hollow laughter wheezed out of my mouth. "That's exactly how I feel—dashed on the rocks. And I thought you might have taught me how to step among the stars."

He cocked his head roguishly. "That's the easiest thing in the world." Gliding to me, Scot placed his arm around my shoulder and led me out of the yard, down the road and to the shore. We listened to the gentle tide and watched the dark water, now free of evening mist. A blanket of shimmering starlight was reflected on the surface of the sea. "There you go," he sang.

I gazed out to the reflected stars and felt a wind drift to me from the water. Or was it a star-wind that would coax me forward, into an abyss? The more I looked outward, the more beautiful the sight became. "Will you come with me?"

He shook his head. "Nah. Not now. Perhaps in time. I am still a moonstruck poet, you see, and although my pen has stopped I still have lips with which to utter poesy to the spheres. I still have dreams in which I feast on fungi sprouting on distant Yuggoth, wherein I sense the perfume of undreamt continents beneath alien moons. I linger within earthly gardens, seduced by perfumed winds just as sweet as any cosmic nectar from a fallen star. I have Kingsport, a realm unto itself, as perfect as the strangest nightmare vision. I need no other place or time."

I offered him his book of verse, which he refused—but as he backed away from me he sang a snatch of verse that I recognized from one of the book's poems:

> "The midnight constellation calls my face
> As I stargaze into eternity
> Wherein I find a more congenial pace
> Undreamt of by dim, dull humanity.
> Far from mortal days I ache to soar,
> Far from flesh, this squalid weight of mud
> That forms this prison-husk I so abhor,
> This useless husk of skin, of bone and blood."

I heard them call above and beyond me, the shifting stars that swam the sky and were reflected on the water. Clutching the book of poetry to my chest, I moved into the water and walked the spaces between the stars. As I moved, my weight altered, as if I might surrender it and freely float into some dark abyss. I was submerged, but by water or black welkin I could not ascertain. And although other things, shapeless and soundless, floated by me, I had never felt so utterly alone. I opened my mouth and drank the liquid fire of a star, and thus my vocal chords were so transformed that I could chant poetry as never before. A strong current (of water or of air I did not know) seized Scot's book from my hand and I watched it drift and disappear into the audient void. It did not matter, for the verse lived within me and danced upon my tongue. I opened my mouth with music and sang the liturgy of nothingness to the darkness that listened and accepted me.

XV.

It rose before them on the apex of a snow-covered hill, like an object found in deep dreaming, the ruined edifice with its three towering pillars. Something in its circular shape reminded the woman of an artifact that she had seen in a museum at Miskatonic University, of an outré triple crown. Peering at the ruins so intently had a curious effect on Josephine Broers, for she imagined that she could see some queer winged shape perched atop one of the three columns; but then the thing fluctuated, separated, and drifted away as dark cloud. She watched as Mateo marched before her through deep snow up the precipitous hill, and after a slight uncertain pause she followed him, struggling through the snow as they climbed together toward the lonesome place. They had been prepared for the severity of weather, and they knew that the region was a place of uncanny legend; and yet they had not pondered the psychological effect that confronting the ruins with the naked eye would cast on them. Thus, mingled with the discomfort of deep snow and icy air was a sensation of almost primordial terror, some ancestral and psychological warning bell that could be felt in blood and bone. What overwhelmed Josephine was a feeling that they were utterly alone, in a place of unfathomable isolation.

Completing their arduous trek, they stood before the mammoth ruins and trembled—and they were uncertain what it was that caused their bones to shake and their hearts to shrink, the coldness in the air that grew more definite, or the indefinite alienness of the ruins before them. The thing looked prehistoric, and the place was so shunned by neighboring localities that there were no legends concerning its origin or race. It was a place that had existed since primordial time, epochal in a way that could be intuited if not comprehended. What Josephine sensed was more than presentiment—it was like a deeply buried racial memory that had been shocked into wakefulness by the sucking in of chilly oxygen. The ruins before them stood like some defacement out of time, a thing that should not be—or should no longer exist. She watched as Mateo, much smaller than herself, stepped through the snow into the circular place wherein the tremendous statue crouched upon its monument. Josephine did not want to approach the thing, for the workmanship that had created it had been monstrously exact. She thought, initially, that it had been created from dark brass of incredible age; but now she suspected that the enormous statue had been chiseled by expert hands (or that which answered for hands) from a gigantic piece of black jade. It was in form an exact replica of the amulet that Mateo had shown her on the night he had convinced her to journey with him on this trek, the amulet of a crouched hound or sphinx that wore a semi-human yet daemoniacal face. She knew that the young man was wearing that amulet on this journey, although he was careful to keep it hidden beneath his shirt.

She looked again at the grotesque statue and noticed one peculiar thing: it was naked of snow, whereas all other objects had been coated with inches of the stuff. At last she followed her companion to where he stood brushing snowfall from an idol that stood in a row with others. She marveled at the look of wonder in the young man's eyes. "It's the Seven Dreamers! I can't believe it. It's one thing to read of them in the *Necronomicon;* but to actually find them here, as physical things—amazing!"

"I've never seen anything like that godless divinity," she told him, staring with eyes aghast at the beast above them. "You expect it to spread those wings and fly off at any moment, it is so lifelike."

"Did you ever read that play by, I think, Dunsany—about the jade gods who were thought to have departed from their mountaintop thrones? He could have been writing about this magnificent devil, which looks ready to vacate this place in search of mayhem. How spectacular to confront a thing of whispered legend."

"I know that the world overflows with freaks—but *why* would anyone want to worship such a ghastly thing?"

"No, this is not exactly a deity, Josephine. It's—a kind of soul symbol, mostly identified with a cannibalistic cult that is rumored to be but quasi-human. Freakish indeed. There are some who think this thing is a representation of the Hounds of Tindalos—but those fiends are 'hounds' in title merely. They're more like an amorphous black shadow or mist, similar to Shub-Niggurath. We can't really understand these things, since they filter down from a dimension that has no semblance to terrestrial matter. They are utterly *other*." He smiled at her incomprehension. "I haven't explained a lot of this to you because I wanted you untarnished by lore and legend. My hope is that your mediumistic endowment can connect with the transcendent nature of the magick that was here evoked."

"I've explained to you that my abilities are merely instinctual. I've never had much interest in them until I saw their potential for bringing me money. I'm little more than a media sensation."

He squinted his eyes at her and curled his lips sardonically. "I know that's your line, your prosaic pose. But no—you're far more than what you allow publically. You see, I *am* experienced with such things. Intimately so, if I may so phrase it. I recognized at once your authenticity when I attended your performance and blew your mind, although you hid your dumbfounded reaction well from the others in your audience. I knew you needed guidance, and I confessed I needed abetment. Thus, here we are."

"It was your money that seduced me, Mateo—not your mission. I am your harlot absolutely. I had no real interest in traveling to this alien land and trudging to this godforsaken place."

"And yet you're captivated. You can taste the aura of the place; I can tell by the look in your eyes. Now I want you to help me evoke its alchemy so that I can name it in formula and become the sorcerer I was meant to be. It's not enough to conjure smoke and wind and shadow—such picayune elementals. I want to elicit the slumbering necromancy that can educe something as tremendous as that atrocious monster. I want to raise fiends with whispered words of thaumaturgy, perform the miracles forbidden in the *Necronomicon,* and taste the occultism that blessed Abdul Alhazred with rich madness. I want to see beyond the pale auroras and faint suns into those other dimension and find unearthly nourishment in their secrets, as the beings represented by these pigmy idols did. Oh damn, it's beginning to snow again. We've little time."

Josephine sighed. "What would you have me do?"

"Commune with this rare realm."

She shivered at the thought, for such secret conference had already found initiation. Some remnant of the region's past had conjoined with her brain and planted vision. She moved before one of the stone idols, knelt deep in snow before it, and pushed away the white stuff with which it was covered. Her gnomish companion gasped at what was then revealed, for the idol wore a mask of gold on which an emblem had been etched upon the brow. Josephine studied the totem's mask for some moments, and then she clutched it with gloved hands and pulled it free. The rough-hued face thus revealed was ghastly, ferocious, quasi-human—yet vaguely familiar. "It resembles you, Mateo."

He did not seem to hear her. "Put it on," he whispered. "Let it meld with mortal flesh."

"No," was her firm reply as she turned to lift the mask to him. "This was not meant for my kind. Only they of your ancestral blood may don the yellow mask. You were right to bring me here. I have communed with the prehistory of this realm—it plants pictures in my brain and sensation in my flow of blood. How odd to taste a memory of carnage on my tongue. Strange aeons have now passed, and old hunger must be answered. Let us satisfy it now."

She brought the mask to her mouth and kissed it, and her companion saw the crimson beads with which her lips bequeathed ceremony. Again, she offered him the mask. He removed his gloves and took hold of it, and he shuddered at the sudden rush of ancestral memory. Turning to acknowledge the beast of black jade, Mateo pressed the mask against his face as the snow continued drifting from the sky. As he peered through eyeholes he imagined that the silver snow turned crimson. A stench of sacrificial slaughter choked his throat and made it difficult to breathe, to speak. No matter. She spoke for him, to the red wet air. He saw the thing that answered her, the smoke that rose from the jade devil, that sentient shadow-cloud with jaws stretched wide; the thing that, drifting to him, clouded vision.

She watched the mask fall from the place from which his face had been eaten away, but before his corpse collapsed she snatched the amulet from around his neck and tied its split cord around her own. Bending to her knees in gathering snow, she fondled the mask and lifted it above her head, allowing the glistening gore in which it had been bathed to rain upon her famished mouth, her glistening teeth.

XVI.

We went, we three, to seek the secrets of the haunted place, to pierce its mystery. We had learned of it in a madwoman's dream diary, which she had kept while confined at Arkham Sanitarium. Sonia Orne was a poetess and dream-biographer of dead versifiers, and we had been enthralled by her imaginative recollections of Justin Geoffrey and Edward Pickman Derby. She was of ancient Arkham heritage, her great ancestor none other than Jeremiah Orne, who imparted the books and funds that led to the establishment of Miskatonic University. It was Samuel among us who had been intensely drawn to her history, being a poet of peculiar cast himself; and it was he who had secured Miss Orne's private diary from the fellow who had stolen it from the madhouse wherein he had once himself been confined. The fellow was still slightly mad, and Maurice feared that the bloke might destroy the diary because of the bad dreams it evoked within the madman's prosaic skull. Samuel, having inherited a fortune from his wealthy Jewish sire, had easily procured the secret diary for an exchange of golden coins. There was no indication in Miss Orne's chronicle as to how she had discovered the existence of the forgotten burying ground, although there is mention in her journal about the dreams that caused her to don a dress of yellow silk and a death-head's mask and dance in a local cemetery where, exhausted, she fell onto the ground and dined upon its dirt. (It was such behavior that convinced her relations to enshrine her at the asylum.) Strangely, the freak who sold Samuel the diary was also fond of dressing in a yellow frock and wearing a pallid mask, and it was he who suggested that he, too, knew the whereabouts of the secret mound and its sarcophagus that had been mentioned in Sonia Orne's diary. Indeed, after one sexual incident, this fellow lunatic had drawn a map indicating how to find the forgotten burying ground and its mound on which a spectral woman was said to dance by light of moon.

We journeyed to the edge of Arkham in Maurice's old jalopy, down a narrow road that became more and more treacherous, until we reached the place where the road had been split as if by some subterranean upheaval. Moe parked his car and we packed our gear and walked until we reached the spectral hollow, entering into it as the heavens turned a curious shade of hazy blue-violet. We trekked until we found, at last, the lonesome place, where we could feel an incredible ancientness in our mortal bones. The mound was half-hidden by a thick growth of willows, but the fading light was enough to reveal the queer catacomb that had been built into it, the stone of which might once have been white but was nigh black with hoary age. Diseased growths of grass and vines dangled over the edge of the roof and mingled with thick webs. Three stone steps three inches in height led to an iron gate, and it took all three of us to coax the thing to swing on its protesting hinges. The vault's cramped chamber was chillier than the air outside, and I lit my antique lantern so as to illumine darkness and aid us in our investigation of the single granite coffin that lacked lid or occupant. What was that draught of cool air that breathed upon my ankles? Hunkering beside the crypt, I found the crevice through which a chilly zephyr issued.

"Fellows," I spoke as I stood, "your assistance please." They gazed at me uncomprehendingly as I indicated the oblong cist and, leaning against it, began to push one end of it with sturdy hands. Still puzzled, my companions came to my aid and we struggled until the coffin began to slide over the floor's smooth stone; and Samuel let out a yell when he came close to tumbling into the pit that we exposed. I wrinkled my nostrils and coughed. "That is the effluvium of the very pit. No, Maurice, don't shine your modern flashlight's beam into the depths; for my antique lantern's glow is far more apropos in aiding our descent. Use caution as we traverse those cracked and narrow steps; they were not designed for our clumsy feet." I held my beacon high as the others slipped their torches into their packs, and I smiled as Samuel removed Sonia Orne's diary from a pocket and held it as if it were some treasured talisman. Entering the aperture and setting one unsteady hand against a cold and clammy wall, I began my descent into the labyrinth.

"I feel as if we've entered one of your wild stories," Maurice told me, and he tried to laugh although the noise was not convincing.

"Or one of my dreams," I responded as I peered into the pit. It was unnerving, I confess, that the journey into the abyss took so long a time, took us so deeply down into the under-earth and seemed to warp time itself. The wretched airstream continued to hurl its foetor into our faces. When at last we reached level ground I shouted at the cavernous space encountered and the litter of yellow bones therein. Numerous dimly discernible archways led in a plethora of directions. "This is a dream indeed," I whispered, "a veritable phantasm."

I moved toward one earthy archway and stepped over bones as we traversed damp sod, earth that was at times so soft that I feared it would sift beneath our tread and open to drag us down to deeper nightmare. The draft of nefarious effluvium had somewhat dissipated, but its nastiness clung to our clothes and hair, so that we resembled an assembly of shuffling cadavers who followed a death-light to some obscure destination. And then we entered another eldritch area, and we shouted in amazement at the sight before us; for it was nothing less than what remained of a decrepit building of disintegrating wood. The silence was absolute as I approached the narrow tilted plank that was all that remained of a door, and I spat disgust as the wood crumbled at my touch.

"You're not seriously going inside, Howard," Maurice protested. "The place will crumble on top of you, just like a House of Usher. The floor will split beneath your foot. Fah, I've never seen anything so dirty

and diseased. It's a veritable carcass. What have we stumbled on—
some forsaken town in which something so vile occurred that it was
necessary to build new ground over it and hide it from sane sunlight?
A place of buried transgression, a madness out of time?"

Samuel's voice sang to us. "It *is* a burial of time, where tomorrow
will never come." Maurice cried out as the young Hebrew pushed past
me and entered the edifice. I did not hesitate to follow him into what
appeared to be a kind of parlor where the few furnishings were crumbling grime-coated antiques such as I had never encountered. In the
dim place beyond were three narrow hallways, into one of which my
youthful friend had trod. Sighing, I advanced after him as he passed a
number of rooms, each of which contained a bed. I was annoyed by
the sound of Moe's rough laughter and his hand on my back.

"It's a bordello!"

"So it appears," I quietly concurred, watching as Samuel reached
the end of the hallway and pushed open one final door. He vanished
into the adjoining room, from which a pale illumination gradually filtered. He had turned on his flashlight. Maurice rushed past me and entered the room, but I was hesitant; for I sensed that whatever the room
held would be an eerie key to the mystery upon which we had been
guided by the diary of a dead woman. But at last I gathered nerve and
crept toward the room, where my fellows were shining their torches
onto a small bed and its occupant. I surveyed the petite mummy that
was attired in a tattered gown of yellow silk. A wig of deepest crimson
covered its dome, and its eyelids were weighted shut with tarnished
coins. I frowned at the soft sound of Samuel's lamentation, which I
could not comprehend, but said nothing as he switched off his flashlight
and floated to my side. Raising the Orne diary to my lantern's firelight,
he turned its leaves until coming upon a poem that had been scribbled
in faint script. He touched the page with caressing fingers as he recited.

> "I amble to your dark and quiet room
> And kneel before your bed of final rest.
> I wear a splash of your preferred perfume
> As in your yellow party frock I'm dressed.
> I see my shadow pirouette and lift

My silhouetted arms to hidden skies.
Oh, take beloved's final precious gift—
I kiss the pennies pressed upon your eyes.
I clutch your glossy tresses with one hand
And move into the daemon danse you taught.
I listen for one final hushed command.
I twist your wig into a tighter knot.
I bend to press unholy lips to thine.
My last embrace will be your ever-shrine."

My lamplight caught movement as Maurice glided to a small table and picked up the quaint object found thereon, an antique music box composed of white gold. How loud it clicked as he wound it, and how impossible it seemed that the relic began to play a delicate melody. I watched as Samuel handed me the Orne diary and shuddered as he pressed his lips to mine for one sweet kiss. Moving from me, he reached for the dead thing's crimson wig and slipped the filthy thing over his hair. Lifting his graceful arms, he moved in time to the sound of the music box. How queerly his silhouette moved across the walls, and how the entire room trembled at his tread. The melody from the box subsided—yet there was music still, muted and distant. Samuel spun toward one wall, where there should have been a window but was instead a rectangle sealed with solid stone. I quaked at the sight of it, for it suddenly reminded me of a nightmare that had recently disturbed my sleep, a vision of a house of death wherein a window was sealed with such a block of stone. And this evocation of unearthly melody became hauntingly familiar the more I listened to it, and I knew that it was a noise that would herald doom.

"No," I whispered as my fellows touched the sealed window and struggled to push the stone away. At last it moved and fell over the edge to the other side, and we all choked at the stench that wafted to us from the aperture. The noise was now distinct—the hideous piping that mocked the music box's enchanting tune. The space beyond the window's rim was illuminated with black-violet phosphorescence. We could just make out the alien tree that spread its writhing limbs, boughs on which seven buzzing spheres shimmered with unnatural radiance. Below the sentient branches of the unfamiliar dendroid stood a black figure, gaunt and lean and haughty, its outline fluctuating as if it were enshrouded in a robe composed of midnight. I could not make out any facial features except the octagonal eyes that shimmered as would golden coins. The uncanny composition commanded my attention and my eyes tried to focus on the shifting things that squatted on the ground before the eidolon and pressed cracked flutes to amorphous mouths. Now and then weird streams of diminutive lightning sparked among the seven spheres of the alien tree, flashes that revealed a vortex of nothing beyond the daemon and its tree, a hungry void.

"No," I wept as Samuel lifted himself into the window and crawled through its cavity, falling out of sight for a moment. When he erected himself the wig no longer covered his glossy hair. I watched him drift toward the daemon and stand trembling before it; and then he lowered himself to his knees as the creature offered Samuel its hand, which my friend began to lick. I shook into full wakefulness as Maurice began to move into the window-space. Turning, I fled from the room, out of the crumbling house, through the earthen labyrinth until I found the narrow steps that took me into moonlight and fresh air.

My friends were never seen again. I miss them, and yet there are times when I seem to sense their presence, and the other ghosts with whom they keep company. I sink into an awareness of this especially when I dream, when Samuel's lithe silhouette spins before me and presses his phantom mouth to my cool mortal lips. Other familiars creep into my vision. I feel the air chill over me as they bend above my sleeping frame of flesh, and I do not protest when they place their coins upon my eyes.

XVII.

He heard the tinkling bell that sounded in a distant place and shivered in the cold, thin air. Thus he concentrated on sucking at his Egyptian cigarette and scowling at the scene spread below them. Perhaps, at another time and in a different mood, he would have been able to appreciate the appearance of the sky from the hill to which they had traversed, for the sky wore aspects of Whistler's fabulous *Nocturne of*

Black and Gold, especially its clusters of yellow stars that spilled toward the valley beneath them and gathered as pools of golden ambiance.

"Are you coming in?" one friend inquired, standing near the entrance of the isolated hillside club.

He waved the human pack away with the hand that held his gold-tipped cigarette. "One moment. I wish to commune with this eastern sky. Perhaps I can coax the hidden moon to reveal herself. I adore the moon and her chilly kiss. Proceed without me, and I shall follow anon."

His party shrugged and turned away, and he watched them flow as gathered flesh through the double doors of the hillside edifice. *"Au revoir,"* he muttered, turning his eyes so that they could follow the zigzag line of the pitted wall of stone that looked, to him, like some petrified python that had fallen into a slumber from which it would not awaken. They had to pass through a portal in that massive wall so as to reach their destination, and he wondered why such a wall was required to separate the lonesome hillside from the region of the valley town in which his people were vacationing. At last, exhaling one concluding cloud of tainted smoke, he crushed the remnant of his weed beneath his foot and turned to examine the building's double doors. What had his companions called the place—the Club of Seven Dreamers? The mundane building would never inspire his dreaming, what with its dull and weathered planks so poorly put together. How it tilted and sagged, and how hesitant he was to enter its confines.

The sound came to him again from some distant place—tinkling bells. Turning to investigate, he scanned the other regions of the hill and detected a figure far away, a being cowled like some dreary monk. Yet as he looked longer, he could not be certain that it was a fellow being at all, for now it resembled an irregular chimney on which a small silver sphere had been painted near its top. Then the image began to blur and sting his eyes, and thus he turned away and shivered once again in the thin air that caused such discomfort when breathed in; and so he approached the double doors and entered the silent club.

He was instantly deflated as he encountered the creature who awaited him, a nude nymph with gold and silver crystals sprinkled onto her pubic nest. Her petite breasts pointed their ruddy nipples to him and he smirked as, fingering one, he whispered, "You should have been a boy." Handing her his heavy coat and wooden cane, he walked past the tables at which figures bent together suggestively, but as he scanned the room for his party he was disappointed by their absence. Perhaps they had wandered into some adjacent chamber. Something caught his attention, the suggestion of a sound, and as he turned to heed it he beheld a figure that transfixed him—a cloaked creature that stood before a wall of obsidian liquid. Beguiled by androgynous beauty glimpsed beneath the figure's hood, he approached the unmoving youth and marveled at its supple limbs, fine pale face, and tantalizing phallus. Moving his hand, he touched the metal bell worn on a piece of cord wound 'round the handsome neck; and he shivered at how soft the metal felt, as smooth as cool new death. Tightening his fingers to the bell, he shook it once and laughed at its tinkling reply; and then, shutting his dazzled eyes, he leaned toward the cowled head and touched mouth to mouth. The phantom's kiss sucked him into the lagoon of night that rippled as liquid wall, and when at last he had imbibed his fill of passion and pulled his face away, he discovered that they had spilled into a dusky chamber wherein seven coffin-shaped urns smoked upon their tripods. Approaching the nearest urn, he peered into its depths and beheld an obscure image that might have been a face composed of fog and shadow, in which yellow eyes ignited. He blinked as these combustive elementals rose in coils of incense and gathered in the dusky aether as a cluster of yellow stars; and as he watched his name was whispered, so that he turned to acknowledge the summons.

The androgynous beast filtered to him through the gathered smoke and shadow, and he could not comprehend its alternation; for the white epicene countenance had altered so as to appear more feminine, and its breasts had horribly expanded, and its golden phallus had sunk from sight. He stood, tilting freakishly, as the cluster of yellow stars blinked about the region of the creature's pubis, glistening in the moist and fragrant mound. Tilting more, he fell onto his knees before the being's sex and sucked in its sharp perfume. As his nostrils expanded, the yellow points that were daemonic eyes trembled with rising and whirled to him until they sank into his own eyes, which were transformed as liquid orbs of altered jelly that peered past mundane dimension and beheld another plane.

A bell tinkled above him. Lifting his eyes to stare at the dead face beneath its hood, he saw the sphere that had once seemed a thing of flesh drift upward as a globe of lifeless lunar dust, the dead illumination of which cooled his dreaming face. He watched that sphere hatch and spill its vision to him, and thus he understood.

XVIII.

I climbed the ancient steps of the moss-thick tower and looked upon the terraced garden of dream, the place for which my weary soul had ached. I found the cavity of ruin in the tower's wall through which I squeezed my paltry flesh and bone, and then I leapt onto the high, sun-soaked wall on which I balanced for a little while until intoxicated by the scent and sight below. Deliberately, I stepped into the air and shut my eyes, but I felt no impression of falling from the wall, felt nothing but the press of hands upon a rough-hewn place. Yet I knew that I had vacated the high and corrugated wall, and so I slowly opened my uneasy eyes and found myself bent over a stony walk within the garden of dream. Ah, the soft sunlight on my entranced eyes! Oh, what beauty in the lullaby of Nature all around! I rose and trod the rough-hewn path and then stepped onto the smooth surface of an arching bridge, stopping momentarily to watch my golden reflection in the gentle water's course. Looking up at last, I admired the handsome structure of a white pagoda wherein a gigantic brass bell hung, and so I crossed the rest of the bridge and stepped onto the other ground. I walked toward the white pagoda and its surrounding trees of delicate blossoms, and when I noticed the obsidian hammer resting upon a pillow of sculpted stone I decided that I would bang the implement against the bell before departing the entrancing place. I knelt to the ground beside the graceful trunk of a cherry tree and lifted handfuls of pink blossoms to the rose and yellow sky. My old dreams had not lied: the drowsy radiance of the place was enthralling, and the conjoined song of murmuring river and whispered breeze lulled me toward an ecstasy of dream within a dream. Yet even as I closed my eyes I could still sense the yellow radiance of the sun upon my lids, an aura through which rose-hued shadows blossomed. Tears of joy trickled down my blissful face.

I cannot recall the seduction of slumber, but suddenly I felt a chill upon my lips. I awakened in a terrarium of nightmare, my aching back against the trunk of a dead and fungous thing, my mouth against a barrier of glass. The still air was haunted by the echo of a mammal's wings. I staggered to my feet and tripped along a chilly path of broken stone, past the grey and splintered pagoda whose tarnished brass bell had fallen and lay lopsided on the ground. I hobbled to the rough-hewn wooden bridge, and midway over its rotting surface I bent over to glare aghast into the stagnant pool below. Sallow moonlight revealed my countenance of diseased yellow skin, a transparent sheath pulled tightly over the skull that held my desiccated brain. The wall was gone, replaced with an unending surface of glass coated with night's slime, an ichor that made climbing an impossibility. I wept until I heard the clanging of a cracked bell, and when I turned to peer at the damaged pagoda I beheld the eidolon that stood beside the tarnished bell, an implement in its hidden hand. Ah, perhaps I could use the black hammer to shatter the wall of glass! I flew to the phantom with rage and determination pounding my withered heart, but the creature did not fight me; rather, it handed me the mallet and seemed to study me, although I could detect no face beneath its cowl. I staggered to the wall of glass and smashed my tool against it, and so ferocious was my madness that the wall began to crack and splinter. I heard the cool air before it caught me, the suction from Outside that plucked me through sharp shards of damaged glass that once had been a wall. I fell into a void of nothingness, wherein the spectres of dead stars churned around the pallid sphere that was my mortal face. Those liquid stars, my eyes, grew dry and lost their luster. I reached out toward emptiness, wherein I crept, a blind and useless memory.

XIX.

I hear the faint far ringing of a deep-toned bell as I carry you up the black mountain in this midnight wind. I have heard the call before, in deepest dreaming; but I do not imagine that I am dreaming now, this witching hour, for I feel too bitterly the sharpness of the trumpeting tempest; and I feel too sharply a pain in my ankles as I traverse toward the apex of the spectral peak with my burden in my arms. You seem to reassure me with your wide and frigid smile, and I bend to kiss your eyes in which I see reflected frosty starlight; and thus, although exhausted, I continue my trek beside the centuried wall that meanders along the mountainous region. The pealing vibrations have ceased their sound, and now the thin and chilly midnight air is still and lonesome as, at last, we reach our journey's termination. Gently, I set your body onto the solid ground and lean, breathing deeply, against the antediluvian wall on which queer symbols, here and there, have been engraved; and I wonder at the sight of the occasional towers atop that unending length of masonry, and cannot guess their function as, reaching toward the lunar sphere, they pierce the midnight air. And as I study one erected pylon, I imagine that a nameless fiend, winged and without visage, glides to the conical point and, hanging there while grasping onto the tower's tip, makes motions to the moon with other paw.

I frown at the slender archway that serves as aperture leading through the centuried wall into another place, and at the coaxing of a midnight moan from some distant pocket of shadow I grasp your pale hands and pull you through the slit in stone, into another realm where wind and earth contain a deeper chill. I glance again at the tower on the wall, which casts its phallic silhouette on garden's ground, but do not see the imagined fiend without a face, and thus I turn to contemplate the holes with which the ground is pockmarked; and as I tilt beside the nearest burrow I smell a memory from deepest dreaming, and my mouth remembers strange remorseless appetite. I smile at you as one large hand claws the loose earth of the burrow and brings a palmful of aromatic debris to my face; and I sigh as I wash the filth into my flesh as I raise my other hand to the moon. I creep to you, my adoring wretch, and you do not complain as I touch you with my grimy hands and lift you so that your face, once more, is sheathed in ghastly lunar light; and, overwhelmed by your beauty, I bury my face within your hair as I tread the garden ground. Here is a weird white tree whose bark is as smooth as cadaverous skin, and so I set you beside its trunk and perform a dance in moonlight for your pleasure. Ah, your grin is wide; and I think that you would laugh if only you could recollect how to stretch your jaws.

I move merrily over an expanse of garden ground until, exhausted, I rest one hand against the centuried wall; and as I pant I see the huddled thing nearby, and when I approach this other inhabitant the moonlight reveals it to be a ruined thing of pulp and petrified bone, with a skull so cracked that one might imagine it to have been smashed against a wall of glass; and as I bend over its remains I am overwhelmed by the rancid aroma of its ruination. I study the marks that perforate the exposed bone, and I close my eyes so as to taste dregs of recollection. But then the midnight wind whispers at my ears and brings the scent of rank vegetation and your sweet fragrance. Returning to where you rest, I fall before you and bless your mouth with lover's passion, and then I fold your arms about my neck and lift you once again as, suddenly, bleak rain slips onto us from stormy sky. But do not fret, beloved, for there in the distance is the silent pagoda composed of crimson posts and roof of jade. We need but cross this wooden bridge to reach its shelter; but let us pause for just one moment and peer into the squalid pool below us and marvel at our sodden shadow on its liquid surface. Ah, the rainfall increases and savages our dreaming visages, and so we rush into the shelter of the pagoda. This ivory pew, as lovely as the skin that sheathes your bones, will serve as couch until the storm has passed, and you look so lovely as I lay you onto it. Yes, I am intoxicated by the violence of the storm, and you smile at my clownish antic as I fling my limbs into the liquid air and dance on soggy sod. Then, returning to you, I notice the wooden mallet on its pillow of sculpted ebony, and with that mallet in my hand I approach the massive bell of brass that hangs from its post within the pagoda. I touch the surface of the bell and examine the figures embossed thereon, those devils poised like furtive apes. I lift the hand that holds the mallet and wink at you, and then I bring it down.

Ah, the deep-toned reverberation! It seems to shake the earth into which its vibrations sink as summons. I pound the massive bell once more, and its heavy sound dispels the storm so that, once more, we see the daemon moon; and in that dead sphere's suggestive illumination I watch the shaggy shadows that ooze from out their earthy pits within the garden ground. I see them raise their canine snouts to Luna's influential light and move into a bestial kind of danse. They pour through pits and call to me, their cousin. Some climb the wall and mount the ancient spires so as to adore the moon with eyes of jade and paws that move symbolically. Some seep toward the remnant of flesh and bone that stains the dirt near one portion of the wall, and the stench of that mortal husk so clutches them that they raise their snouts to howl deliriously. And one last shape lopes toward us, my love, and grins rapaciously as it sniffs the aura of your decay; and then together, kindred creatures, it bends with me to feast upon your chilly breasts.

XX.

I creep along the wide surface of the high and ancient wall. Below me, in the ghoul-haunted garden, a north wind begins to rush through the high grass; and I welcome that wind as, rising, it moves the fabric of my yellow gown and frolics with the coils of my scarlet hair. My arms, outstretched, wave hands among the o'erhanging branches of those slender trees nearest the pale wall, branches on which enigmatic emblems had been etched; and I allow one talon of my left hand to pierce my right arm and carve a similar sigil into its ebony flesh. Ah, the odor of my peculiar blood as its beauteous liquid drips onto the ledge on which I stand in sheer moonshine! I move my nude feet a little in slight danse onto the smears of blood that stain the boundary wall on which I balance, and then I lower myself to my knees and, reaching into a deep pocket of my yellow gown, bring forth the shard of charcoal that nestles in its depth. The charcoal has been prepared from an essence of rare vegetable and animal, and its alchemical properties are persuasive when combined with the chemistry of my spilled blood. I press its porous substance onto the surface of the wall and hum an antique tune, drawing an emblem that evokes a vision of dreamland, that mystic otherwhere I wish to waft unto.

I rise and stand on naked feet, lift my arms to cool moonlight, and hum my antique tune. Returning the shard into its pocket, I raise my hand and make movement to the moon, forming my fingers into an Elder Sign. My eyesight catches the black shape that sails through cosmic aether, the lean descending thing that stretches bat-like wings as it circles to our mortal world; and as it falls unto our speck of temporary dust each star touched by its tip of wing dims a little, or dies entirely. Ah, how it seems to ride a beam of lunar light, to me; and although its wings are wide they make so sound at all, and I marvel at how its black rubbery flesh seems to drink in the moonlight as the night-gaunt perches on one of the basalt turrets of the ancient wall. Although the blood beneath my foot congeals, its sister liquid rushes hotly in my veins.

I stand on my insignia of charcoal, move my fingers to the moon, and fancy that the beast observes me; although how it could do so I cannot comprehend, for it wears no countenance. Yet as I peer at the flat surface where there should have been a face, I suspect a suggestion of some sentient force within the area of blankness, and as I gaze more deeply into its nothingness my eyes grow heavy and my mind begins to mist. Before my eyes completely close, I see the stretched wings of the dreamy beast, and the whole night is eclipsed by the obsidian silhouette of the night-gaunt. I laugh at the talons that torment me as I am clutched and carried from off the ancient wall, into thin air. My jaws stretch wide with rapturous howling as I voyage far from mundane time and space, beyond the wall of sleep, into an undimensioned region that is a product of my intimate nightmare. I sense the spectral atmosphere protest as one of flesh and blood presumes to invade the land that accepts naught but dreaming psyche, and I relish the subtle catastrophe to the chemistry of dreamland that is the result of my nameless voyage. I open my eyes at last as our movement slows, as I am set before the ruins of a castle that I had known in deepest dreaming; and as I ponder its charred remains, a flock of smooth black beings emerge from its cavities—the kindred of the night-gaunt that has stolen me from the waking world and brought me to my realm of dream-delirium. They spin over me, around me, and some draw so near that I can feel their prehensile talons in my hair. I turn to the nearest gaunt and press my lips onto its slate of facelessness. They take hold of my black hands, the texture of which is so close to theirs in hue, and lead me into danse beneath the vault of heaven. My bones tremble within their husk of corporeal flesh because they sense they do not belong in dreamland, where only phantoms of our mortality haunt in pockets of places conjured by human whimsy. But I am not human; rather, I am a monstrous mongrel bred of a diversity of madness, formed as a whole entity by my elder brother, Nyarlathotep.

I dance, and my coiled hair of flame spins in the wind aroused by the flapping of wings that make no sound. We promenade from before the ruined castle and skip down a path that takes us into a necropolis in which thick white willow trees droop vines. Upon one dilapidated seventeenth-century slab of white marble, which has been partially engulfed by the trunk of a willow next to it, sits a figure that sucks unwholesome nourishment from a remnant that has been excavated from hoary charnel earth. The night-gaunt that has liberated me from the waking world approaches the feasting creature and extends one impossible paw, to which the ghoul tilts so as to kiss what passes for palm. I watch the gaunt shudder in ecstasy and then lift itself into the midnight aether, where it joins others of its brood.

"Richard," I call as I approach the white slab; for I have known this fellow in intimate dream inspired by the study of a canvas on which he worked his art when human. He gazes at me queerly, for it has been a length of time since any voice has so saluted him, and the sound of my physical tone has startled the surrounding air of dreamland and splintered the fellow's brain with semi-recollection. Sitting beside him, I exhale my witch breath to his mouth, silently forming his mortal name with my lips; and finally his wide mouth moves, in mimic of the motion of mine own.

His broken speech is guttural, as if spoken in difficulty and pain. "I . . . have known your eidolon. You have haunted me as phantom when I was delirious with fever. But you are no ghost now, for I can smell the chemistry of your blood. You . . . corrupt our realm with your blood and bone, and the weird sugariness that emanates from you changes the fragrance of dreamland air."

"That is the sweetness of Sesqua Valley, and it is but one component of my combination skin. You know the valley, for you visited its boundaries when you were of the waking world."

The nude ghoul frowned. "I have . . . no recollection."

"Do not fear me, or be intimidated by my physicality. I come to give you memory of your mortal art, as I have bequeathed new remembrance of human speech. You once possessed a sinister gift, which you have lost in maladroit ghoulishness. Sometimes, in one pocket of what remains of your human heart, you feel an ache, and your fingers itch to hold once-cherished implements. Give me your hand."

He hesitates for one moment—and then holds out his monstrous hand, into which I place the shard of charcoal that I have retrieved from my deep pocket. The ghoul studies the object with uncomprehending eyes. I take it from his palm and press its porous substance across a small section of the white slab on which we are assembled. Standing, I return the shard to his hefty hand as he stares at the name that I have written on the slab. "Pickman," he reads, and his human name is echoed on the rising wind. His green eyes gleam with dim memory, and he speaks his name once more. Hesitantly, he presses the charcoal onto the slab and begins to work. When he is finished, we both admire the semblance of the face he had once worn in the waking world. It is a fine likeness, for portraiture had been his forte.

"When we met in dream," I whisper, "you led me to an archway through which I caught a glimpse of an audient void wherein one might encounter Crawling Chaos. You spoke intimately of these things, for one of the two books that you brought with you from the waking world was a rare sixteenth-century Greek text of the *Necronomicon,* and no matter how inhuman you become, the memory of that manuscript never leaves the remnant of your mortal brain. Do you remember that archway, Richard?"

"I do."

"Show me the place again," I command.

The ghoul sighs, then shrugs. "It is but a little distance." Pushing off the slab, he lopes inelegantly through the burying ground; and I follow, past an ancient stone church with crumbling spire, past tombstones and fallen obelisks, until we come at last to a solitary mausoleum. We enter through a grating of ornate iron and descend some few stone steps into a vault of marble in which I observe three oblong boxes in various states of ruin. On one of these coffins I espy the two books that Richard Pickman brought with him from the waking world—the manuscript of Alhazred and an edition of Edgar Allan Poe. My companion drops to his knees and begins to struggle with one section of the stone floor, working it with tough inhuman fingers until at last he pries open a portion of that floor that proves to be a flat block covering an aperture. Violently, he hurls the square of stone from him and then bends over the edge and inhales, drinking in the potent odors that waft to him from the pit. Raising his face to mine, he smiles—and I notice how his face has started to change, resembling more the artist he once had been. Not speaking, he climbs into the aperture and begins to scale its rough stone wall. I follow, and together we climb down a cylinder of rock, finding whatever holds we can for hand and hoof. My witch eyes adjust easily to deep darkness, and I laugh at the playful bats that flock about us. The air breathed in grows weighty and moist the deeper we descend, and the entire atmosphere takes on a peculiar quality that my mortal lungs relish. How curious, the elements of dreamland, that I should experience them as physical stimulant. The things of dream defy all sense and reason.

We touch, at last, a surface of damp earthen floor, and I study the vault and its debris. The ghoul turns me to and inclines his head to one side. "You know my name, but have not spoken your own."

"I am Marceline Dubois, sorceress of Sesqua Valley. But only one portion of my being is the spawn of Sesqua's shadowland; for my ever-changing eyes reflect the other realms from which I have taken physical being, and I am here, in this impossible place, to reacquaint myself with cosmic birthright. Show me the archway of which I have spoken."

Pickman stands and nods thoughtfully; and then he creeps to one corner of the room, toward what I mistakenly assume to be an archway leading into a chamber that is identical to the one in which we find ourselves. But then I behold the blurry semblance of my ghoul companion, and Richard's hand, outstretched, touches a surface of polished glass.

XXI.

I approached the standing mirror before which the nude ghoul posed and admired its tarnished frame, and when I stood before my reflection I noticed the rare and precious symbols that had been embossed on the metallic framework, glyphs that were emblematic of occult things. Scrutinizing my familiar in the mirror, I disliked how the refulgence of my yellow gown clashed with the murkiness of the crypt; and so I pulled my garment from me, stepping out of it as it fell to earth. My ebony flesh looked most appropriate in my surroundings, matched as it was by the dusky tissue that was the hide of the ghoul beside me. I moved behind him and snaked my arms around his neck, pressed my body against his nakedness, and whispered into his awful ear. Together, we spoke his human name, and he watched, spellbound, as his face continued to transform, to become less ghoulish and resemble more and more the ominous fellow he had been in the waking world. His expression so amused me that, laughing, I kissed the back of his neck as I lowered my hands to his loins; and then I sank to knees and kissed his buttocks, which caused him to shudder just a little. I drank in his rank aroma, that stench of graveyard filth and feast, and then I turned him around and tongued his impotent sex. He knelt so as to join me, and our mouths met. Biting into my lip, he sipped my little stream of blood, and then he raised his bloodstained lips a little higher and kissed my eyes. The world before me was a crimson blur, and to that visual distortion I spoke the exceptional formula that had been embossed on the mirror's gilded frame. As I spoke I moved so as to see our embracing figures on the glass, our reflections that rippled queerly. Blinking blood from my eyes, I pushed Pickman from me and crawled into the mirror, and thus entered another gulf of dream. Looking behind me for a moment, I watched Richard try to find me in the mirror's reflection; but all he could see was his altered physiognomy, and the way his dark rubbery skin had grown smooth and pale, more akin to the man he once had been. Whispered he:

> "'All that we see or seem
> Is but a dream within a dream.'"

I stood and turned to face the void. A figure stepped out of nothingness, and the crown perched on his dome seemed composed of an identical metal as the mirror's splendid frame. The Black One from Outside offered me his hand, which I took and licked.

"You have debauched the dreamland with your mortal presence and have altered the very fabric of its air with your sugar-stench of Sesqua Valley. Yet I cannot help but be fond of you, sister of my soullessness. You have come to me at last, in this realm between dimensions, from which a portion of your essence has been formed."

I bowed my head in reverence as my eyes twinkled in adoration. Tugging at my chin with one beautiful hand, the Crawling Chaos breathed onto my eyes, and I shivered at the infernal revelation that consumed my boiling brain. His hot hand moved into the coils of my crimson hair, as indistinct fiends formed above the Strange Dark One and paid homage to him with the terrible music produced on cracked flutes pressed to amorphous mouths. A multitude of cosmic winds thronged about us and wailed of unearthly things. Nyarlathotep brought his other hand to my hair and smiled magnificently. Ah, the sensation of his working hands as they manipulated my mortal flesh and molded me into a black sphere of dust. The Crawling Chaos howled insanely, his noise accompanied by the baleful piping music produced by his hellish acolytes, and then he pressed together his appalling lips and bathed me with his breath, that potent exhalation that worked into the sphere I had become, and blew my dust away.

I awakened beneath moonlight, on a hill in Sesqua Valley, to the sound of eldritch piping. The daemon before me was familiar, and I watched Simon Gregory Williams as he filled the valley air with alchemical music produced on his paranormal flute.

XXII.

The madwoman climbed the endless stairs that took her to the choking room that contained one single inhabitant, the notorious mystagogue of whom all Arkham had been whispering. They who had witnessed the disturbing exhibition spoke of it with fear clouding their uneasy eyes, and as she contemplated the troubled murmurings of the crowd, the madwoman heard a buzzing of recollection within her cracked skull; for she had once been a professor of esoteric poetry at Miskatonic University where she had dwelt on the fantastic poets such as Justin Geoffrey, Clark Ashton Smith, and Edward Pickman Derby—seers who had also spoken of fantastic things. The intriguing rumors shared among Arkham folk were very similar to the themes evoked in the poetry of those bards, whose books she had managed to hold on to when madness had cost her the position at the college and forced her into a homeless existence, in which her nights were spent in a shelter beneath the steeple of an ancient church. Curiosity often pricked her questing lunacy, and it was always charming to locate a new hovel in which to hide during daylight; and so she climbed the endless stairs that took her to a little room in which a tall, gaunt woman of exotic beauty stood, a creature whose burnished hair of deepest red fell below her back. The eccentric wretch liked the warmth of the modest room, and she cherished its cozy silence, which served as contrast to the obnoxious world of men. She enjoyed looking at the enchanting woman whose gown of yellow silk clung seductively to a sensual figure, and she pondered the talisman that hung from its cord at the lady's bosom—an amulet that depicted a faceless idol beside which two winged figures genuflected.

"Welcome," the woman spoke as she stood before a wall-sized screen on which dream-like images prophesied of mortal doom. "Please sit here, in this chair before me, and let us commune. You have appetite, I know. Look, on that table there—a tray of sustenance from which you will win a multitude of nourishment. Yes, set your thin book on the chair next to you and let me place this salver on your lap. Excellent." The lunatic marveled at the sight of the tray and its contents, for she had never seen anything like the seven iridescent apples of peculiar blush; and when she took one spherical object in hand and chomped into it, she was overwhelmed with awe at the taste that spilled into her mouth as the choked room darkened. She bit into the flesh again, as images began to move upon the walls, circulating pictures that coalesced into one single representation of an alien tree on which seven prismatic globes of fruit hung on writhing limbs before a backdrop of absolute obscurity. The quiet little room became haunted by a subtle song of windstorm that might have issued from far galaxies, a tempest that took on potency and attacked the tree, the substance of which deteriorated as scattered dust, although its seven spheres remained aloft in nothingness which they enhanced with rapid brilliance that burst from them as cosmic sparks. And then they too were caught within the cyclone and, spinning, they became a vortex of extraterrestrial tint, a spiraling pandemonium into which a madwoman might be sucked.

And so she was, drawn into a non-dimension that was awash with streams of violet illumination that glittered with the golden wreckage of seven dying suns. Yet she was not alone, for the magnificent black woman stood beside her as escort and took her melting hand as she was transformed into a perishing bubble without form or place. Yet still some semblance of paltry human psyche remained extant, as mercury that spilled from black inhuman palm and leaked into another realm, wherein it frolicked before the features of daemonic camouflage that clothed Ultimate Chaos and danced to the playing of cracked flutes held in monstrous claw. Ah, glorious—the idiotic wail of that which transcends time, the fury without form or meaning, around which the transformed lunatic whirled as eternal advocate.

"That's a wondrous book." The sepulchral voice awakened the unfortunate one from dream's dimension.

"Yes, I used to teach it at university," the madwoman replied as she placed a protective hand over the book. She laughed scornfully as memory emerged. "I had to pretend that it was symbolic—but my dreams had informed me otherwise, as only they can. The poet Derby was in fact a furtive campaigner of dark and secret things unknown to the plebeians who savored his lyrical aptitude alone, which they heightened because of his youth. Potent visionaries, the young. His art was a seductive force, as you are; and to sing his lines is to enter into an intimate relationship with sorcery."

She took up the volume, kissed it, and pressed it to her bosom, from which her heartbeat sounded as a delicate throbbing in the gloom. She opened the book and peered at what she could make of the yellowed page; but she did not need to see the lines, for they dwelt inside her unhinged mind. However, before she could begin to recite, her hostess uttered song.

> "I see the impish flock that moves in danse
> About the Nameless Eikon so adored.
> Their outlines play upon a ruined manse
> As ghastly silhouettes of daemon-horde.
> Oh, devil-horde that spreads membranous wings,
> That seeps from out the manse of ill-repute
> And flocks as nightmare's brood, obscene hatchlings
> That move in an expression of tribute
> About the Nameless Eikon of smooth stone,
> Their embassy of Chaos absolute,
> A monster mundane time cannot disown,
> A deity dull man dare not refute."

The madwoman lifted her eyes in astonishment as the other sang the syllables of printed poetry; and then she shut her eyes and spoke the final couplet:

> "And I, once dead-yet-dreaming, now awake
> And reach into rich bedlam, and partake."

The black one smiled and removed the tray from the madwoman's lap. "What are you named?"

"I am Geraldine Worthington."

"Ah, Geraldine—look here, an ornamental hashish pipe from mystical Egypt. Now, let me ignite it with this length of match. Let me suck. Isn't that a sweet aroma? No, don't rise. Take this in your pretty mouth and let it transport you to a realm of delicious delirium and language. Heed not the sparks that flit between those incandescent suns, ignore the cosmic storm that weaves into your hair. Draw upon that stem and feel the coils of alchemy that curl into your skull, and then suck these lips I offer thee and taste of untold things."

Miss Worthington took the pipe and placed it in her mouth, drawing on the wooden stem so that airy nectar seeped into her mouth as a cloud that floated to and claimed her brain, which hatched with vision. Smiling idiotically, she pressed her mouth to the other's and drank the elixir that was siphoned through her lips—that intoxicating lava. The seven suns turned above her head and sank into her eyes, with which she found new revelation. Her mortal essence moved through antediluvian forest until, at last, she stood before an obsidian obelisk that tilted over the obscene rubbery fiends that pranced around it. Some distance behind the black pylon stood a ruined manse through which a chill wind played through cracks and fissures, wailing as freakish intonation to which the dog-things danced. The madwoman ached to ape the dancing of the brood, one of which held horrid nourishment to its mouth; and she felt a tinge of unfathomable exhilaration as the ghouls raised filthy paws to the enormous moon whereon shifting clouds formed a thousand faces. She watched the terrible beams of that lifeless sphere of lunar dust fall onto the inhuman physiognomies, which it seemed to bleach and blur with reconstruction; and when those reformed visages turned to her the madwoman recognized them as the poets with whom she had been intellectually intimate. Wafting to them through shimmering aether, she took hold of hands and joined in their danse, shouting with them to the forlorn moon. At last exhausted, they ceased their movement, and she turned to the Frenchman's severe face, the stormy eyes of which she kissed. Noticing the bit of infant's brain that blemished the perfection of his mouth, she plucked it from him and held it to soft light. The poet smiled as he took it from her grasp and placed it below his nostrils, and he closed his eyes as he drank its sweet bouquet; and then, smiling, he moved it to the woman's mouth and placed it on her tongue.

The mystagogue stood before the obelisk and raised her countenance to moonlight, and the lunatic marveled as she watched the black face melt into a million more until, at last, it utterly diminished. Raising one magnificent midnight hand, the strange Dark One caught residue of lightning that sparked between seven bursting spheres and aimed the voltage to the obelisk, the bulk of which began to split. Bat-winged brutes oozed from the cleft in stone and flowed aimlessly about the ruined mansion as other fiends, formless and fearful, took shape in mid-air and drifted to the black enchantress, before whom they genuflected as they raised cracked flutes to formless mouths. The coruscation emitted from the shimmering spheres melded with the melting black stone and reshaped it as the idiotic Lord of Chaos to whom the bat-fiends flew in adoration.

Stepping to the Faceless One, that triumphant avatar of ultimate pandemonium, the madwoman bowed so as to join the nebulous creatures in their adoration as their piping pierced the universe; and bending low she pressed her mouth to dark daemonic foot—the foot that, rising, contemptuously struck her mortal head.

XXIII.

My sense of wonder palpitates as I stand before the house wherein you lived when you penned your sonnet cycle, those poesy-dreams of alien fungi. Perhaps you were lured into the writing of your poems by Klarkash-Ton's sublime verse—for who could resist such influence? Or perhaps it was Melmoth's midnight vision that worked as aesthetic enticement. I stood before your home, wherein you dreamed of Dunwich and of Yuggoth, and I placed my hand upon the 10 with which the house was numbered—and I was overwhelmed with such potent emotion, such elevated sublimity, that I have not yet come down from ecstasy. It overwhelms me now, as I work on this sequence with which I pay honor to you, my Ever-Muse.

At times it seems impossible that you actually existed, so much has my life been affected by the wondrous things you wrote. You seem mythic and remote, a Muse that visits only in my memory. The world in which you lived has drifted down Time's unending stream, and as I try to visualize it in the violet-misted sky I see nothing but my own paltry era. The shimmering sun is a spectral disc within mauve heaven, a beacon that I follow down the rutted road that takes me to the isolated church, ancient and white-steepled, from which chimes no longer sound at death of day. I follow the slates until I find your name, which I whisper as I fall to bended knee. My bones shudder within their husk of wearied flesh as tears blur your name that is etched on weathered stone—the name to which I pay homage with my art. When they sank you into your futile depth of earth, you felt a failure in all things and sensed you would be forgotten for all time; but the Old Ones you awakened with your pen have never slept, and (dead-yet-dreaming) haunt the world anew, generation after generation. I seem to see one now, a blot within the violet-misted sky, an eidolon of chaos crowned by whorls of dead stars that it siphons from the universe; and as I gaze its strange dark hand catches a cluster of those cosmic embers and plants them deep within my mortal eyes. Thus aided, I behold strange towers and curious rivers as I dance through labyrinths of wonder beneath some vault of dream. And seeing this I ache to hold my pen and join you in eldritch song of Literature, to weave the words that express my sense of wonder. And from some pocket of this dream I feel the kiss of phantom wind that carries the evening chimes that reverberate from some ancient and white-steepled edifice in a land both alien and intimate, wherein I can see the mystic mirage that is conjured by the perfection of your literary art.

XXIV.

You called the individual names of the harpies that followed you through the streets of clay between tall and vacant buildings inhabited by regretful shadows. You relished the daemon-wind that whined betwixt the shards of shattered windows and matched the unholy litany of your antique violin with which you seduced the vixen at your heels. Ah, they followed you to the black canal and drank in the rich decay of its stagnant oily current, the sludge that oozed like black blood in some monstrous vein. Your hags, some of whom had lost their tattered wings, crept near you on their clumsy feet, their gnarled hands raised gracelessly to the daemon-wind, an element of which they caught and swallowed in their awful mouths. You led them past the tall and vacant buildings to the arch of displaced stone that spanned the black canal, and then you stopped midway in crossing it so that they circled you with jerking limbs and moaned an accompaniment to your violin's wretched tune. Stupidly, your vultures lifted legs that pirouetted in the idiot wind and moved to the edge of the arch of displaced stone, on which they balanced for one moment before falling over and into the stagnant slime. You laughed at their swampy song and continued to perform your heartless intonation as the daemon wind rose with what was left of your maladroit harpies: their yellow masks. You watched that cluster of false faces whirl from you toward the tall deserted buildings that rose like time-lost haunts of clay, and as you watched and grinned another element of wind bubbled upward from the thick canal. It claimed you as it caught your violin and snatched it from your hands; and as you reached impotently for your tool its strings were played upon by the daemon-wind, and at the squeal of that lullaby you moved your feet with following, coaxed once again into the city, above which arose a yellow mask of fog that spoke your miserable name.

XXV.

I awoke to daemon howling, and to the rattling of a tattered blind that flitted like some great bird's broken wing at the shattered window. I was not sad to see the pane's destruction, for I remembered witnessing an image on it that disenchanted me. I pushed myself with hands that pressed on shattered glass and rose erect. I combed my length of hair with fingers so as to rid it of splintered glass and other sullage. The thin air of the tall and vacant building that I inhabited had suffocated my dreams, and thus I vacated the choked room and climbed cautiously down the rough stone steps that took me from the urban tower, into untenanted lanes. An expanse of low and filthy cloud resembling a rippling yellow mask so unnerved me that I fled out of the dead city toward the stagnant canal just beyond the limits, the length of which I followed in my attempt to escape the infested metropolis and its pallid mask of cloud. I did not drop until the cityscape was a distant blur, and then I fell to knees on one cement ledge above the length of canal water. My eyes followed the serpentine flow until I saw the distant bridge that crossed over it, to a shelter of woodland. Something in the dark-

ness of the woods beguiled my imagination, and thus evoked my day-
dreams summoned me to crawl beneath the mauve sky to what remained of an antique basalt bridge, over which I crept as the water
beneath me coaxed with weird whistling. I had never known water to
coo in such a way, and so I paused at the other end of the bridge and
listened, until I learned the whistled tune, which I tried to imitate by
pressing my cracked lips together. The second sound ceased at the in-
filtration of my descant and was replaced by a slithering that approached from underneath the bridge, from the hidden spot from
which the structure's troll emerged—the hairless hermaphrodite who
held a thin black reed in one bleached hand. I was about to bend so as
to sniff the rank aroma of the creature's double sex when, from some
deep place within the woodland, there came a low metallic sound that
summoned me.

"Be wary of that false chime," my hobgoblin playfully counseled,
but I refused to heed its coy admonition and, rising to my slippered
feet, padded along the path into the labyrinths of woodland, past thick
dark trees and gigantic boulders on which moss and fungi flourished. I
could see, when lifting my eyes to the tops of trees, that the mauve sky
had deepened into indigo, and I fancied that I could hear again, above
those trees, the muted wailing of a banshee wind. The way sloped
downward and led into a glade through which a river of blue and silver
water frolicked, although it made no sound. But I could not watch that
water because I was entranced by that which stood above the wall of
rock on the river's other side; and as I gawked a peal swept toward me
from the black spire that tilted over its edifice of stone. I paid no heed
to the voice behind me that murmured, "Beware the false chime!" I
climbed the hill of grassy patches and slate that led to the rotting
wooden bridge that spanned the river and its rocks, and I tripped
across the splintered wood and followed a narrow path until I touched
the tabernacle. The high hills behind it were lush with silent growth
that rose to the darkening welkin in which dim starlight began to wink.
Bending to one square of deftly placed stone, I touched my mouth to
the rough surface and shivered as its chilliness sank into me; and then I
pushed away from wall and approached the entrance, where brass

doors, hoary and unhinged, had fallen to the ground. I crossed the threshold and was instantly encased by an antediluvian aeration that christened my physiognomy with subtle moisture. Shadowed by my epicene mutant, I was propelled through thick gloom and passed into an uninhabited chancel. The outside light was extinguished and thus I could not see my way too clearly, and so I reached for guidance to the wormy pews that smelled of perished prayers. I approached the silhouette of an altar as a sudden effulgence of moonlight beamed through the stained-glass window high before me; yet as I studied that window I could not comprehend its image, which might have meant to convey some unrepentant creature pent in hell. And yet—something in the form of that dark figure composed of dusky glass seemed familiar, and I tried to study it until a cloud obscured the lunar light and the window's image became a nebulous afterthought.

I heard once more the moan of daemonic wind from outside the edifice, and as I peered into obscure corners I finally noticed the second threshold, narrow and obscure. Wandering to it I discovered a circular stairway of rough-hewn stone that rose to the hidden place above. As I began to climb I heard again, more loudly than before, the pealing of some great bell. I paused to hear another warning from the freak that followed me, but instead there came the eerie piping of a flute. Ignoring the noise, I climbed until I reached the third threshold that led me into the belfry. The choked compartment was closed by three walls on which were fitted arched and unstained windows of impressive size. I could smell the grey thing that leaned against one enormous bell that was savaged by a crack in its metal. The amorphous shape sniffed the air and pushed away from the bell, and as it flowed to me I fancied that it was a breathing eidolon of the image I had detected on the stained-glass window above the altar. Pressing its significant nostrils to my shroud, it drank deeply of my decay; and then it spun me around and thrust me toward one arched window, upon which was reflected my remains. I moaned as black memory awakened and the chamber echoed with the ghastly piping of some flute that was accompanied by the mocking wind outside the tower. I shuddered as my husband wrapped his rubbery arms around me and buried his wide face into my hair.

XXVI.

None in our artistic circle had seen or heard from John in the nine months since his return from Prague, and although we had grown accustomed to his reclusive ways we had begun to wonder. John had inherited the old Whateley place on a hillside about one mile from town, a residence that aided his hermitage. Through laziness or indifference he had allowed the place to run down, not seeming to mind the dilapidation; for John existed primarily in his imagination, the way some artists do, and neglected the outside world entirely when he could. However, he and I were friends, and he had promised that upon returning to the States he would begin work on a new piece for my museum of decadent art. I had grown anxious to see what, if anything, he had come up with, and so late one stormy afternoon I drove up the hill to his silent house and pounded on its door. I stood there for a little while as the wind washed a fine drizzle onto my face, but eventually I heard movement and saw a shadow form behind the door's window. The door of oak opened and he stood before me, and I could tell from the fevered light that smoldered in his dark eyes that he had been at work on some great thing.

"Gerald," he breathed, stepping aside and allowing me entrance into his demesne, "I've been meaning to call you. I've been laboring on the new project and I'm fairly satisfied with what I've managed to do." The calm tone of his voice did not fool me; I knew when he was in the throes of artistic ecstasy. But I said nothing as he took my jacket and placed it on a peg. "I did write you from Josefov, didn't I?"

"Yes, where you drank a toast to Kafka for me. Your card—I suppose you were too preoccupied to write an actual letter—mentioned something that you had found, some interesting item. That was the last I've heard from you in this length of time."

"Yes, I had found something inside a hidden alley shop. You know I have a talent for sniffing out the lost and obscure haunts where one may stumble across some fabulous thing."

"The kind of shop where you find your extraordinary books."

"Exactly. That's always been a handy ancestral attribute, but I possess it to a keen degree. But come, let's go up." Thus we climbed the stairs to the second landing, from where I could detect the spicy fragrance of scented candles from the attic rooms above—John refused to work at art in electric light. I always cherished my hours in the attic rooms where the ceiling was so low that it almost touched my dome, for it was a realm in which I felt absolutely at home—a world of grotesque art, where beauty and terror dwelt in happy cohabitation. Portions of the wall contained built-in shelving on which hundreds of books were packed, and there were other tomes that rose as twisted columns from the floor. A small bed with rumpled covers testified that John had been nesting in the attic, as was his habit when possessed by creativity. I peeked through the arched opening that led into a second chamber and saw the easel on which a large painting had been covered with an expanse of yellow silk. Always unable to contain my curiosity, I stalked through wavering light, past the threshold, and into that other space.

"Is this your new thing, John?"

"It's recent—but no, that's not what I'm working on." I clipped fingers to the silk and lifted it from the canvas, and then I whistled. "Interesting, isn't it? Ring-around-the-roses is one of childhood's oldest games, internationally so. You know the commonly held notion that it represents the Great Plague of London in 1665, with the children aping death when they 'all fall down'—but that idea is now widely disputed. The so-called 'symptoms' described in the popular versions of the song don't fit well with the actual agonies of plague. You'll notice that I've made the faces of the innocents rather grim and mature, although I've tried not to make them overtly malignant. Still, their effect is unnerving, I hope."

"Yes, it's superb. But the attention is riveted to the desiccated figure around which the infants play, especially its uninviting face. You've captured in that stiff expression a kind of pure ecstasy, which is the direct opposite of the face of the one child who looks out at the painting's viewers. Most disturbing. One hardly notices the other subtle touch—those two blurs in the background that take on form the more one notices them and begin to suggest contemplative griffins with wings folded on their humped backs. Whatever do they represent?"

The artist shrugged. "Haven't a clue. They're the one aspect I imagined on my own. You see, this oil is a modification of another— work." He hesitated for some few moments, and then he ventured into one dark corner and removed a rectangle from its wall. Returning to me, he handed over the large and heavy framed image, and I held its plate of glass to candlelight so as to study the yellowed photograph beneath. "That's what I wrote to you about from Prague, after finding it at a small shop in the Jewish Quarter. It's obviously quite old, yet its faded image commands attention. At first I thought it must be an etching that had been cleverly designed to mimic early photography, but now I think it's an actual print."

"It reeks of paganism."

"Doesn't it? Deliciously so. The figure looks like a thing carved from smooth pale wood, except for the skull, which looks real enough. But, god, what expertise it took to make that sculpture so resemble an actual corpse! The technique astounds me. Of course, the wee creatures haven't joined hands as in my painted representation; rather, they seem engaged in some form of maypole dancing, with each paw clutching a twisted strand of silken hair. At first I mistook the gnomes for naked children, but one can't when seeing the imp that has turned to glare into the camera's lens. I've never seen such savagery in a face. Those twisted features—ugh! It looks an embodiment of purest evil."

"Yes—it's vile. I must hang it in my forthcoming exhibition. You'll lend it to me, of course."

"Um—no. I have something else in mind for you." He grinned at my little pout, took the photograph, and set it onto a table. Then he took up a candlestick and crossed to the attic window, which he cracked open. "The tempest has passed, and the wind is pushing the clouds away from the new moon. Ah, the air smells magical after a storm. Let's go out back and I'll show you what I've been working on." So saying, he held the candle aloft and followed its guiding light to the steps that took us down to the second landing, where the bright lights offended my eyes. I followed John down the stairs and through a hallway that took us to the kitchen, and then we exited through a back door into a spacious yard, a place I loved because of its relics. Here was the rusted antique automobile that had belonged to John's grand-father. There was the crude homemade guillotine that a suicidal cousin had constructed in his successful search for extinction. I followed John toward what looked like a canopy that he had erected at a place where grass did not deign to grow, and I heard him laugh softly as a rush of wind extinguished his candle's flame. Entering beneath the tarp that was the structure's roof, my friend stood beside a figure that had been draped with a covering of heavy fabric. "Help me with this, will you?" he asked as he dropped the candle to the dirt and took hold of one section of the fabric. Together, we lifted the covering from the statue beneath it, and I shouted a little at what was there revealed. The artist laughed again as he stood and admired his creation. "I knew that I didn't have the skill to duplicate the smoothness of that pale wood in the photograph, so I used bleached calfskin. Calfskin's perfect because it assimilates hide, and as you know I like to have my sculptures touched as a part of the spectator's experience of art. Go on, feel it. Sensual, in a ghastly sort of way. Isn't the wig fabulous? I had it made by Keziah, whom you'll no doubt recollect."

"What, that wretched transvestite performer we encountered in Arkham?"

"Just so. She's a marvelous wig-maker, and I paid her a fortune for this. It's human hair, of course. It needs to feel authentic, not synthet-ic. It reaches almost to the ground, just as the hair on the thing in the photograph would were it not clutched by those goblins."

"And where are *your* imps?"

He hesitated. "I've—yet to construct them. Actually, I can't decide how they should look, what would seem more decadent. Those freaks in the photograph are certainly grotesque, but I rather like what I've done with my painting—those gnomes with childlike faces. I'm just about to start work on a second canvas to see what else I can come up with before I begin to build the rest of this piece."

He smoothed a hand over one artificial arm as I leaned nearer to examine the sculpture's skull, which looked odd in the lack of light. Bending low, I retrieved the candle and flicked my lighter to its wick. Bringing the flame near to the death's-head, I examined its surface with my fingers. "What the hell—is this a mosaic of, what, bits of bone?"

"Of course it is. The entire object had to be a construction of art. It took me a while to figure out where to find a deposit of bone fragments, but then I remembered when we drove through Dunwich and you stopped so that we could climb that domed hill where that weird altar site was littered with fossils."

"You're saying that this skull is composed of bone fragments from Sentinel Hill? That explains its discoloration in places."

"Yes, some of the fragments were oddly charred or melted. Combined with others, they form a nice yet subtle chiaroscuro."

A patch of cloud obscured moonlight, and I was glad to have the candle's feeble glow. Glancing at my friend, I noticed his playful expression in the eerie light. Reaching out, he clutched a rope of silky human hair. Smiling, I did likewise, and then I followed him as we circled the statue, dancing in the darkness to which we chanted.

Three weeks later, John's body was found in the backyard. Death had come as a small dagger that had been plunged into an eye socket. An acquaintance from the police force interviewed me and told me more details than perhaps he should have. The only fingerprints on the weapon were John's own. I was shown a photograph of the dagger but didn't recognize it as belonging to John's collection of occult ritual paraphernalia. John and I, one drunken evening, had decided to arrange to be each other's beneficiaries in case of death, but I was startled to discover he had made good on the joke. Thus I inherited his habitat and its contents, and I spent that first week after his death sleeping on the cot in his attic. My exhibition was now to be a memorial to my friend and his artistic genius. I had taken the eerie yellowed photograph and hung it on the wall above the bed—gawd, what a delirious effect that had on my dreams! Going through his things in the attic rooms, I was slightly disconcerted to discover a folio of sketches that were studies of the evil gnome in the photograph; and yet I understand how such an image could engross a macabre artist, for the beast was like nothing one had ever witnessed. Studying the sketches made me remember John's statue, which I hadn't looked upon because of its close proximity to his place of demise. Now I ached to be near it, to touch my fingers to the silky hide and woven hair. So I stalked down the steps, out of the house, into night.

The high moon cast its silver glow on the ground but could not penetrate the canvas that was the canopy's roof, and so I savagely uprooted the poles that held the structure up and let the lunar beams bathe the phantasm of flesh and bone and hair. Pressing my mouth to the thing's solid grin, I exhaled hot mortal breath into the cavity of bone, and then my hands clutched lengths of woven hair as I danced idiotically around the statue, my eyes awash with moonlight. I whistled at the two puffs of curious black cloud that drifted near the moon, and then I dropped to my knees and wept. My hands, pressed upon the dirt, found the curious indentations in the ground, prints that might have been the footfalls of malformed children that encircled the statue. My mouth made love to a leather foot that was effectively secured to the platform that kept the figure erect, and as I reclined I wrapped my arms around the creature's ankles and succumbed to dreaming.

Awakened by soft movement, I opened encrusted eyes and peered into the gulf of night. The moon was farther from me, and the black clouds had escaped the sky. I could see the prancing shadows in the corners of my eyes but could not yet directly acknowledge them. Instead, I shut my eyes again and pushed up onto my knees. Blindly, I sought one leather hand, and bending to it I kissed its palm. When again I opened my eyes I saw the distant place to which the two dark clouds had drifted, where they had settled so as to stretch their great black wings. The gnomes circled me in danse, and I shuddered to see the naked malefaction of their wretched faces. The one I recognized from the yellowed photograph held a small dagger in his malformed mouth, and I did not dare to move when at last he approached and touched his mouth to mine. Thus was the exchange completed. They stood dead still in the awful lunar light and waited. I lifted my eyes for one final glance at the mosaic death's-head, which bent so as to smile down on me. And then I removed the dagger from my mouth and lifted it to my eye.

XXVII.

The artist, deaf and mute, had been my childhood friend, and it was he who taught me how to sign; and it was from him that I found the inspiration to become a poet, an artist of language as he was an artist of imagery. We had remained close up until the time of my unhappy marriage, and after my divorce I visited him infrequently. I had been so emotionally drained and defiled from personal torment that I became extremely reclusive, remaining alone after returning home each work day from my secretarial duties. When, at last, I began to work on a new collection of verse, I experienced a longing for artistic companionship, and so I made my way to Philip's small house and pushed the doorbell. The live-in housekeeper/cook answered my summons and led me to the wide ladder stepway that took one to the upper attic rooms where my friend did most of his work. I found him sitting before a canvas in bright electric light, and that puzzled me as it had always been Philip's habit to paint in candlelight. We signed our greetings as I pulled a chair next to his and took his hands in mine, and then I studied the painting on which he was employed. It was a night scene, but one so exceptional that I was instantly captivated. The main image was that of a titanic three-sided lighthouse erected on an expanse of large flat rocks that spread as far as eye could see. No body of water was in sight. A full moon shot one solid beam of light to the top of the tower that contained the lantern room, although the lighthouse itself was entirely dark. What struck me so powerfully about the work was the combination of effects the image evoked. The plane of large flat stones, the moon, and the myriad pinpoints of stars looked entirely realistic; but the structure itself contained a quality of otherworldliness that perplexed me. It was like some fabled construction of biblical myth that had usurped a location in historic fact.

Philip turned to study my reaction to his work. "It's strange and effective," I told him as he watched my mouth. "Wherever did you come up with the conception?"

How odd, his timid smile. "I saw it in a dream," he signed; and as I clasped him I thought I detected a slight trembling of his hands, as if he had been moved by queer emotion. And then an especially weird occurrence took place. I heard a most peculiar sound outside the small attic window. How can I describe it? It began as a high-pitched ringing sensation deep inside my skull that grew in depth of sound and transitioned to some place within the gulf of night outside the window. It then deepened into a kind of low moan not unlike wind, or whispering, and within its sound one could almost detect an idiotic alien summons. Something in the unfathomable sound of it stabbed like splinters in my skull, and I cried out in dismay. I turned to Philip, to see if he had detected my alarm, although he obviously would not have heard my cry; and I grew cold with a kind of fear when I saw that he was staring at the attic window with an odd expression on his face, an aspect of *listening*. Rising, I released his tight hands and walked to the small attic window, which I opened. Cool air brushed my face as I stared into dark heaven, and at first I could not understand what I imagined was before me—a void of illimitable blackness that contained a kind of undulation, as if I stared at waves of liquid sea that moved from me toward cosmic nothingness. Sensing Philip at my side, I turned to gawk at him, and although his face was at first extremely serious, he slowly forced a smile and leaned so as to kiss my face. Then he turned to peer out of the attic window, and when I followed his gaze I saw that there was a moon and myriad stars.

That was the last time I saw my friend. His mysterious disappearance caused much talk in our circle of bohemia, especially when it was learned that he had left a list of instructions in which I was bequeathed his final painting. That these instructions had been legally arranged suggested that he knew he would be disappearing, and many expected to find his body in some lake or isolated location—but his escape from the world was absolute and he was never found. I arrived at his home, which had been left to his faithful companion, and she presented me with the large canvas, which had been wrapped with sturdy paper and twine. I was surprised, upon returning home and removing its cover, to find that what I had was either an alternative painting of the same scene or a reworking of the original canvas. It was identical in many ways, except for the moon, which was now a decayed grey globe; and the lighthouse was no longer dark but illuminated with a kind of black-violet light that oozed from the lens of the lantern room into space, toward the dead lunar sphere. All starlight had extinguished. As I studied the image I was overwhelmed with a feeling of intense loneliness, and with a futility toward all aspects of reality. It was a depressing work, and it made my brain cold with a kind of horror for mortal existence. I was overwhelmed with a longing for escape, for some way to vanish as completely as Philip had.

I hung the painting, that night, over my bedpost. It had snowed that day and my apartment was chilly. It is my habit to sleep in the nude; I liked the feel of flesh against flesh, my legs wrapped around one other, my hands at breast or thigh. I went to my closet and found the heavy eiderdown that I kept there for chilly winter nights, and thus I was fairly comfortable when at last I retired. But it was a sharp chilliness that awakened me, and I could not understand why no blankets covered me. I felt cold terror when, gazing upward, I did not see bedroom ceiling but rather an expanse of midnight sky in which a cold moon gleamed. I pushed myself to a sitting position on the large sheet of rock on which I had reclined and shivered in the wintry wind that assaulted my nakedness. The triangular tower of stone tilted above me, and out of its pharos there shone a blurred beam of dark radiance. Rising, I walked along the rocks to the tower's archway and crossed the threshold, into a place of ice-cold basalt. I climbed the many steps of smooth stone that took me to the top, where my nakedness was bathed in eerie anti-light. The sentient radiance moved in circular fashion, like some revolving behemoth eye, and the pulsing beam of black light shot out toward the moon. I stepped out onto the circular balcony and was surprised to find no metal lattice to keep me from falling to the rocks below. I gazed outward as the moon began to decay in the outer darkness, and as I beheld that dying globe I felt an uncanny need to touch it. Thus I reached out, stepping into the path of black and violet illumination that beamed toward the decrepit globe. I walked into the aether, toward the dying moon, as cosmic mistral frolicked with my hair and encased my mortal nakedness. The blackness all around me began to ripple like waves of an ocean, and I smiled as this nameless undulation washed me outward, toward an infinity of naught.

XXVIII.

He left his apartment at around twenty minutes to midnight on August 29th, with a yellowed newspaper cutting in his hand. It was his hope that most of the Caucasians that inhabited the section of the metropolis where he had found a hotel would be inside at so late an hour; for he had grown to hate the suspicious glances from their pallid faces when they noticed him, and he loathed the way they infested the sidewalks, oozing like puffy pale maggots as they chattered in high nasal tones. Thus he rushed beneath the bright windows of occupied buildings that were hideous in their modernity, and he scowled at the bleating voices and obnoxious contemporary noise that was the music of the age, squeezing from out those windows and maddening him. He had rushed quickly and was soon breathless, and so he finally ceased his scurrying and leaned beneath one antique lamp post that looked different from the ones that illuminated the populated places, and as he calmed his lungs he brought the cutting to the light and examined it anew. It was because of the article he had found in the old newspaper, and more specifically the accompanying photograph, that he had come to the city; for in the photograph he saw a thing that had visited him in his most fantastic dreams, a statue carved of dark wood that resembled a bestial black goddess, a loathsome thing of Africa. In his fantastic dreams he was one among a throng of the very old folk that worshipped this effigy of twilight, and it astounded him to discover, quite by accident in the bookshop where he was employed, on a page of newspaper that had lined a box of books that were a part of a dead man's library, the image from his midnight dreams. The books in the box were decades old and of little value, and he had been bored to death as he plucked them from the box and listed them in his notebook; he had barely noticed the folded sheet of newsprint at the bottom of the box until its photograph seized his attention. He read the article that spoke of the old abandoned section of a city, and of its courtyard where a mysterious pagan statue stood like some icon of secret myth. Thus he had come to the ugly modern city, determined to discover its neglected older corners and the courtyard with the aid of a street map.

As he leaned against the lamp post the midnight air was graced with a soft low sound—a bell was tolling in the centuried church he could dimly see in the distance—and the genteel pealing helped to take him away from the neoteric clamor of the city and its plastic inhabitants. He followed the sound into the shadowed confines of the older section, where he was suddenly overwhelmed with a sense of keen expectancy; for he felt that another world was opening before him, an elder realm of old wood tainted by strange sunsets and ghastly moonfire, where one could encounter neglected deities, forgotten gods. Paved sidewalks were replaced by cobblestone that led him, at last, to the arched threshold and the sacred place beyond it. Lured, he stepped into an older shadow and breathed another air that was fragrant with spice and marvel, and in that air he thought he could detect half-heard songs—a paean of rapture that called the thing, darkly divine, whose worship had elapsed, the thing whose idol was suddenly before him. He knelt below the hoary figure of a goddess carved of obsidian and ached to chant the half-heard mantra that haunted his skull. He breathed the alien language and drifted into an incorporeal place disembodied from mundane reality. The hand that stroked his hair was as smooth as polished marble, and as chilly. Taking that hand in his, he kissed it; yet as he stood to drink in her spectral beauty, his eyes were burned by the awful whiteness of the moon above them. He stared at her with prayerful eyes, and so she turned from him and moved a hand into distant air, forming a rift in reality beyond which he could see the others of his ancestral kin, the strange dark folk who hungered to dance around their goddess. Taking his hand, she led him through the threshold of dream, into which, happily, there would be no return.

XXIX.

Simon Gregory Williams sat in the fragrant place of fern and bloom and scanned the majestic mountains of South Asia. The region contained a lush and antique beauty that rivaled that of Sesqua Valley, and Simon's silver eyes flashed as they drank in the scenery. "I have never witnessed such a singular vista," he told his companion, "outside my homeland. The beauty seems almost prehistoric, and there is such variety. The distant mountains have about them an air that comes close to cruelty; and yet here, in this meadow, these tall stems with their flowers of delicate pink wear a charm of innocence."

His neighbor gestured to the platter of fruit that he held. "Will you have a slice of mango, Beast? We must consume an infinite diversity of fruits if we are to nurse the Seventh Eidolon of Chaugnar Faugn."

"Is that so?" Simon queried as he frowned at the slices of fruit and bowls of rich red pomegranate nectar. "I rarely imbibe of mortal sustenance. However, in the case of arcane ritual, I bend to tradition." He reached for one of the mangoes, tore off a slice, and popped it into his wide mouth. Chewing on the fruit's flesh for some moments, he nodded and swallowed. "It is luscious to the taste and complements the fragrance of this wondrous mountain aether. Really, your mountains are superb, and to gaze upon them is to drink their daemonic potency with one's eyes."

The tiny fellow beside him nodded anxiously. "Great things are done when Men & Mountains meet."

"Ah," Simon cooed, "you're familiar with Blake. Yes, immortal poetry should be uttered in such a place. But we are not men, Ronzie. I am the spawn of shadow and mist; and you, although you were once a man, are now quite transitioned." Simon regarded the Asian at his side and admired the fellow's ears, so extended and webbed. Where an ordinary human would wear a nose, Ronzie possessed a loathsome green-hued trunk almost one foot in length. A charming fellow, Simon assured himself, and highly proficient at necromantic skills.

"This is your first visit to this part of the globe, Mr. Williams?"

"It is. I have long ached to visit India, but life has kept me busy elsewhere. Too, I dislike tropical weather, and it has always been my prejudice that India is hot. Your own environment is quite pleasant. But tell me, what is the significance of the bowls of juice?"

"They represent the blood on which the Old One loves to feast."

"Just so. Of course, it is a mistake to regard the daemon as a Great Old One, or even an Outer God. He is deliciously enigmatic, having filtered from some unfamiliar dimension, in similar fashion to Yog-Sothoth yet not nearly so potent. Indeed, his lack of potency is what drew me to your region. I had read hints of your temple in a volume of forgotten lore; but it wasn't until a sorcerer acquaintance sold me some of your especial incense that I tasted your peculiar clime in dream and knew that I had to practice here. I am devoted, you see, to the secret places wherein the covert ways are observed. I almost never dream, but as I sucked in the fumes of your abnormal incense, I was violated with mental images such as I have experienced but once before, when an acolyte of Great Chaugnar summoned an aspect of that daemon to our hills. I have never located an actual temple to the forgotten god, as he is sometimes titled. This will prove an exceptional experience. Why do you frown and look uncertain?"

The sky became tinted with gold and pink and green, like unto the skin of the unsliced mango that nestled on Ronzie's platter. The Asian priest watched the setting sun. "You have confessed to not being human."

The beast frowned. "Is that a complication?"

"You are intimate with the legends of those who fell to Earth when the planet was raw and yet unformed. You have scanned the legends that whisper that humanity was the creation of those antediluvian forebears, who conjured forth the chemistry of blood that slinks within mortal veins. The tomes and stones and scrolls have hinted of the uncanny allure that human blood has for some of those that frolic between the stars and are without form or dimensions. I sense that you are a kind of Immortal, and thus I doubt that the liquid in your veins will contain the required components so as to awaken the forgotten god that slumbers as eidolon within our antique temple. What assurance can you give me?"

Simon turned his own gaze skyward and watched as the colors of sunset succumbed to inky darkness. "Yes, I am inhuman. But I have combined the corporeal qualities of Sesqua Valley so as to clothe my essence within a semi-mortal husk. I have planted within my breast a fabulous seed that rooted veins throughout new limbs and washed those veins with a semblance of human blood. Mine is a rare elixir, such as Great Chaugnar has never known. But it is not merely the taste of blood for which the neglected god hungers—it is slaughter. I am well versed in ritual murder. The daemon will be satisfied. You will be a magnificent sacrifice. But these are merely words I utter. I can give you something more. Let me take up that ritual dagger with which you have sliced your consecrated fruits. See how I slice its point into my wrist, just so. Ah, how provocatively my liquid bubbles forth, thick and dark, speckled with hues of amethyst and gold. Partake."

The small priest quivered with desire. He unwound his trunk so that its fanged disc fastened to the stranger's flesh. Shutting his slanted eyes, he supped. The beast of Sesqua Valley moaned passages that he had learned from ancient books, and his rare outrageous language seemed to shake the firmament wherein stars began to form. Silencing his chanting, Simon took his arm away. Ronzie shuddered where he sat, in ecstasy; and then he pushed himself to a standing position, uttered arcane words to the twinkling gems in heaven, and led the way to the secret temple, and to unholy ritual.

XXX.

I followed the heartbeat of my vision, out of raw reality and into another place beyond the rim of time and space. The plastic city of mortality crumbled behind me, a lifeless memory, and there spread before me mists of light that clothed an elder realm, a town where centuried roofs huddled beneath golden sunset beams. This was a locality where I could catch exhausted exhalation and drink with lungs a senescent elixir of unearthly mist, where the shadows of my eyes, no longer writhing in agony at the sight of neoteric glare, could blend with deeper darkness. I stood upon a hill from which one was rewarded with a panorama of a sunset city where ancient houses crowded centuried lanes, where wraiths of shimmering radiance played among the Georgian steeples of slumbering oratories in which pilgrims uttered prayers. Oh, how I longed to articulate such rare language, to chant to elder gods; but I had no tongue with which to pronounce such benedictions, and my only vocal sounds were hateful hiss and moronic moan. Thus I backed away from the edge of the hill on which I stood and looked, following the path of sod that took me out to the lane that led me to the another kind of sacred house—the residence in which my god of fiction had penned his poetry and prose. It rose before me, the grey Victorian house, which I had seen in waking, but to behold it here, in dream, was an added enchantment; for this was a demesne in which time and space did not exist, and I knew that the house would still be standing here, enshrouded with the orange and amber rays of sunset, when humanity's little world was naught but burned-out cinder. For dreams can never die. I saw that the door of the lower room, where he had lived and worked, was open, and I could feel the keen imaginative lure coax me to it; but I did not need to enter its confines in order to drink the rich elixir of imagination and art, because that art was its own entity, existing in the mundane world of mortality as well as in this realm. His weird fiction was devoured by eyes of flesh and spoken by mouths of mortal tissue; it tainted the minds of women and men and sank them into a void of phantasy such as they had never known. It brought them here, to the place where I stood, beguiled.

I shut my phantom eyes and remembered his work, as encroaching twilight darkened the abyss above me. I entered a dream within a dream, wherein six strange stars winked awake as they clustered around a sallow moon. As I pierced that gulf of night with my eye-beams, I saw a portion of its gloom drift to the place before me, where there was no longer a house of wood but rather a site of nameless ritual where seven pillars tilted over an altar around which six shadow-figures stood. The essence of my dreaming self sifted through dark aether toward the altar, and soon I was reclined upon its smooth and chilly stone.

One of the figures, hooded and obscure, was taller than the others, and it bent its lean and blurry form to me as it spoke. "Ah, the seventh dreamer. We have awaited thee from dusk to dusk. We require you to join our chorus and bless the alignment of stars, so that their chaos may envelope the time of mortal men. Speak with us the chant that we now teach you." One by one the other apparitions flowed to me and bent their mouths to mine; and as they whispered into that cavity, my mouth, I felt the fabric of their fantastic language spill beneath my teeth and seek the tongue I did not own. I made my paltry moan in answer to their prayers as sorrow stabbed my soul and slipped as water from my eyes. But then the tall and faceless effigy bent above me, and I saw that it was composed of purest nightmare, black and proud and alien. It was the sublime and dripping eidolon that was one aspect of that genius who was my god of fiction, a phantasm of horror elevated unto the heights of literary art. Ah, how my mouth ached so as to howl adoration in honor of this devil now bent over me—but I had no tongue with which to form unholy idiom, and thus I whimpered.

"Your agony is a form of prayer," the old one said with words that issued from him as smoke and ash that drifted to my mouth and coated my face. I watched as the being lifted one dark hand and reached beneath its hood to a place where it should have worn a mouth, and when that hand emerged from the faceless void it held a portion of some black tongue that licked the being's palm. That hand dipped into my mouth and planted the thing of writhing muscle behind my teeth; and I felt the dry rough thing root itself beneath my mouth, a mouth that, now transfigured and bewitched, spoke the prayer of the seventh dreamer, as a strange star formed above us in the haunted place beside the jaundiced moon, a star that began to crawl in assembly with its kindred in honor of our dread lord.

XXXI.

Ashton read the letter over a second time and laughed. How delightful to be insulted! Usually the telegrams that he received concerning the publication of his poems, books that were illustrated with photographs of his outré sculptures, had been empty-headed in their prosaic praise; thus this new response was a welcomed change. "A friend gave me a copy of your *Cthulhu and Others in Stone* as a Yule gift. You are one sick bastard. God knows from what mental cesspool you dredge your polluted ideas." Laughing again, he crumpled the paper and tossed it into the hearth, and as he bent toward the flame the amulet worn around his neck swung against his breast. His hands found the cord and pulled the thing over his head, and he held it to the firelight so that he could admire his work—this icon that he had sculpted from dinosaur bone. Gazing at the fluid object he whispered to it, "Where do I get my ideas? From Outside, and its secret inhabitants." Delicately, he pressed one hard edge of bone against his forehead and moved it so as to inscribe a kind of sigil into his skin, and as he did so he imagined that the firelight dimmed a little, although no current assailed the cabin room. Turning his eyes to one dim corner, he admired his newest work, a figurine fashioned from volcanic rock. It was larger than his usual study in stone, and in the darkness of its corner its wavering silhouette blended easily with other shadow. The longer he studied it, the more it perplexed him, as did its five kindred—for its nebulous figure would not keep solid form; rather, it seemed to undulate and re-form itself suggestively. Like its kindred, its design had not been planned; it had instead indicated itself beneath his tools and hands, revealing its odd self as he watched with a sense of wonder shining in his captivated eyes. Yes, it had inspired marvel—and subtle fear; for it was a ferocious icon that conveyed a kind of hunger that he could not comprehend. Entranced, he laughed a third time as he arose and stalked toward the statuette.

Ashton pressed his hand to the idol's soft stone, and then he took it up with both hands and cuddled it to his chest, where it pressed closer so as to listen to his mortal heartbeat. The poet walked out of the cabin's doorway, into twilight, and found the path that took him into the foothills that were his intimate haunt. He climbed until he reached the stretch of land where a low burial mound rose above the grass, and then he stopped and frowned at the dead tree atop that mound, a dendroid corpse that drooped withered branches to the ground. It annoyed him to see the black woman who leaned against the tree and chiseled into its dead bark with ritual blade. She turned to him and motioned that he should join her, and thus he reluctantly crept up the mound until he could smell her fragrance as it washed to him on the wind that moved the soft silk of her yellow dress. She smiled, and he shuddered at how the dead moonlight glimmered on her wet teeth.

She saw the figurine that he held to his chest and cooed. "Ah, the sixth dreamer. Set it in the ring among its fellows while I complete the sign." There was command in her gentle voice, and he yielded to it, falling to his knees next to where the other figurines formed an incomplete circle. What warm emotion he felt as he examined the other creatures of sculpted stone, as if they were familiar cronies who welcomed him as their own. How wonderful to watch their weirdness as it was complemented by ghastly moonglow, as that awesome disc spread its illumination in the meaningless vortex of night. Ashton heaved his moan into the gathering wind that caught and took his uttered sound upward, to the lifeless lunar sphere that grinned down upon the scene. An essence of his moan echoed among the stars.

"Rise," a voice instructed, "and help me nourish this elder creature with mortal wound." Weirdly, he was lifted to his feet, which dragged themselves to the sorceress. He watched her remove her dagger's tip from the tree and studied the emblem that had been engraved upon the bark; and then he watched as the woman showed him her palm, into which she pressed the dagger's blade and etched the arcane symbol into her flesh. The wind blossomed into tempest that caused the woman's long red hair to billow as she floated to him and pressed her wet red hand against his mouth, which drank her acrid blood, the taste of which coiled through his lips and, rising, taunted his brain with scalding vision. Her mouth, so close to his, breathed alien language into his own, and then her fingers clutched at his hair and smashed his face against the dead tree's husk, which he bathed with blood. Ashton wrapped his arms around the trunk and held steadfastly as the creature beside him tore his shirt from his body and bit into his back. He felt her alchemical hands knead his flesh. "We welcome the seventh dreamer," she informed him as his flesh shifted and reshaped. She firmly held his altered form to the moon, and then she planted him in the circle among his kindred, with whom his now liberated limbs moved in danse. And as he capered he could see the shifting of starlight and hear reverberations from beneath the mound. He saw the centuried tree that moved with them, twitching its branches as they grew thick and dark with resuscitation. He beheld the globes of searing unearthly color that flowered on those branches, spheres that resembled seven mocking suns; he watched them hatch and scorch the atmosphere with fire that burned the woman's face away, revealing her nothingness that was a representation of future time. Spitting laughter, she joined the seven dreamers in celebration of the Old Ones who, finding portal, filtered beyond dimensional rim from Outside.

XXXII.

The black skyscraper towered above him in all its hideousness, reaching toward the filthy smog as in the streets a myriad of cars filled the air with hateful honking. His need to escape became paramount, and thus he rushed from this modern activity toward the old and neglected portion of town, a place that was shunned by most because of its dilapidation, its stench of decay that came, in part, from the place at the bottom of one steep hill where a charnel canal dragged its water through a realm that was always dark with mist and shadow. He tripped down the hill, past the vacant buildings with shattered windows, over pavement littered with grime and shards of broken glass. Slowing his pace, he listened to the silence of the place, which was another reason why the city's mundane inhabitants did not like it—for they found a kind of safety in their clamor, whereas quiet was a thing they could not comprehend, a thing that drove them to distraction. Even the dark water of the lean canal refused to make a noise, and he gazed into its current as he gradually stepped onto the ancient stone of the bridge that crossed the water. Stopping for one moment to study the sluggish flow of water, he saw a pale thing rise to the surface and bump against one side of the stone wall of the canal; and he thought perhaps the malformed thing might once have been human, although he could not be certain as the current caught it and pulled it from his view.

He continued his walk along the other length of old stone and followed the gaunt road that took him to St. Toad's. The pile of stone, black with age, rose within its shroud of fog, a miasma that smelled far sweeter than the foulness belched within the artificial city. He pressed his hand against the squares of rock with which the edifice had been constructed and knew that this stone had not been some false manufacture of mankind—it was an element of earth, cold and real. In calm reverence, he entered St. Toad's and found the statue that awaited him in a place of soft illumination, the chiseled form that wore a pallid mask. She had been expertly composed, and as he kissed one chilly breast he could almost imagine that a pulse reverberated from some place beneath it. Lowering to humble knees, he studied the symbol that had been etched onto her firm palm, a sign that drank the room's pale light and was reflected on his eyes. Shutting those eyes, he tilted to the palm and licked it. He shuddered as the place grew chilly, yet when he went to embrace himself he could not find his mortal frame. He had escaped his husk of solid flesh. Now he wandered through a dimension of dreaming the likes of which he had never experienced. He drifted into a darksome valley and its depth of haunted woodland, beside a foul lake in which suggestive black shapes splashed awfully. The surrounding trees were spotted with unwholesome fungi and phosphorescent patches of moss. Pausing beside the lake he peered into its squalid depths, through which a viscous creature broke, a nebulous thing that wore his face and whistled like a fiend before submerging once again into the undulating perdition.

He rose and watched the illuminated woodland for any sign of movement, but there was none; and yet a presence from the place beckoned and beguiled him, and so he moved into its lonesome places until coming to one tree from which small orbs dangled from low boughs, cloudy globes of crystal with hints of fire at their centers. He saw that these globes were not perfectly round; rather, they had oblate ends that brought to mind a passage he had scanned in a yellow parchment manuscript of the *Book of Eibon,* which told of a wizard who had owned such a spherical crystal in which he could behold some secrets beyond the rim of sanity. Reaching up to touch one low crystal, he peered at the pinprick of light at its center and saw it blossom into a dream within a dream. He watched, bewitched, the thing that pushed out of earth before him—the gaunt tower of black stone, octagonal in shape and some sixteen feet in height. Creeping to it, his attention was caught by the characters etched upon its surface, and he lifted his hands so that they moved over those markings as a blind man's might decipher brail. And as his hands smoothed the stone his palms transformed, splitting open as mouths that mewed the language etched on stone. The sound of those syllables made him giddy, so that he bent backward and fell onto the place where there should have been ground; but all he could feel was a continuation of plummeting as the black obelisk melted into a mound of loathsome sentience, a formless mass of slime and poisonous vapors. To look upon this unfathomable horror was to surrender all sanity and every ounce of remaining humanity. Thus he bubbled as a blind amorphous stream of slime that spilled into the swamp of nothingness, where he splashed among his kindred in a mire of meaningless cosmic mud.

XXXIII.

It wafted to him from the distant harbor, the low and bestial whistling that overwhelmed with desolation. Exiting the café, he stumbled beneath the old roofs that tilted toward the street, past the shuttered windows of strangely tenanted hovels composed of crumbling brick and rotted wood. He paused for one moment before the cloudy window of an antique shop and pressed his face against the cold unyielding glass; and as he peered into the spectral room of forgotten things he thought he could espy a dim silhouette that motioned to him invitingly. Gazing through the dusky glass had always bequeathed a sense of dreaming, as if the place before him were a realm of vision that could melt his solid flesh and pull him into another place; and he would have allowed himself such alteration if the harbor whistles had not sounded a second time and lured him from the glass and down the lane, past the decaying spire of an abandoned funerary chapel, along the twisting cobblestone lanes on which crumbling warehouses slept within their shrouds of mist and spray.

He slipped onto a wooden pier and leaned against its railing as he peered at the expanse of feculent water, trying not to gag at the fumes that coiled from the floating debris among the carcasses of fowl and fish. One piece of litter strangely caught the reflection of the yellow moon, and as he studied it he thought it was some portion of a leather sail to which had been fastened a pallid mask. He looked at it as the moonlight dimmed, imagining that the flat fabric floating on still water began to ripple, to rise slowly and whistle to him. It shaped itself into a naked human form that walked on water toward the pier, so malignant that he had to shut his eyes and clamp hands over ears. He could not, however, block the stench that rose from the water and settled just before him. Wet hands pressed against his wide forehead and played within his scant hair as something kissed his rector's collar and moaned his name. Raising his hands to push the thing away, he touched the heavy breasts that swung before him as something chilly found his ear and whistled once again.

He opened his eyes and beheld the naked thing that wore a pallid mask. Beneath that façade of silk a voice, low and mesmerizing, sighed to him to join with her as she danced upon the water. "Come with me," it coaxed, "and I will plunge thee into a depth of dreaming such as you have never known." He saw the long steel needles that kept the mask in place; and as he watched, a lithe black hand pinched the needle that had been pushed through the mask's mouth and pulled it free. How wickedly the moonlight shimmered on the needle's point, and how cold that needle was as the figure smoothed it across his lips! He watched the hand that removed the other implements that fastened mask to flesh, and when the last needle was removed he raised his hands so as to catch the mask that fell to them. He did not understand why there was no face before him at the place from which the mask had fallen, why there was nothing but smooth black surface that seemed to drink an essence of glimmering moonlight and thus glisten like a pool of oil.

God, how silky was the mask against his fingers! What wonderful fragrance wafted from it, sweet yet pungent, like shards of odor that pierced into his brain. Perhaps if he pressed the mask to his face it would dispel the wretched harbor stench that made him want to vomit. He pushed the perfumed silk to his face and peeked through eyeholes as the black woman's hands drifted to him and began to push the needles that she held through the silken fabric. He uttered no sound as the final pin found his mouth again and pushed through his numbing lips. His eyes remained open as the figure tilted to him and pressed her facelessness against the mask as the wooden pier melted beneath his feet. He thought he could see vaguely through the shadow that engulfed him, see the water on which he danced with his spectral mistress in his arms, the enchantress who kept her promise and dragged him downward, into a realm of immortal nightmare.

XXXIV.

I examined the dead city as our raft drifted down the gaunt canal, and did not like the way its outline suggested awful things that one may witness in diseased dreaming. One could not believe that such a place was inhabited—and yet there came from someplace deep within a sound of muffled and monotonous drumming, deliberate and persistent. I could just see, beyond the filthy fog that hovered over the decaying towers of the metropolis, the expiring orb of day sinking in the darkening sky. Our raft was sailing slowly, and yet it disturbed me to see Bobby standing boldly near its edge, holding on to nothing but the enormous grimoire that he had found in an antique shop somewhere in the necrotic megalopolis. We had almost reached the city's end when I beheld the stone bridge ahead of us that spanned the gaunt canal. I thought that the dark figure who stood at the center of the bridge was waving at us, but as our craft neared her I saw that she was gesturing to the risen moon; and it disturbed me, as we approached the bridge, to see Bobby raise one hand and imitate the dark woman's motion. I peeked to where her face should have been, but all I could discern was undulating shadow beneath the length of rich red hair, and then she was blocked out by the rotting stone with which the antediluvian bridge had been erected.

The city was behind us, and gradually our craft drifted more slowly still, until it floated to an outcropping of rocks and stopped. I marveled at how my young friend hopped nonchalantly onto those slippery rocks and climbed their little height to solid ground. Cautiously, I rose to a standing position on the gently bobbing raft and gingerly stepped onto one flat rock; and as I balanced myself on the stony surface the raft behind me moved away, reentering the black canal and drifting from us down the oily water.

"I don't care for this weird trek you've proposed, Bobby," I informed him. "You told me that we were going to visit a haunt of spectral dream such as I experienced during last night's slumber. Thus far this is nothing like my delicious nightmare. Why you've brought that cumbersome tome is quite beyond me."

It was then that the little imp turned to me and smiled as he had never smiled before, and he opened the heavy book so that its sheets of parchment were illuminated by beams of moonlight. I could not decipher the words that had been etched thereon in minute script, and to stare at it oppressed me with headache and dizziness. I had of late been plagued with an unaccustomed ocular trouble that prevented me from reading fine print, and as I peered at the page I experienced a renewed tugging of nerves and facial muscles. "Look here, Howard," he squeaked, "this is an elaborate description of the way to our desired destination, a diagram of language. It's easily deciphered. Come on, old man—follow me!"

He scampered ahead of me, almost skipping, and I limped after him along the way that led down a dark, half-wooded heath where boulders wore patches of phosphorescent moss. I followed the young creature who was impelled by some obscure sense of quest, until we came to a dark and seemingly familiar woodland, into which we walked. Time passed and at last we came upon a miasmic swamp that seemed to excite my friend. Pointing to an alien-featured tree across the foetid quagmire, he shouted, "There—we need to stand before that tree!" He studied the squalid water and then, to my astonishment, walked onto it, laughing at my yelp of caution. When I saw that he did not sink into the depths I approached the dank surface and saw the path of large flat stones on which my friend was walking. "Are you coming, Howard?" he called; and so I timidly stepped onto one flat rock and held out my arms in an attempt to balance myself as I followed Bobby across the water. Yet the rocks, large as they were, were slippery with slime, and just as I had almost reached the other side I lost my foothold and fell into thick water. Bobby, standing on grassy ground, shook his head as if I were some pathetic clown, and then he set down his book and offered me his hands, which I took as he pulled me out of the swamp. How strange that other hands beneath the surface, phantasmal and determined, seemed to try to hold onto my ankles and drag me to the nadir of foul water.

Bobby helped me to the solid ground, on which I dripped. "You're a damn mess," he sadly informed me, and then he seemed to forget my existence completely as he turned to the unfamiliar tree and touched a hand to one of the black spheres that was attached to a low branch. Why on earth did he begin to hum to that queer object, and why did his humming sound so unnatural? How curiously he bent to that black sphere and touched it with his mouth. I began to step toward him and foolishly trod upon his monstrous book, the binding of which was warm and wet. Bending to pick it up, I was appalled to see that the hide serving as binding seemed to be perspiring, which caused a cry of disgust to escape my mouth. My noise caught Bobby's attention, and he filtered to me with drowsy motion and relieved me of my burden.

"We're almost there now," he pronounced as he chewed upon the black flesh of the sphere into which he had eaten. I did not like the alteration of his intonation, how it was laced with a kind of buzzing articulation. Nor did I like the way his mouth had widened when he smiled. "I have devoured knowledge and can show you your habitat of vision. Follow me." Although wearied of this game of "follow the leader," I held my tongue and moved my feet, my legs weighed down by the heavy fabric of my soggy suit. Eventually we emerged from the woods on to a table-land of moss-grown rock lit by faint moonlight, and something about the place did indeed seem strangely familiar. Even more recognizable were the rusty tracks of a street-railway, which we followed until we came upon a yellow, vestibule car, such as I had discovered in my unfathomable dream. It was untenanted, as in my dream, and we cautiously boarded it. Bobby, before me, had opened the tome and was reading from it in his peculiar buzzing drone, and the snatches of formulae that he uttered aloud were so frightful that I begged him to stop. He turned to me and revealed the monstrous malformation of his face, which was now a mere white cone tapering to one blood-red tentacle. My mouth was frozen with terror, and I could not understand why his clothes were as drenched as my own, or why the heavy book was in my grasp. Feeling faint, I staggered forward, toward the archway in which the other figure stumbled until its visage touched my own. Howling bestially, I plunged into and through the yielding door of glass, the shards of which ripped my atrocious visage from me. Blind and idiotic, I stomped on the floor of our temporary globe, the blasphemous book pressed against my breast, as I raised my facelessness to the cold and primal stars.

XXXV.

She escaped the hidden, silent place of old woodland and saw the sunset over the city's towers. The crimson face of the setting sun bathed her eyes with beauty, and soft wind wafting over the canal came to her, moved into her long red hair, and frolicked with the folds of her yellow gown. From the woods behind her she heard a faint buzzing that reminded her of something dismal, and so she fled to the stone bridge and began to cross over the canal, stopping midway so as to watch the raft that floated toward her on the water. Of the two figures on the raft, the teenage boy standing near the craft's edge ignored her as he studied the heavy book he held, but the other fellow was staring at her with such a helpless expression that she raised her hand to wave at him. How strange that her motion seemed to increase his worry! This so annoyed her that she did not turn to watch the raft emerge from under the other side of the bridge, but continued her way toward the sunset city. She stopped for a moment to study the faceless statue that stood a little ways from the bridge, and wondered at the book of stone it held in basalt hands. How curious were the symbols etched onto what passed as the leaves of the statue's book, and how her fingers tingled as she ran them over those etched characters as a blind woman would in reading Braille. Finally she turned from the curious statue and advanced toward the city, running her still-tingling fingers against the softness of her silken gown.

She entered the city and walked its oddly narrow cobblestone streets, until she came to the extraordinary edifice that was a funerary chapel whose façade was decorated with carvings of fantastic beings that could exist in dream alone. When she entered the place she was surprised to encounter the smoke of incense, for the place appeared absolutely deserted. Pushing one door of scrolled wood, she entered the chapel chamber, wherein she found seven stone coffins instead of pews. Upon each oblong box of stone reclined a sculptured figure so life-like that one could imagine they were the slumbering dead with hands pressed in prayer to some dread lord. She pressed her own cool hands together and whispered words that she had remembered from some obscure book of myth, and it confused her how her language spilled from her as mist that floated upward, to the roof of beams from which six skeletons swung from lengths of hempen rope. As she watched the subtle danse, the risen moon appeared behind one arched window, throwing its beams onto the things of bone and casting their silhouettes above the altar place.

Wind hummed through crevices in the rotting walls, like some low moaning of lost souls. She watched the skeletal shadows on the wall, above the spreading sculpture of a tree; and when she stepped onto the altar place she marveled that the fruit hanging from sculpted boughs was real. She plucked one pomegranate from its branch and bit into its tart white pulp, and then she laughed to see the pale worm whose flesh she had almost nibbled. Carefully, she chomped again into the flesh of fruit, as the lengthy maggot fell onto her palm and writhed about until it resembled one of the curious symbols that she had observed on the faux page of a book of stone. Lifting her hand, she smoothed the creature into her hair and felt it fall onto the fabric of her neck, where it stretched itself into a fleshy rope that coiled around her and lifted her into the quivering air, to where the others hung.

XXXVI.

I loved the ancient things, for in them I found a trace of some dim essence beyond time and space, a portion of the past that is more alive to me than this dull neoteric age that fancies itself so clever and unique. And so I sought and found the olden city whose legend had been whispered among devotees of dark things. I was not disappointed. It was almost impossible to believe that the place had ever been a modern site, for its desolate towers and cobblestone lanes were the very epitome of dead eras. I was enchanted by one forlorn edifice that, upon entering, I discovered to be a kind of funeral chapel. I passed into its nave where there were no aisles but rather seven coffins of stone. The ceiling was covered with a macabre fresco of seven skeletons engaged in danse around a monstrous white worm. I stepped onto the altar, and there I found a large book bound in red leather; but when I opened the book I saw that the script on its yellowed pages was too faint to be read. Turning the brittle leaves, I discovered a faded photograph tucked into the book, and I studied its image as well as I could, concluding it to be some kind of faceless icon wrapped in a crimson robe. I shut the book and looked around but could not locate the physical representation of the photographic image. Whistling a remembered hymn, I strode out of the building and continued my investigation of the cobblestone lanes, until I came upon what must once have been an antique shop but was now obviously an abandoned ruin. There was no door, and the large window was fissured with age. Peering through the cracked pane, I was startled to see that the cramped room beyond it was still packed with fabulous items. Dim moonlight above me threw my shadow into a dusky corner of the establishment—at least I thought it was my shadow, although some trick of illusion made it fluctuate with movement as if it were beckoning me to enter inside its confines.

I crossed the threshold and breathed in the tenuous aether of the silent room. I looked around at the objects from another time, and seemed transported through dimensions that, unlocking, pulled me into other years. The awful glow of the pale, pitying moon crept through window cracks, and in that strange light I sensed another realm press upon my mind, as if I had entered a phantasy of dream. I walked until I found the nameless eikon carved from crimson wood, and it shocked me to realize that it was a representation of the photographed being I had beheld within the church of death. I could not fathom what it might represent, or why its countenance was veiled. I carried it with me as I continued my exploration of the room, and I laughed with delight when I found a kinetoscope with a winding handle, which I rotated as I pressed my face against the viewing screen. Oh, the unearthly light that began to bloom within the box, an outré illumination in which I beheld the flickering image of six gnomes that capered within a circle of squat stones! They danced like lunatic freaks and banged the backs of their hands to those of their neighbors, and as their talons struck each other there was a play of sparks which irradiated a figure in the background, a thing out of Poe, tall and lean and wrapped in fabrics red as sunset flame. I watched as the figure raised one beckoning hand as the sparks tapped against the glass through which I peered, the surface of which began to crack as had the window of the dismal shop. I felt those sparks spill into my eyes as my hair stood up on end, and for a moment I was blinded by a blackness that seemed to pull me into it. I shut my burning eyes and pushed away from the machine, but as I steadied myself the air around me altered, and the silence of the place was haunted by the faint beating of insistent drums that was accompanied by another throbbing sound, as if I were surrounded by things that danced. And when I opened my eyes I saw the beasts that moved in slanting moonbeams, the creatures of which I was the seventh. We twirled upon the haunted hill, in ghastly light, as the fixt mass that was our world disintegrated into a cloud of dust upon which the Strange Dark One exhaled until we drifted into some unknown gulf of night.

Fungi from Yuggoth

by H. P. LOVECRAFT

I. The Book

The place was dark and dusty and half-lost
In tangles of old alleys near the quays,
Reeking of strange things brought in from the seas,
And with queer curls of fog that west winds tossed.
Small lozenge panes, obscured by smoke and frost,
Just shewed the books, in piles like twisted trees,
Rotting from floor to roof—congeries
Of crumbling elder lore at little cost.

I entered, charmed, and from a cobwebbed heap
Took up the nearest tome and thumbed it through,
Trembling at curious words that seemed to keep
Some secret, monstrous if one only knew.
Then, looking for some seller old in craft,
I could find nothing but a voice that laughed.

II. Pursuit

I held the book beneath my coat, at pains
To hide the thing from sight in such a place;
Hurrying through the ancient harbour lanes
With often-turning head and nervous pace.
Dull, furtive windows in old tottering brick
Peered at me oddly as I hastened by,
And thinking what they sheltered, I grew sick
For a redeeming glimpse of clean blue sky.

No one had seen me take the thing—but still
A blank laugh echoed in my whirling head,
And I could guess what nighted worlds of ill
Lurked in that volume I had coveted.
The way grew strange—the walls alike and madding—
And far behind me, unseen feet were padding.

III. The Key

I do not know what windings in the waste
Of those strange sea-lanes brought me home once more,
But on my porch I trembled, white with haste
To get inside and bolt the heavy door.
I had the book that told the hidden way
Across the void and through the space-hung screens
That hold the undimensioned worlds at bay,
And keep lost aeons to their own demesnes.

At last the key was mine to those vague visions
Of sunset spires and twilight woods that brood
Dim in the gulfs beyond this earth's precisions,
Lurking as memories of infinitude.
The key was mine, but as I sat there mumbling,
The attic window shook with a faint fumbling.

IV. Recognition

The day had come again, when as a child
I saw—just once—that hollow of old oaks,
Grey with a ground-mist that enfolds and chokes
The slinking shapes which madness has defiled.
It was the same—an herbage rank and wild
Clings round an altar whose carved sign invokes
That Nameless One to whom a thousand smokes
Rose, aeons gone, from unclean towers up-piled.

I saw the body spread on that dank stone,
And knew those things which feasted were not men;
I knew this strange, grey world was not my own,
But Yuggoth, past the starry voids—and then
The body shrieked at me with a dead cry,
And all too late I knew that it was I!

V. Homecoming

The daemon said that he would take me home
To the pale, shadowy land I half recalled
As a high place of stair and terrace, walled
With marble balustrades that sky-winds comb,
While miles below a maze of dome on dome
And tower on tower beside a sea lies sprawled.
Once more, he told me, I would stand enthralled
On those old heights, and hear the far-off foam.

All this he promised, and through sunset's gate
He swept me, past the lapping lakes of flame,
And red-gold thrones of gods without a name
Who shriek in fear at some impending fate.
Then a black gulf with sea-sounds in the night:
"Here was your home," he mocked, "when you had sight!"

VI. The Lamp

We found the lamp inside those hollow cliffs
Whose chiselled sign no priest in Thebes could read,
And from whose caverns frightened hieroglyphs
Warned every living creature of earth's breed.
No more was there—just that one brazen bowl
With traces of a curious oil within;
Fretted with some obscurely patterned scroll,
And symbols hinting vaguely of strange sin.

Little the fears of forty centuries meant
To us as we bore off our slender spoil,
And when we scanned it in our darkened tent
We struck a match to test the ancient oil.
It blazed—great God! . . . But the vast shapes we saw
In that mad flash have seared our lives with awe.

VII. Zaman's Hill

The great hill hung close over the old town,
A precipice against the main street's end;
Green, tall, and wooded, looking darkly down
Upon the steeple at the highway bend.
Two hundred years the whispers had been heard
About what happened on the man-shunned slope—
Tales of an oddly mangled deer or bird,
Or of lost boys whose kin had ceased to hope.

One day the mail-man found no village there,
Nor were its folk or houses seen again;
People came out from Aylesbury to stare—
Yet they all told the mail-man it was plain
That he was mad for saying he had spied
The great hill's gluttonous eyes, and jaws stretched wide.

VIII. The Port

Ten miles from Arkham I had struck the trail
That rides the cliff-edge over Boynton Beach,
And hoped that just at sunset I could reach
The crest that looks on Innsmouth in the vale.
Far out at sea was a retreating sail,
White as hard years of ancient winds could bleach,
But evil with some portent beyond speech,
So that I did not wave my hand or hail.

Sails out of Innsmouth! echoing old renown
Of long-dead times. But now a too-swift night
Is closing in, and I have reached the height
Whence I so often scan the distant town.
The spires and roofs are there—but look! The gloom
Sinks on dark lanes, as lightless as the tomb!

IX. The Courtyard

It was the city I had known before;
The ancient, leprous town where mongrel throngs
Chant to strange gods, and beat unhallowed gongs
In crypts beneath foul alleys near the shore.
The rotting, fish-eyed houses leered at me
From where they leaned, drunk and half-animate,
As edging through the filth I passed the gate
To the black courtyard where the man would be.

The dark walls closed me in, and loud I cursed
That ever I had come to such a den,
When suddenly a score of windows burst
Into wild light, and swarmed with dancing men:
Mad, soundless revels of the dragging dead—
And not a corpse had either hands or head!

X. The Pigeon-Flyers

They took me slumming, where gaunt walls of brick
Bulge outward with a viscous stored-up evil,
And twisted faces, thronging foul and thick,
Wink messages to alien god and devil.
A million fires were blazing in the streets,
And from flat roofs a furtive few would fly
Bedraggled birds into the yawning sky
While hidden drums droned on with measured beats.

I knew those fires were brewing monstrous things,
And that those birds of space had been *Outside*—
I guessed to what dark planet's crypts they plied,
And what they brought from Thog beneath their wings.
The others laughed—till struck too mute to speak
By what they glimpsed in one bird's evil beak.

XI. The Well

Farmer Seth Atwood was past eighty when
He tried to sink that deep well by his door,
With only Eb to help him bore and bore.
We laughed, and hoped he'd soon be sane again.
And yet, instead, young Eb went crazy, too,
So that they shipped him to the county farm.
Seth bricked the well-mouth up as tight as glue—
Then hacked an artery in his gnarled left arm.

After the funeral we felt bound to get
Out to that well and rip the bricks away,
But all we saw were iron hand-holds set
Down a black hole deeper than we could say.
And yet we put the bricks back—for we found
The hole too deep for any line to sound.

XII. The Howler

They told me not to take the Briggs' Hill path
That used to be the highroad through to Zoar,
For Goody Watkins, hanged in seventeen-four,
Had left a certain monstrous aftermath.
Yet when I disobeyed, and had in view
The vine-hung cottage by the great rock slope,
I could not think of elms or hempen rope,
But wondered why the house still seemed so new.

Stopping a while to watch the fading day,
I heard faint howls, as from a room upstairs,
When through the ivied panes one sunset ray
Struck in, and caught the howler unawares.
I glimpsed—and ran in frenzy from the place,
And from a four-pawed thing with human face.

XIII. Hesperia

The winter sunset, flaming beyond spires
And chimneys half-detached from this dull sphere,
Opens great gates to some forgotten year
Of elder splendours and divine desires.
Expectant wonders burn in those rich fires,
Adventure-fraught, and not untinged with fear;
A row of sphinxes where the way leads clear

Toward walls and turrets quivering to far lyres.
It is the land where beauty's meaning flowers;
Where every unplaced memory has a source;
Where the great river Time begins its course
Down the vast void in starlit streams of hours.
Dreams bring us close—but ancient lore repeats
That human tread has never soiled these streets.

XIV. Star-Winds

It is a certain hour of twilight glooms,
Mostly in autumn, when the star-wind pours
Down hilltop streets, deserted out-of-doors,
But shewing early lamplight from snug rooms.
The dead leaves rush in strange, fantastic twists,
And chimney-smoke whirls round with alien grace,
Heeding geometries of outer space,
While Fomalhaut peers in through southward mists.

This is the hour when moonstruck poets know
What fungi sprout in Yuggoth, and what scents
And tints of flowers fill Nithon's continents,
Such as in no poor earthly garden blow.
Yet for each dream these winds to us convey,
A dozen more of ours they sweep away!

XV. Antarktos

Deep in my dream the great bird whispered queerly
Of the black cone amid the polar waste;
Pushing above the ice-sheet lone and drearly,
By storm-crazed aeons battered and defaced.
Hither no living earth-shapes take their courses,
And only pale auroras and faint suns
Glow on that pitted rock, whose primal sources
Are guessed at dimly by the Elder Ones.

If men should glimpse it, they would merely wonder
What tricky mound of Nature's build they spied;
But the bird told of vaster parts, that under
The mile-deep ice-shroud crouch and brood and bide.
God help the dreamer whose mad visions shew
Those dead eyes set in crystal gulfs below!

XVI. The Window

The house was old, with tangled wings outthrown,
Of which no one could ever half keep track,
And in a small room somewhat near the back
Was an odd window sealed with ancient stone.
There, in a dream-plagued childhood, quite alone
I used to go, where night reigned vague and black;
Parting the cobwebs with a curious lack
Of fear, and with a wonder each time grown.

One later day I brought the masons there
To find what view my dim forbears had shunned,
But as they pierced the stone, a rush of air
Burst from the alien voids that yawned beyond.
They fled—but I peered through and found unrolled
All the wild worlds of which my dreams had told.

XVII. A Memory

There were great steppes, and rocky table-lands
Stretching half-limitless in starlit night,
With alien campfires shedding feeble light
On beasts with tinkling bells, in shaggy bands.
Far to the south the plain sloped low and wide
To a dark zigzag line of wall that lay
Like a huge python of some primal day
Which endless time had chilled and petrified.

I shivered oddly in the cold, thin air,
And wondered where I was and how I came,
When a cloaked form against the campfire's glare
Rose and approached, and called me by my name.
Staring at that dead face beneath the hood,
I ceased to hope—because I understood.

XVIII. The Gardens of Yin

Beyond that wall, whose ancient masonry
Reached almost to the sky in moss-thick towers,
There would be terraced gardens, rich with flowers,
And flutter of bird and butterfly and bee.
There would be walks, and bridges arching over
Warm lotos-pools reflecting temple eaves,
And cherry-trees with delicate boughs and leaves
Against a pink sky where the herons hover.

All would be there, for had not old dreams flung
Open the gate to that stone-lanterned maze
Where drowsy streams spin out their winding ways,
Trailed by green vines from bending branches hung?
I hurried—but when the wall rose, grim and great,
I found there was no longer any gate.

XIX. The Bells

Year after year I heard that faint, far ringing
Of deep-toned bells on the black midnight wind;
Peals from no steeple I could ever find,
But strange, as if across some great void winging.
I searched my dreams and memories for a clue,
And thought of all the chimes my visions carried;
Of quiet Innsmouth, where the white gulls tarried
Around an ancient spire that once I knew.

Always perplexed I heard those far notes falling,
Till one March night the bleak rain splashing cold
Beckoned me back through gateways of recalling
To elder towers where the mad clappers tolled.
They tolled—but from the sunless tides that pour
Through sunken valleys on the sea's dead floor.

XX. Night-Gaunts

Out of what crypt they crawl, I cannot tell,
But every night I see the rubbery things,
Black, horned, and slender, with membraneous wings,
And tails that bear the bifid barb of hell.
They come in legions on the north wind's swell,
With obscene clutch that titillates and stings,
Snatching me off on monstrous voyagings
To grey worlds hidden deep in nightmare's well.

Over the jagged peaks of Thok they sweep,
Heedless of all the cries I try to make,
And down the nether pits to that foul lake
Where the puffed shoggoths splash in doubtful sleep.
But oh! If only they would make some sound,
Or wear a face where faces should be found!

XXI. Nyarlathotep

And at the last from inner Egypt came
The strange dark One to whom the fellahs bowed;
Silent and lean and cryptically proud,
And wrapped in fabrics red as sunset flame.
Throngs pressed around, frantic for his commands,
But leaving, could not tell what they had heard;
While through the nations spread the awestruck word
That wild beasts followed him and licked his hands.

Soon from the sea a noxious birth began;
Forgotten lands with weedy spires of gold;
The ground was cleft, and mad auroras rolled
Down on the quaking citadels of man.
Then, crushing what he chanced to mould in play,
The idiot Chaos blew Earth's dust away.

XXII. Azathoth

Out in the mindless void the daemon bore me,
Past the bright clusters of dimensioned space,
Till neither time nor matter stretched before me,
But only Chaos, without form or place.
Here the vast Lord of All in darkness muttered
Things he had dreamed but could not understand,
While near him shapeless bat-things flopped and fluttered
In idiot vortices that ray-streams fanned.

They danced insanely to the high, thin whining
Of a cracked flute clutched in a monstrous paw,
Whence flow the aimless waves whose chance combining
Gives each frail cosmos its eternal law.
"I am His Messenger," the daemon said,
As in contempt he struck his Master's head.

XXIII. Mirage

I do not know if ever it existed—
That lost world floating dimly on Time's stream—
And yet I see it often, violet-misted,
And shimmering at the back of some vague dream.
There were strange towers and curious lapping rivers,
Labyrinths of wonder, and low vaults of light,
And bough-crossed skies of flame, like that which quivers
Wistfully just before a winter's night.

Great moors led off to sedgy shores unpeopled,
Where vast birds wheeled, while on a windswept hill
There was a village, ancient and white-steepled,
With evening chimes for which I listen still.
I do not know what land it is—or dare
Ask when or why I was, or will be, there.

XXIV. The Canal

Somewhere in dream there is an evil place
Where tall, deserted buildings crowd along
A deep, black, narrow channel, reeking strong
Of frightful things whence oily currents race.
Lanes with old walls half meeting overhead
Wind off to streets one may or may not know,
And feeble moonlight sheds a spectral glow
Over long rows of windows, dark and dead.

There are no footfalls, and the one soft sound
Is of the oily water as it glides
Under stone bridges, and along the sides
Of its deep flume, to some vague ocean bound.
None lives to tell when that stream washed away
Its dream-lost region from the world of clay.

XXV. St. Toad's

"Beware St. Toad's cracked chimes!" I heard him scream
As I plunged into those mad lanes that wind
In labyrinths obscure and undefined
South of the river where old centuries dream.
He was a furtive figure, bent and ragged,
And in a flash had staggered out of sight,
So still I burrowed onward in the night
Toward where more roof-lines rose, malign and jagged.

No guide-book told of what was lurking here—
But now I heard another old man shriek:
"Beware St. Toad's cracked chimes!" And growing weak,
I paused, when a third greybeard croaked in fear:
"Beware St. Toad's cracked chimes!" Aghast, I fled—
Till suddenly that black spire loomed ahead.

XXVI. The Familiars

John Whateley lived about a mile from town,
Up where the hills began to huddle thick;
We never thought his wits were very quick,
Seeing the way he let his farm run down.
He used to waste his time on some queer books
He'd found around the attic of his place,
Till funny lines got creased into his face,
And folks all said they didn't like his looks.

When he began those night-howls we declared
He'd better be locked up away from harm,
So three men from the Aylesbury town farm
Went for him—but came back alone and scared.
They'd found him talking to two crouching things
That at their step flew off on great black wings.

XXVII. The Elder Pharos

From Leng, where rocky peaks climb bleak and bare
Under cold stars obscure to human sight,
There shoots at dusk a single beam of light
Whose far blue rays make shepherds whine in prayer.
They say (though none has been there) that it comes
Out of a pharos in a tower of stone,
Where the last Elder One lives on alone,
Talking to Chaos with the beat of drums.

The Thing, they whisper, wears a silken mask
Of yellow, whose queer folds appear to hide
A face not of this earth, though none dares ask
Just what those features are, which bulge inside.
Many, in man's first youth, sought out that glow,
But what they found, no one will ever know.

XXVIII. Expectancy

I cannot tell why some things hold for me
A sense of unplumbed marvels to befall,
Or of a rift in the horizon's wall
Opening to worlds where only gods can be.
There is a breathless, vague expectancy,
As of vast ancient pomps I half recall,
Or wild adventures, uncorporeal,
Ecstasy-fraught, and as a day-dream free.

It is in sunsets and strange city spires,
Old villages and woods and misty downs,
South winds, the sea, low hills, and lighted towns,
Old gardens, half-heard songs, and the moon's fires.
But though its lure alone makes life worth living,
None gains or guesses what it hints at giving.

XXIX. Nostalgia

Once every year, in autumn's wistful glow,
The birds fly out over an ocean waste,
Calling and chattering in a joyous haste
To reach some land their inner memories know.
Great terraced gardens where bright blossoms blow,
And lines of mangoes luscious to the taste,
And temple-groves with branches interlaced
Over cool paths—all these their vague dreams shew.

They search the sea for marks of their old shore—
For the tall city, white and turreted—
But only empty waters stretch ahead,
So that at last they turn away once more.
Yet sunken deep where alien polyps throng,
The old towers miss their lost, remembered song.

XXX. Background

I never can be tied to raw, new things,
For I first saw the light in an old town,
Where from my window huddled roofs sloped down
To a quaint harbour rich with visionings.
Streets with carved doorways where the sunset beams
Flooded old fanlights and small window-panes,
And Georgian steeples topped with gilded vanes—
These were the sights that shaped my childhood dreams.

Such treasures, left from times of cautious leaven,
Cannot but loose the hold of flimsier wraiths
That flit with shifting ways and muddled faiths
Across the changeless walls of earth and heaven.
They cut the moment's thongs and leave me free
To stand alone before eternity.

XXXI. The Dweller

It had been old when Babylon was new;
None knows how long it slept beneath that mound,
Where in the end our questing shovels found
Its granite blocks and brought it back to view.
There were vast pavements and foundation-walls,
And crumbling slabs and statues, carved to shew
Fantastic beings of some long ago
Past anything the world of man recalls.

And then we saw those stone steps leading down
Through a choked gate of graven dolomite
To some black haven of eternal night
Where elder signs and primal secrets frown.
We cleared a path—but raced in mad retreat
When from below we heard those clumping feet.

XXXII. Alienation

His solid flesh had never been away,
For each dawn found him in his usual place,
But every night his spirit loved to race
Through gulfs and worlds remote from common day.
He had seen Yaddith, yet retained his mind,
And come back safely from the Ghooric zone,
When one still night across curved space was thrown
That beckoning piping from the voids behind.

He waked that morning as an older man,
And nothing since has looked the same to him.
Objects around float nebulous and dim—
False, phantom trifles of some vaster plan.
His folk and friends are now an alien throng
To which he struggles vainly to belong.

XXXIII. Harbour Whistles

Over old roofs and past decaying spires
The harbour whistles chant all through the night;
Throats from strange ports, and beaches far and white,
And fabulous oceans, ranged in motley choirs.
Each to the other alien and unknown,
Yet all, by some obscurely focussed force
From brooding gulfs beyond the Zodiac's course,
Fused into one mysterious cosmic drone.

Through shadowy dreams they send a marching line
Of still more shadowy shapes and hints and views;
Echoes from outer voids, and subtle clues
To things which they themselves cannot define.
And always in that chorus, faintly blent,
We catch some notes no earth-ship ever sent.

XXXIV. Recapture

The way led down a dark, half-wooded heath
Where moss-grey boulders humped above the mould,
And curious drops, disquieting and cold,
Sprayed up from unseen streams in gulfs beneath.
There was no wind, nor any trace of sound
In puzzling shrub, or alien-featured tree,
Nor any view before—till suddenly,
Straight in my path, I saw a monstrous mound.

Half to the sky those steep sides loomed upspread,
Rank-grassed, and cluttered by a crumbling flight
Of lava stairs that scaled the fear-topped height
In steps too vast for any human tread.
I shrieked—and *knew* what primal star and year
Had sucked me back from man's dream-transient sphere!

XXXV. Evening Star

I saw it from that hidden, silent place
Where the old wood half shuts the meadow in.
It shone through all the sunset's glories—thin
At first, but with a slowly brightening face.
Night came, and that lone beacon, amber-hued,
Beat on my sight as never it did of old;
The evening star—but grown a thousandfold
More haunting in this hush and solitude.

It traced strange pictures on the quivering air—
Half-memories that had always filled my eyes—
Vast towers and gardens; curious seas and skies
Of some dim life—I never could tell where.
But now I knew that through the cosmic dome
Those rays were calling from my far, lost home.

XXXVI. Continuity

There is in certain ancient things a trace
Of some dim essence—more than form or weight;
A tenuous aether, indeterminate,
Yet linked with all the laws of time and space.
A faint, veiled sign of continuities
That outward eyes can never quite descry;
Of locked dimensions harbouring years gone by,
And out of reach except for hidden keys.

It moves me most when slanting sunbeams glow
On old farm buildings set against a hill,
And paint with life the shapes which linger still
From centuries less a dream than this we know.
In that strange light I feel I am not far
From the fixt mass whose sides the ages are.

Acknowledgments

"Within Your Unholy Pit of Shoggoths," first published in *Conqueror Womb,* edited by Scott R. Jones and Justine Geoffrey (Martian Migraine Press, 2014).

"Your Weighing of My Heart," first published in *Surreal Grotesque* #13 (October 2013).

"The Tomb of Oscar Wilde," first published in *Horror for the Holidays,* edited by Scott David Aniolowski (Miskatonic River Press, 2011).

"These Harpies of Carcosa," first published in *In the Court of the Yellow King,* edited by Glynn Owen Barrass (Celaeno Press, 2014).

"An Ecstasy of Fear," first published in *Bohemians of Sesqua Valley* (Arcane Wisdom, 2013).

"Darkness Dancing in Your Eyes," first published in *Fresh Fears,* edited by William Cook (James Ward Kirk Publishing, 2013).

"Beyond the Wakeful Senses," first published in *Lovecraft eZine* #32 (August 2014).

"Ye Unkempt Thing," first published in *Encounters with Enoch Coffin* (Dark Regions Press, 2013).

"Half Lost in Shadow," first published in *Black Wings IV,* edited by S. T. Joshi (PS Publishing, 2015).

+ ACKNOWLEDGMENTS

"Circular Bone," first published in *Eye to the Telescope* #6 (October 2012).

"Jester of Yellow Day," first published as chapbook by Dunhams Manor Press (May 2014).

"This Splendor of the Goat," first published in *Bohemians of Sesqua Valley* (Arcane Wisdom, 2013).

"Monstrous Aftermath," an earlier version of which was published as "To Kiss Your Canvas" in the *Lovecraft eZine* (March 2015).

"An Element of Nightmare," first published in *Searchers After Horror*, edited by S. T. Joshi (Fedogan & Bremer, 2014).

"Some Unknown Gulf of Night," earlier version published by Arcane Wisdom, 2011; this revised and expanded version contains several thousand words original to this collection.

www.ingramcontent.com/pod-product-compliance
Lightning Source LLC
Chambersburg PA
CBHW050338030726
47303CB00008B/2515